Spellbound

Hex After 40 Book 2

Shelley Dorey

DEDICATION

To the women
Worn out or blind-sided,
Who rebuilt their lives
The Happiness and Joy
Does come back
With a richness and depth
That will surprise you!

CONTENTS

ONE

It was a bittersweet drive back from the airport in Albany, seeing the twins off for their return to college. Twins...huh. They picked opposite coasts for their respective schools: Jessica in New England, while Thomas chose California.

The Christmas week together had passed at warp speed. When we weren't skating on the frozen lake, we were inside playing Monotony by the fire while sipping mugs of hot chocolate. But now it was time to get back to normal.

Back to the renovations, tackling the rest of the cabins in the resort I'd inherited from my Aunt Maeve. The main house was pretty well done, thanks to my efforts since the Fall when I'd moved in.

I smiled, remembering how pleasantly surprised Jessica had been when she'd first stepped inside the old two-story house. Even pragmatic Thomas had seen the beauty of the clapboard home nestled in the forest. What they hadn't seen was the ghost of my Aunt Maeve, a fact that I was grateful for. She'd been there the whole time, watching and giving nods of loving approval. But only I could see her.

Which reminded me of my New Year's resolution—the Witching Well and really getting into this magic stuff! There was no doubt that it worked. Okay, the results of my first attempts had nearly ended in disaster, but I had no clue what I was doing. That was going to change! My Christmas gifts to myself were a bunch of books on the subject. Now that the kids were back at school, I'd be able to devote my time to my own education on casting spells and all the rituals.

Aunt Maeve, despite the fact that she was perfectly able to communicate with me via text, wasn't helpful. When I asked her to show me how to do a simple thing, such as just lighting a candle, she sent me a damn text! And it read the following:

> Shannon, as much as I love you and hate to see you make mistakes, I am not going to hold your hand through this learning process. You have a born talent, yes, but it's your responsibility to learn the ways of White Magic on your own. Your place in the Cosmos is unique to only you. And so you mote, MOTE take care when you attempt to bend it to your will. These lessons will be difficult, but they mote be learned in your heart as well as in your head. And that's up to you to do so.

Thanks, Aunt Maeve, thanks a lot. Instead of having an Obi-Wan showing me the way, I'm stuck with C-3PO; chatty as hell, but not helpful. So, under my bed was a small stack of books I found online that I wanted to get through now that the twins were back in school.

A few light flakes of snow hit the windshield, and I thanked my lucky stars the storm hadn't started until I was about a mile from home. While I was used to dealing with snow from my former life in Pittsburgh, this was my first winter in the Catskill Mountains with its icy, winding roads. And this storm was forecast to be a real doozy. I flipped the turn signal on and turned into the long driveway leading to my house.

Movement on the long front verandah caught my eye. I leaned forward peering out the windshield. Oh my God. It was a bobcat! My breath caught in my throat. Not just any bobcat but that same one missing the tip of one of its ears! He eyed my truck as he slowly ambled across my front porch.

I wheeled the truck into my parking spot and turned it off, still keeping my eye on that big cat. He'd hopped down from the verandah into a foot of snow in the side yard. But what the hell was it doing out there in the open? From what I knew about these wildcats, he should be hightailing it into the cover of the forest.

The cat sauntered slowly through the powder and stopped ten feet away from the old-growth fir and maple trees. His good ear twitched, and his yellow eyes blinked leisurely before lifting a paw, cleaning it with his tongue.

My heart beat fast as I peered at him. Or maybe the cat was a *her*? Did she have babies nearby and was out prowling for food? It was hard to tell if it was male or female with the shaggy, spotted fur. Framed in the pristine white, the animal was beautiful, but it was also pretty dangerous, from what I read about them since I first saw this creature. Hell! It might even be rabid, judging by the bold way it was acting, taking a leisurely bath, instead of beating a path into the forest.

The distance from my truck to my front door was almost fifteen feet. Could I make it there if that beast decided to attack me? As if reading my mind, it dropped its paw and peered straight at me now! I was in a staring match with a giant, wildcat? It seemed like hours that we both locked eyes, but it was probably only a few minutes. Finally, the cat leaped up, bounded through the snow, and disappeared into the trees.

I let out a long sigh through pursed lips. *You better get moving before it changes its mind, Shannon!* My fingers trembled as I threw the door open and raced to the front door.

As I reached for the lock, I noticed a bunch of pine cones next to the welcome mat. My face squinched in puzzlement, seeing the pile of them neatly arranged in a small pyramid. What the hell? Pine cones in a forest weren't that unusual, but seeing them organized on my porch like that was odd. Who would do that? They hadn't been there when I left with the kids that morning.

I slid the key in and looked over my shoulder before

3

entering the house. The only person who might have done that was my neighbor, Steve. But why would he do that? I glanced over at the forest where the cat had disappeared before closing the door. That bobcat had been sniffing around those cones when I'd driven in.

My cell phone beeped with a text, and I fished it out of my pocket. The screen showed a picture of my daughter, Jessica. I smiled. Of course, she was checking in to see that I made it home okay.

After shedding my boots, I wandered into the kitchen to plug in the kettle for a cup of tea. I read the text message,

> My flight was late although Thomas got off okay. Figures. Just boarding now. How was the drive?

My finger typed a quick reply,

> Good. No snow until I arrived in Wesley. Had a welcoming visitor—a big bobcat! Pretty awesome, until he ran off.

I wandered into the living room to get a fire going. The place looked big and empty without my two teenage kids lounging around. It would be a long time until spring break when hopefully they'd visit again.

When the fire caught, licking flames around the cedar log, I pulled out my phone and sent a text to Steve Murphy.

> Hi! Home safe and sound. Did you stop by my house today and leave me some pine cones?

The whistle of the teakettle rose to a shrieking whine, jolting me to go to the kitchen to make my tea. While it steeped, I peeked out the window for any sign of that bobcat. Maybe I should have mentioned it in my text to Steve. The only movement outside were branches swaying in the gusts of snow-whipped wind. The cat was gone, but considering its odd behavior, that was good.

Why was it so interested in those pine cones? And who put

them there anyway? It just had to be Steve. Maybe there's some "country courtin'" tradition in the Catskills I didn't know about or something.

And that bobcat… I could tell by the point missing from the top of one of its ears that it was the very same one I first saw on my drive to Wesley in September. I'd never forget that! It had leaped out onto the road and I'd almost ran over it! If not for my Aunt Maeve's intervention, wrenching the steering wheel from my grasp, it would have ended up as roadkill.

And I'd seen it a couple of times after that when I was going to the glade where the Witching Well was. It was the SAME bobcat! I mean, this bruiser had been in a few fights to have lost an ear. How many cats like that could there be in these mountains?

The phone buzzed, and I read Steve's reply.

> **Thanks for letting me know you made it okay. Don't know anything about your pine cones. A secret admirer leaving gifts? LOL**

Hmmm. As I poured my tea, the scent of lilies with an overtone of patchouli oil filled my nostrils. When the air next to me shimmered, I grinned but kept fixing my tea. "I wondered how long it would be before you materialized. Things are back to normal, Aunt Maeve."

"Not quite, Shannon."

I leaned back against the counter, sipping my tea as my gaze met hers. She looked exactly like she had in the summers when I had visited as a teen. The same azure-blue eyes peeking out from her messy platinum hair, and her closed-lipped smile, bordering on being a smirk.

"You liked my kids, huh? Aren't they amazing?" This time I couldn't help the grin that spread over my face, thinking of Thomas and Jess.

"Of course. Why wouldn't they be amazing? Aside from Ass-hat's genes, they're *Burkes*." Her form wavered a little, and she kind of drifted in the air, floating over to the window. "It's about the bobcat, Shannon. It seems he's taken a liking to you."

My head tilted to the side as it hit me. Of course. That cat was somehow connected to the magic of this place—*literal* magic as in what had awaited me when I first visited that strange Witching Well in the glade of trees.

I blew out a sigh. I should have known. "It left the pine cones? I thought cats left presents like mice or birds. He must be a vegetarian, or maybe he's not a very good hunter. Probably the latter after seeing that mangled ear."

Her head turned, and she scowled at me. "It's not a joke, Shannon. That bobcat is *drawn* to you. You've read about witches having familiars, haven't you?"

I made a face at her. "Yeah, I *read* about it. You could have told me about it."

She made a short wave with her hand. "Don't be sassy. I already told you that you need to put in more work learning."

I stuck out my tongue, just like I used to do when I was a teenager spending my summers with her.

Now it was Maeve's turn to sigh. She shook her head and crossed her arms. "I can tell you this. Cats have strong psychic energy. I should have recognized it was extraordinary when it jumped into the path of your truck." She waved her translucent hands in the air. "But I was still getting up to speed with all this *spirit* stuff."

"Wait a minute, Aunt Maeve. I'm not a cat person. I'm not even all that fond of dogs. I certainly don't want some giant *fleabag* hanging around, scaring me to pieces."

When I saw the look of shock come over her features, I backed off a little. "Okay, he's an amazing sight, but he's *enormous*. If I had to have this"—I made air quotes with my fingers—"*familiar*, why couldn't it be something smaller? Maybe a frog or an owl? An owl would be cool. I'm okay with birds."

"Holy doodle, Shannon! You don't get to *choose*! A familiar chooses *you*! And just to set the record straight, not all witches are blessed with such beings to help them." Her lips pursed, and she looked away.

Okay. Now I was getting to the meat of it. Aunt Maeve had practiced witchcraft when she was alive and living here, but she'd never had a familiar. It was time for a little tact—not my best quality, I'm afraid.

"Aunt Maeve, maybe it's here for *you*? Better late than never? You said yourself, you're still learning this spirit stuff. Maybe Bob is drawn to you? He could have left those pine cones for—"

"*Bob?*" She rolled her eyes. "Trust you to trivialize that magnificent creature with a name like that!"

"Come on! Bob The Bobcat? Pretty catchy, isn't it?" I winked at her before continuing, "Okay, say you're right, and this feline has chosen me. What does a familiar do? I mean, can he cast spells, help me with learning this magic stuff? Anything actually useful?"

"A familiar *protects* you. As I said, they're psychic. They can sense if you are in danger or if someone has cast a negative spell on you. They can even protect you from *yourself*!"

She shimmered and then swept across the floor to hover next to me, wagging her finger in my face. "The night of the party when you were so distraught, thinking the magic of the well had destroyed your relationship with your kids… you were hell-bent on destroying the well. On your way there, you heard your familiar in the forest, snarling at you."

My face tightened. "But he didn't *save* me! Burning the well could have had disastrous consequences, but it was Libby and Mary-Jane who stopped me! And that was because YOU sent them! Bob didn't do anything but snarl!"

"Do you honestly think they would have found you on their own? Bob showed them the way to the well, lighting the path with fireflies." Her head tipped to the side. "You should be grateful to have him! I know *I'm* thrilled for you."

With that, her image shimmered and then faded to nothing.

My chest tightened as I stood at the counter sipping my tea. She'd made it sound so...so *special*! And the fact that she never had a familiar of her own was pretty sad. If anyone should have been blessed with one, it should have been Maeve.

But I couldn't change the past any more than I could have chosen what kind of familiar I could put up with.

I rinsed my mug and rummaged in the fridge for the leftover ham to make a sandwich. As I sliced the meat, I glanced over at the window. The snow was falling harder now, whipping up swirls of white confetti across the yard. It wasn't a fit night outside for man nor… oh man…*beast*.

I rolled my eyes. Why was I letting myself get sucked into feeling anything for that bobcat? But…

"Okay!" I hacked off two thick slices from the ham and plunked it in an empty pie pan.

As I headed to the front door with it, I couldn't help but grumble, grudgingly. "This is just for one time, Bob! Even if you could hunt, you'd have a hard time in this storm."

I opened the door and set the pan next to the pile of pine cones. "Consider this your reward for 'protecting' me, if that, in fact, is what you're doing. I'm not sure I buy that, but whatever."

There was no sign of Bob at the edge of my lawn or even in the trees when I peered over there. The snow falling faster, forming a sheet of white, wasn't helping to see him. I shivered and went inside quickly, closing the door and locking it after me.

I finished making my supper and took it into the living room to eat while I wrote in my Grimoire. It had been almost two weeks since I'd had a chance to make any entries. And now I had a fresh one to include in my journal of magic.

Bob, apparently my new familiar. I let out a snort.

Normal people have guard dogs. I have a guard cat.

Just another day at the office, right?

TWO

The next morning my eyes pried themselves open at the sound of a vehicle outside. Squinting at the window, the first reddish streaks of dawn glowed on the pane of glass. A glance at my cell phone showed the time as 6:14. Oh my God! It felt like the middle of the night after two weeks of sleeping in over Christmas vacay.

A series of thuds now joined the sound of the vehicle's motor outside. What the hell? Who would be out at this time, and what were they doing? I threw the comforter back and grabbed my robe before hurrying over to peek out the window.

A black truck—Steve's—with a snowplow blade mounted on the front backed up, before pushing another path of snow to the edge of my verandah. Even from the second-story window, I could see that the storm had continued overnight, leaving a dump of eight or so inches. Thank goodness for neighbors with plows!

Plows... Yeah, I got a nice tingle. Oh man...*that man* is plowing my yard... mmm...

"Shannon!" I admonished myself out loud. I needed a cold shower.

I hurried downstairs and flipped the switch on the coffeemaker. The least I could do was offer the guy a cup of joe for helping me with the driveway! Hopefully, he'd have time before he headed off to work to come inside and join me. That was the neighborly thing for me to do in turn, to thank him.

Just being a good neighbor, that's all. Nothing to do with the fact that he was easy on the eyes, not to mention fun to hang with. Nope. Not even going to think about his dark-blue eyes or the dimple in his sculpted chin, or the way he filled out a pair of jeans so nicely with a tight ass and…

I felt my lower half grow warm along with my cheeks. As I watched him finish the space next to my truck, I shook my head. Sure, he was great looking, and it had been almost a year since I'd had sex, but still! Talk about a case of raging hormones!

The budding romance (lust?) between us had ended even before it had actually started. We'd both agreed to put any kind of relationship on the backburner, at least until I had my life squared away. It wasn't just my kids to consider; I needed time to be me. After twenty years of marriage, I needed to stand on my own two feet and figure out what *I* wanted, not just trying to please the cheating Ass-hat or being Supermom.

Steve parked his truck, and when he stepped out, there was a snow brush in his hand. My eyes opened wider, seeing him begin to clear off the snow from my truck. That was too much! I went to the front door and yelled to him.

"Thanks for clearing my drive! But never mind my truck; I'll get that. Come in and have a coffee with me."

When his head turned to me, the hood of his jacket fell back, showing dark curls of hair plastered to his forehead. "It'll only take me two minutes! But sure, I'll take you up on a coffee!"

I tugged the sides of my robe tighter together, rolling my shoulders from the crisp winter air as I stood in the doorway. It was then that I noticed the glint of the aluminum pie pan sticking up in the snow at the end of the verandah. There was no sign of the ham, which meant that Bob had probably found it. Either that or some other animal had scored a free meal.

Steve tossed the snowbrush into the cab of his truck and grinned as he walked over to me. "Who needs a gym when you live in the mountains? It sure gets the blood pumping."

As he stepped closer, it struck me once more how tall he was. And with the dark-brown parka, he looked like a big, burly mountain man. Like Leonardo DiCaprio in that movie. It was more than adrenaline pumping through my veins at the sight of him. Even the fresh scent of his aftershave didn't go unnoticed.

I fanned my neck as I stepped back, inviting him into the warmth of the entry. "Glad to be of service! You can plow my drive anytime you want." As soon as the words left my mouth, my cheeks grew warm. This was too reminiscent of the flirty double entendres that had happened between us months ago.

All hopes that he hadn't picked up on that vanished when he chuckled. "Kind of like checking out your chimney? How many other tasks need my attention, Shannon?" A warm smirk twitched his lips as he slipped his coat off. "I guess I earned a…coffee."

"For sure!" I hurried into the kitchen, calling over my shoulder, "So Byron's back to school today? Or does he get a snow day? Back in Pittsburgh, this would have closed the schools."

"Not here. That's not even a foot, hardly anything. Nope. He'll be at school." He took a seat at the table. "How about your kids? Did they get back okay?"

As I poured two mugs of coffee, I nodded. "Yeah. It's sure going to be quiet around here without them."

"They're great kids, Shannon. I'm glad that things worked out so they were here for Christmas." He watched me with a small smile as I placed the mug before him and took a seat. "So, what are you tackling next? It's pretty cold to be working on any of the cabins. I mean, they don't have heat, aside from electric space heaters."

I sighed. "Yeah. I may have to postpone for a few weeks. I hate doing that. I really want the cabins ready for Memorial Day. A lot of families take extended vacations that weekend."

With Ass-hat threatening to scale back on monthly support, the rental income from those cabins was definitely needed. As it was, the small nest egg from the divorce settlement was shrinking fast.

"That's five months away! I wouldn't worry too much. You'll have them done in no time, once the weather warms. Take some time for yourself. Christmas was fun, but it was also exhausting. To tell the truth, I'm happy to get back to the store and work."

"I don't think I have much of a choice about the cabins. But it's going to mean some very long days here. Almost like hibernating." I sipped my coffee, wondering how I'd manage without getting stir-crazy. It was lucky that Aunt Maeve popped in now and then from the cosmic ether.

"If you're looking for something to do, you could work for me."

My gaze shot to him. "You need another person at the store? I've never worked retail—"

"No! Not there. Particularly not at this time of year. It barely warrants my part-timer, Jody." His chin dropped, but his eyes locked with mine. "No, I was thinking about my house. I've been meaning to repaint the living room, and since you did such a great job here… well, I'd pay you."

My head dipped to the side, scowling at him. "You come over and plow my driveway and expect me to take money for helping you? Not going to happen, Steve. I'd be happy to paint your living room. I know where you can get a good discount on paint!"

"Not Mountain Hardware! You can't trust that guy who runs it."

I laughed. "That's what the scuttlebutt is. He's much better at snowplowing than mixing paint." Placing my hand over his, I leaned closer. "Seriously, I'd be happy to help with your living room. Just make sure you have a really sturdy ladder with those cathedral ceilings, okay?"

"You do the walls and leave the high stuff to me." His eyes narrowed. "Actually, knowing you, I'd better be there to make sure you don't tackle them. Working alongside each other, we could probably have it done in two days."

For a few moments, all I could do was stare at him. Was this some kind of play he was making to resume where we'd left off? That night I'd spent at his place when there were septic problems at my house, had ended with a kiss that had made my knees feel like cooked spaghetti. If he hadn't broken the kiss to go to his own room to sleep, I'm pretty sure we would have ended up in bed together.

Was that such a bad thing? Why couldn't we be friends with benefits? We were adults and not hurting anyone.

A bloodcurdling yowl broke the stillness in the air outside. I knew that yowl! I leaped to my feet, pulling the curtain back from the window to scan the yard outside for Bob.

"Holy shit! That's a bobcat!" Steve jumped up and raced to the front door, calling out, "I've never actually seen one! I've got to get a picture to show Byron!"

Movement in the periphery of my line of sight caught my eye. The big cat emerged from behind a cedar and stood gazing from Steve's truck to the house. The snow was up over his haunches, while his white-rimmed, green eyes blinked slowly.

Steve's footsteps pounded across the front verandah, and he sped by, coming to a halt at the edge. Now his body blocked my line of sight of Bob. I went higher and leaned to the side but still couldn't see the cat. I got up and raced to the front door.

Just as I got there, another high-pitched yowl filled the air. Steve held his cell phone out in front of him, filming the cat as it bounded through the snow. Oh shit! It was coming toward the house.

"Steve! Get back here! He's coming!" My heart leaped into my throat as I watched the snow kick high from the cat's feet.

"Hang on! Almost…" Steve took a step backward but still held the phone high. The cat was only ten feet away, crouching lower as if to spring at him.

"Bob! No!" I sprinted across the deck, coming to a stop when I was between Steve and the cat. The bobcat hunkered even lower, staring back at me. Only his head with the golden eyes and that tuft of dark hair on the tip of his ear showed in the sea of white he lay in.

"Shannon!" Steve grabbed my arm, tugging me back. "What are you doing? C'mon! Let's get back in the house."

I couldn't tear my gaze away from the cat as I took a step backward. The cat let out a small howl before flopping over onto its back and wiggling deeper into the drift of snow. I leaned forward watching the cat's movements. What the hell? It swished from side to side, rubbing itself in the snowdrift like…like I'd seen housecats do, playing with their owners!

Steve tugged at my arm. "You called it Bob. You've seen this cat before?" He took a step so that we stood together gazing at the cat cavorting in the powder. "Being so close to people… That's not supposed to happen. Maybe that cat's sick with rabies or something."

At his words, the cat practically did a flip, springing high and landing closer to the verandah. And this time he wasn't stopping, leaping through the snow to get to us.

Before I was even aware of it, my hand rose. "Stop! That's close enough!" My arm tingled but felt detached, all at the same time, as I locked eyes with the cat.

The bobcat came to a halt in a swirl of snow, sitting there about six feet away with his one good ear flattened on his head. His lip curled up displaying pointed incisors as he stared at us.

This time, Steve practically dragged me across the wooden floor, heading for the door. "That cat shouldn't be doing that, Shannon! We need to call animal control or maybe even shoot the damned thing. It's dangerous! A wild animal—"

"No!" I yanked my arm from his grip, glaring up at him. "No one's gonna shoot that cat! Not you or animal control." My forehead knotted. "They actually have that in this town?" I shook my head, getting my focus back. "You're gonna leave that cat alone! It's my property and my—"

"Your what… Your *cat*?" His eyes were like golf balls, scowling at me. And then he noticed my feet. "Oh shit! You're going to get frostbite coming outside in your bare feet! We'll talk about this once we get you warmed up."

I wasn't even aware of the cold on my feet! All I could think of was Steve's attitude, trying to "fix" what he thought was a problem. He didn't have the first clue about that cat and his "go-to" was to *shoot* it?

"I'm fine!" I pushed by him, stomping into the house, my feet now stinging from the cold. I went to the kitchen sink and ran hot water before soaking the tea towel in it. When I wrung it out, I went to the kitchen table to wrap my feet in the warmth, ignoring Steve all the while. The heat prickled my skin before I could feel it seeping deeper.

"Shannon? That's a wild animal, not some kind of pet! I don't like it hanging around here. The next time it might attack you instead of…" He shook his head. "When it charged, why didn't it keep coming? It was like it listened to you. There is something strange about that bobcat. It needs to be put down."

I jumped to my feet and almost tripped on the tea towel, walking over to him. "That isn't for you to decide, Steve." For a moment I was reminded of how he'd treated me when Devon Booker tried to fix the septic problem in the fall. Steve had gotten all huffy trying to *mansplain the problem*. Well, I'd had a bellyful of *that* in my former life with Ass-hat. I wasn't going down that road again!

"Thanks for plowing my driveway, Steve, but this is my house, and I make the decisions about what happens here. And that includes the wildlife."

His eyes grew bigger, and his head drew back. From the twitch in his jaw muscle, I could tell he was as pissed off as I was. When he spoke, his voice was icy. "Fine. You're making a mistake, but it's *your* business as you so clearly pointed out."

He turned and walked out of the kitchen, with a parting shot drifting behind him, "Don't trouble yourself with helping me paint. I'll find someone else." With that, the door banged shut behind him.

Well, that was childish. What is it with men? Well, if there's one thing I've seen in my forty-plus years, it's men getting all huffy like that and storming off to man-sulk.

Whateverrr.

I raced to the window to see if the bobcat was anywhere near. But only the dent in the snow from when it rolled there, and the path to the trees could be seen. The cat had gone.

Along with Steve.

THREE

It took me a while to calm down after Steve left. But there's a plus side of anger; it can be energizing. I finished my housework and showering in record time. After smudging a bundle of sage, wandering counterclockwise around my living room to cleanse the space, I sat cross-legged on the wooden floor.

With the book of witchcraft I'd started the night before propped open on the footstool, I took a deep breath. This was it. My first formal spell. The items I needed to "cast a circle" and start my first ritual, honoring the Divine Mother and asking for her blessings, were assembled next to me.

The diagram in the book showed a pentagram made by securing two different-colored lengths of yarn. Taking the pink one, I spread it out, creating a triangle and securing the points with small pieces of masking tape.

Next, I spread the green yarn, overlaying the first one with the top tips of the triangle pointing in opposite directions. Checking that all six points were more or less even, I smiled at the pentagram. It looked fine. I placed tea-light candles on each of the points and then placed the glass bowl containing the thick, white candle in the center.

After lighting each candle, I reached for the small satchels of herbs to have them handy.

Raising my right hand to follow the directions of my words, I began, "I call to the North. I call to the South, I call to the East. I call to the West. As above, so below, the circle is complete." There. I'd cast my circle.

For a few moments, I gazed into the flame of the large candle, consciously breathing slowly. From a series of jars beside me, I took a handful of herbs and sprinkled rosemary leaves into the bowl around the candle. "Rosemary for protection of myself, my children, and my friends."

Reaching into another jar, I said, "Bay leaf for wisdom and strength," while adding those herbs to the rosemary.

From another jar, I took a healthy pinch of ginger and added it, saying, "Ginger for success and personal power."

My eyes closed, and I envisioned myself growing stronger, learning, and being at one with the universe. It was hard at first, as random thoughts tried to snag my intent, but gradually I managed a few pure, deep breaths, keeping my focus. A feeling of peace settled into my core, spreading out until my hands and feet felt heavy and warm. The quiet calmness in my body was such a lovely sensation that I wondered why I hadn't tried this before.

After one last long breath, I opened my eyes. Taking the candle snuffer that I'd found in one of the drawers in my aunt's dresser, I extinguished all the candles, setting the spell.

For a few moments, I continued sitting there cross-legged on the floor with my palms resting on my knees. I'd done it! My first spell ritual to help me on my journey into this magical realm.

I grabbed my Grimoire from the coffee table to make an entry about my actions, noting the feeling of "rightness" that I'd experienced. When I was done and about to clear the items away, the air near the window shimmered, and I smelled my aunt's perfume.

It didn't take long for her form to become visible, showing a warm smile as she gazed at me.

"Good. I'm glad you're finally starting to put work and

discipline into this." Her figure wavered and then drifted closer. "You will find this becomes even more rewarding as time goes on, Shannon."

When I stood up, my knees didn't creak the way they usually did. I even felt lighter, like I could float in the air as my aunt was doing. My hand rose to touch her cheek, but, of course, it passed right through her. "Yeah. Y'know, I *feel* it deep inside. No more erratic spells for *this* woman! From now on, everything I cast a spell for will be with intent. I can't wait to tell Libby and MJ about this."

"They're coming tonight? It's the new moon. That's propitious. And just so you know, when I was alive doing moon magic with my sisters, we didn't always go to the Witching Well for that, especially not in the dead of winter. The backyard, next to the lake, is fine. What matters are your intentions."

I nodded. "From what I've read, it always comes back to that. After a rocky start in the world of magic, I'm willing to keep things simple and absolutely do no harm to others. There's no way I want to mess with the power of three. I don't need anything bad boomeranging back at me, threefold. No thanks. I've learned my lesson."

"Attagirl! That's the way!" She floated, leading the way to the kitchen, and paused at the front window. "It looks like you're about to have company."

I went over and saw a cargo van pull up next to my truck. The US Postal Service insignia was etched on the side of the truck. "Hmmm, I don't remember ordering more parcels. I wonder what this could be."

When I turned to my aunt, of course her form had already dissolved. At the tap on my door, I left the kitchen to answer it.

The delivery guy, bundled in a navy-blue parka, handed me an envelope. "Registered mail for Shannon Burke. Can I get your signature?" He thrust an electronic box, with a plastic pen attached, at me, and I scribbled my name.

My chest tightened as I wrote, wondering if this letter was

from Ass-hat's lawyer. He'd threatened to reduce the support I was receiving, and maybe this was my notice. But when I closed the door and scanned the return address on the envelope, it showed the Town of Wesley, Property Tax Division. That was weird. Why would they send this by registered mail?

When I ripped it open and scanned the letter, my mouth fell open. This couldn't be right. I reread it, more slowly.

> Dear Ms. Burke,
>
> An appraisal assessment on the property, 41 Lakeshore Lane, Tract 12, Section 2, Township 46 East, Wesley County, New York, was finalized in November 2018. As assessed value is based on the current market of comparable property, it has been determined that your property taxes have subsequently increased. Comparable properties range from $923,000 at the low end to a high of $1,240,000.
>
> Therefore, taxes due February this year, are in the amount of $9, 238.42.
>
> Please submit full payment within thirty days of receipt of this letter. Please visit our office or contact us if you have any questions.
>
> Yours truly,
> Harold Ainsley
> Senior Auditor

Oh my God! I stood there feeling numb from the shock of it. There had to be a mistake. But then I remembered the offer that Devon Booker had made on this property back in the fall. It had been well over a million. So maybe the tax office was correct.

But to hit me like this, all at once! I felt my stomach sink, almost as fast as what this would do to my nest egg from the divorce settlement. I needed that money to finish the renovations on the cabins as well as provide a place for me to live, at least until I could start getting the seasonal income from vacationers.

And the fact it was due next month! How could I manage? I sighed. I'd have to try to find a job. But what job? For over twenty years my focus had been raising the kids and running the house—not exactly what employers looked for on a résumé. The only work experience had been two years as a journalist at the *Pittsburgh Daily* before the kids came along.

Shit! This day—no, correct that—this year, was sure getting off on the wrong foot! First the fight with Steve and now this!

I'd hardly finished my first magic spell before getting hit with this…this *shit*! This wasn't supposed to happen.

So much for magic and protection!

FOUR

Mary-Jane

"Don't tell me you're going *running*, Mary-Jane!" Ray looked up from where he was bent, shoveling snow from the walkway. "I thought for just *one day* you could take a break! You're going to fall and sprain your ankle again with all this snow."

I tucked the edge of the knitted hat over my ears as I walked over to him. "No, I'll be okay. I'm not going to let a little snow stop me." The truth was, I couldn't imagine starting my day without at least a one-mile run. I'd dropped almost thirty pounds in the last few months, and I'd never looked better! That added bonus from Shannon's spell didn't hurt either.

As I was about to set off, Ray grabbed my arm and leaned closer. "I can't keep this up, MJ!" His mouth set in a hard line, his eyes sparking. "You're killing me, y'know."

I grinned. "But what a way to *go*, Ray! Why don't you join me? And after, well…" I bobbed my eyebrows up and down. Yes. The afterwards—mind-blowing sex. It was getting to the point that just the *thought* of exercising got me hot! He hadn't complained when that side effect had first happened.

He shook his head. "No. You aren't listening, MJ. I'm not as young as I used to be. The sex is too much—way too much. And just so you know… I won't be here when you get back. Someone's got to look after the restaurant, and lately, it certainly hasn't been you! We're lucky that Debbie has been able to handle the kitchen, but she's not you! Business is falling off since you've abandoned cooking."

My mind was still ringing with "I won't be here when you get back." That wouldn't work. Not. At. All. I'd be like a cat in heat when I returned home from my run. True, Ray's ardor had cooled, or as he'd put it, "I'm like a trained monkey, performing on-demand."But surely he wasn't making me go cold turkey.

I plastered on my most flirty smile when I snuggled into him. "Come on, Ray. Zoe's at school; it's just us. We can try some new positions. Maybe even do it in the shower. You always liked that."

His hands gripped my upper arms, pushing me away from him. "No! This time, I mean it, MJ. Why can't we be like other couples? Y'know, do it once or twice a week? I can't keep this pace up! I'm going to have a heart attack or something."

My chin rose. "If that's the case, you shouldn't be shoveling snow! Most men would be envious to have the kind of sex life you have." I winked at him. "Maybe you need more of those little blue pills."

"You know those things made me dizzy! When I tried them, I thought I was having a stroke!" Again, a deep scowl creased his face. "No more, MJ! Stop with the exercising and start acting *normal!* Okay?"

Normal? When I'd acted "normal" before Shannon's spell, he'd criticized me for being overweight and out of shape. My eyes narrowed, glaring at him.

"Screw you!" I pulled away from him and started at a fast walk, going up the sidewalk and then onto the street. There was absolutely no pleasing that man! For years I'd put up with his jibes and outright derision about my weight and practically everything else about me. Things had changed for a while after

I'd screwed up my ankle. He'd actually been more like the guy I'd married rather than his usual, smug ass-holery.

He hadn't appreciated what he had until it was threatened. My getting injured had shaken some sense into him. And he hadn't complained when our sex life had gotten a turbocharge from Shannon's spell. He'd been thrilled, at least until about a month ago. That's when the wind had gone out of his sails, so to speak.

Humph! I picked up the pace, heading down the street, dodging any spot that looked like black ice. No way was I going to prove him right by slipping and falling on my ass! He'd probably like that!

My shoulders fell as I crossed to the other side of the street. Would he really not be there when I got home?

But I was kidding myself hoping that he hadn't meant it. When I'd touched him, that message had blared in every cell in his body. Sometimes the "gift" I'd been given when I visited that damned Witching Well could be a serious downer. Like when Old Lady Webb had stumbled into me in the grocery store last week.

What came through her bony fingers clutching my arm was like a foghorn in a sea of mist. She'd been on the brink of tears, wondering where she'd put her wedding band. A picture in high def had flashed in my head of her placing the ring on a shelf in her fridge. Her fridge! Then she toddled off to a sudsy sink, full of dishes. That poor, old soul should be in a nursing home before she ended up setting her house on fire.

I helped her, of course. I stopped by her place to say hi and just "by accident" noticed her wedding band on the shelf. When I handed it to her, she barely controlled herself from bursting into tears. Great, my good deed and all, but this psychometric thing could be kind of sad. And then there was Ray. Shit. He really, really meant it this time.

Double shit! Already with the exertion of running, endorphins flooded my body, along with a surge of hormones.

Maybe I *should* ease back on the workouts. But even as I pondered it, I knew that wouldn't happen. I was addicted to exercising! As bad as a gambler constantly pulling the slot machine's lever but with the jackpot waiting at home, in bed.

"Hey, MJ! Lookin' good!"

My head swiveled at the deep, baritone voice. I smiled, seeing Steve Murphy stepping out from his store, Mountain Hardware. "Hey, Steve!" I swerved from my track and jogged over to him, still running on the spot. "Thanks! It's perfect for a run with all the fresh snow."

"That's one way of looking at it. If you don't have to shovel it or plow it." His smile faded. "Have you seen Shannon lately? Or more specifically her new *pet*?"

"What? She's not a big animal lover, not that I know of. What pet?" With the hormones gushing in my body, it was hard not to notice how ripped Steve's body was, the width of his shoulders, and the fit of his jeans. Not too tight but hugging him in all the right places.

Shit! I was a married woman! I might have teased Shannon about getting it on with Steve, but that was all it was…just *teasing*. Get a grip, MJ!

Steve's forehead furrowed. "I was there this morning to plow her out. Some big bobcat showed up in her yard, and she acted like it was no big deal!"

My feet came to a dead stop, and I grabbed his arm. "A bobcat! What the hell?" Immediately, I could feel his anger. Then the scene of Shannon and him arguing flooded into my mind.

"Shannon doesn't know about the wild animals in these mountains, MJ! What was worse was the way the cat was acting. I'm no Tiger King, but even I know that a bobcat normally avoids contact with people. But this one was crazy!"

"What do you mean?"

His face knotted. "First he rolled and lolled in the snow like he wanted his belly scratched, and the next thing he did was jump up and charge us, snarling!" He shook his head. "I think it might be rabid or something."

My mouth fell open as his shock and fear surged through me, reliving that moment. "That is so not good, Steve. I'll talk to her. But you just can't threaten to shoot animals on *her* property. It's her place."

His eyebrows bunched as he peered at me. "How'd you know that? I never told you that part."

My hand jerked away as if I'd touched a hot ember. Uh-oh! I'd said too much. "Uhh…it's only logical. I mean, you were worried for Shannon. Of course, you'd want to make sure that cat couldn't hurt her. You said it could be rabid, right?"

His mouth snapped shut, and he was silent for a few beats. "Hmm, maybe." He started walking away, still looking at me with question marks in his eyes. "I'm going for a coffee at the Bear Paw. You want to join me, or do you have more running to do? By the way, how's Ray?"

For a second it felt like the tables had been turned on me. But there was no way he could have known about the fight with my husband.

I mustered a smile. "Good! I'd better finish my run. I'll call Shannon later and straighten this out about the bobcat." I sprinted by him, continuing down the street. It looked like I wasn't the only one starting the day on the wrong foot. Men! First Ray, and then Steve trying to run our lives.

I decided to take a detour so that I'd see if Ray had made good on his threat to go to the restaurant. It was true what he'd said about me not working as much in the kitchen. Between my exercise routine, looking after the house, and trying to find some private time to learn more about witchcraft and the paranormal, well, working at that restaurant just didn't hold the same appeal as it once had. Learning about magic was way more exciting.

But, still, I had to get to work and earn my daily bread, right? I headed to the restaurant.

When I rounded the corner to the street where my restaurant, The Cat's Whiskers, was, I paused. A middle-aged couple was talking with Devon Booker on the sidewalk in front of the building. My restaurant and a couple of other stores occupied the street level, and there were a bunch of apartments on the upper floors. As they talked, they kept looking the entire building over, from the storefronts to the upper residences Weird. It was too early for lunch when Devon would sometimes entertain clients at our spot. The couple wasn't familiar either. What was up with that?

As I passed by the restaurant, my eyes opened wider seeing Ray's silver SUV parked in the side lot. That bugger! As if there was any big need for him to be at the restaurant! It was Monday, not our busiest day. Besides, Sylvie and Debbie could handle running things. He didn't *have* to be here.

He *should* have been home.

In bed.

Waiting for me!

My chest tightened. It was clear he preferred being at work than with me.

Damn.

FIVE

Libby

Istepped out of the shower just as my cell phone went off with Mary-Jane's ringtone. Grabbing my robe I answered, but before I could even get in a hello, she blared.

"I'm so mad at Ray, I could spit! He left me hanging in the lurch here, Libby!"

Holding the phone out before my eardrums broke, I asked, "What do you mean he left you?" Then the implication of my words sank in. "No! Not left you, as in separating?"

"No! Not that. Although, considering the circumstances, maybe that wouldn't be so bad; at least I'd have my freedom."

"Slow down, MJ, and tell me what happened." I pressed the speaker button, so I could continue drying off and getting dressed.

"Well, you know how I get when I exercise, right?"

I rolled my eyes. Total nympho? I didn't need her going into details about that! "Yeah, yeah. Go on."

"It was going great for the first few months. Ray was even losing weight from all the bedroom workouts! And he could stand to lose a few pounds."

That was an understatement. The beach ball that was Ray's

stomach looked like a pin could puncture it, sending him flying around the room like a balloon. But I couldn't say that, not to MJ.

"Couldn't we all? Okay, not you, MJ. You're losing too much weight if you ask me. But back to what's got you so fired up."

"He's been slowing down over the past month. It's like he's not even interested anymore. And today he told me he's can't go on like this. He acted like having sex was a burden, and then he just took off to go to work." There was a hitch in her breath at the last sentence, like she was fighting tears.

Much as I felt sorry for MJ, because of Ray having returned to being his snarky self, there had to be more to this. "What exactly did he say, Mary-Jane?" I cocked my ear for her response as I slipped my jeans on.

"He said I'm killing him with all my demands for sex. And that I haven't been working at the restaurant as much as I should be. He's blaming *me* for business falling off."

My mouth snapped shut as I pictured Ray—*the old Ray*—constantly criticizing MJ. Well, a leopard doesn't change its spots, after all, does it? "It's because of you, Mary-Jane, that the restaurant is so successful! It's not just great food, but you visit with customers and make them feel special. Ray works hard, but he doesn't have your…your touch."

"So you think he's right? That because I haven't been working, that business is falling off."

"*Falling off?*" Oh shit. This just got real, or maybe she was exaggerating. "How bad is it, MJ?"

"It's seasonal, Libby! Business always dies off in the winter. I thought I'd take that opportunity to learn more about this witch stuff, y'know? *And* keep with the exercise program. That's important too!"

I breathed a sigh of relief. It was Mary-Jane's histrionics, not their business failing. Not yet. But… "Maybe you need to bend a bit on this, MJ. Scale back on exercising and work in the restaurant more. Maybe try moderation, y'know?"

"I can't! I *need* to exercise!" She was silent for a couple of beats. "But maybe the side effects…you know. Shannon's spell is causing the real problem. I can't keep working out if it's going to make me feel like some horny teenage boy. It was fun at first but… not with Ray acting like this."

"We need to ask Shannon to reverse the spell. It served its purpose, but you don't need it anymore. You've lost weight and you're healthy again! Your doctor is amazed at you."

"But—"

"No, I'm serious, MJ! That spell is causing you problems now. I'll speak to Shannon about this, tonight. You're going to be there too, right?" This was our New Year's resolution, to meet on Monday nights for our Esbat. Since the three of us had come together that Halloween night at the Witching Well, we'd tried to meet once a week. Sometimes it was tough with our varied work schedules, and Mondays seemed to work best.

"Of course, I'll be there. Maybe we'll get to see Shannon's *new pet*."

My mouth fell open as I listened to Mary-Jane's recap of the fight Shannon had with Steve about the wild bobcat. *A bobcat?* I didn't admit to MJ, but I agreed with Steve on this one. You can't tame a wildcat nor should you even try!

When she finished, I commented, "With any luck, that cat has taken off into the woods where it should be." I sighed, picturing MJ. Much as I felt bad for her, I hadn't really been much help.

"If you feel like some company, you can pop over, MJ. I've got a ton of things to do, but we can chat some more if you want."

"No. Thanks, but I'm going to do some research on spells. I might find something that will help with what I'm going through. I'll see you tonight."

When I hung up, I sat there for a few moments thinking of Mary-Jane and Ray. Maybe if Shannon couldn't reverse the spell, she could put one on Ray too? At least then, MJ and her husband would be on the same page…or in the same bed as the case may be. But that probably would spell certain disaster for their restaurant.

Nope. That was one thing I'd learned about spells and wishes. Use them with caution because there was always some weird side effect that could come back and bite you on the ass. I shook my head. Kind of like when Shannon wished impotence on her cheating ex with his girlfriend. It worked, and the skanky pair ended up breaking up. BUT when her ex used their children to try to restore their marriage, it had caused a rift in Shannon's relationship with her kids. That had been a close call.

As I made the bed, I couldn't help feeling just a bit jealous of Mary-Jane's burgeoning power of psychometry. When it first started after visiting the well, it was only snippets of emotions she could pick up from touching an object or a person. Now she could "see" into people. Their memories played out in her mind like a movie, while my powers…

My eyes narrowed, and I pointed at the throw cushion laying on the floor. Keeping my attention zeroed in on it, I envisioned the cushion floating up in the air and settling next to my pillow. A buzzing sounded in my head as a current of energy zapped down my arm and into my finger. I strained harder, focusing. The pillow lifted on one side, wavering there for a few moments before flopping back down on the hardwood.

Shit. Mary-Jane was progressing in leaps and bounds. Shannon could "wish" a spell and she also could see spirits. But what about me? Why wasn't the magic of that well manifesting stronger inside me? Granted, I didn't practice as much as MJ or Shannon, but still.

I grabbed the throw cushion and hurled it at the bed.

SIX

Shannon

That evening...

"So what are you going to do, Shannon? I'd offer to loan you the money for the tax bill, but we took a hit recently with a big car repair." Mary-Jane's hand closed over mine on the table.

I'd told both of my friends about the tax bill as soon as they'd arrived for dinner. And true friends that they were, they were totally sympathetic. I managed a small smile as I answered MJ, "I'm going to have to get a job, I guess. But doing what?"

When neither of them came up with a suggestion, I made a wry grin and continued. "You think I could hang a red light over my door and try the world's oldest profession?" The look on their faces was priceless. I shrugged. "Naw. There's probably not a lot of demand for menopausal women."

"Stop it, Shannon! You do this all the time; you always try to make light of things, but I know this is bugging you!" Libby gave her head a shake before continuing, "Didn't you work as a reporter at a newspaper for a few years when you finished college? Maybe—"

Mary-Jane interrupted, "I know the editor of the weekly newspaper! Wayne and his wife never miss the Friday night special. I could ask if he needs any help? At least you'd be doing something you went to school for. Something you have experience with." Mary-Jane grinned. "Why not go see him and use me as a reference? It can't hurt."

"But I only did that job for two years! And that was over twenty years ago." As I sat there, I thought about those days at the *Pittsburgh Daily*. It was pretty cool. Sure there was the routine stuff of new businesses opening or local personalities making good, but there also were exciting things like robberies and fires and stuff like that.

Libby's voice yanked me back to the present. "It doesn't matter how long ago it was. You can still write and you're smart. The *Wesley Weekly* isn't exactly *The New York Times*. Harold would be lucky to have you write articles or cover local events. You'd get to know more people too!"

I nodded. "I'll go see him tomorrow. But if that doesn't pan out, is there anything at the hospital I could do? I'd clean the floors if I had to."

"We're barely holding our head above water now, Shannon. There's a hiring freeze, except for replacing Edith, the head nurse. She's retiring soon."

Mary-Jane leaned closer to Libby. "Edith is finally retiring! She's older than dirt. Are you going to try for that job? I'm sure it would mean more money."

Libby looked down at the table, toying with the napkin. "I'm not the only one who wants that job. Remember I told you about Jolene?"

I blinked a few times before gaping at Libby. "Jolene, as in the first-class bitch who undermines you every chance she gets? Don't tell me she stands a chance! If you had to report to her, you might as well quit now, Libby." I couldn't believe that Libby was able to put up with that woman's backstabbing, all the while trying to make herself look like God's gift to nursing.

"I'm not quitting. I can't. I need that job." Her eyes met mine. "We've all got problems to deal with. Mine is Jolene.

Yours is the tax office. And don't tell me that Devon had nothing to do with that, Shannon."

I couldn't argue with her. It was just too circumstantial. He wants my property, and reported me to the environmental office when I'd had problems with the septic in the fall. And now that's cleared up, the town was once more being a pain in the butt. How much influence did that bugger have here in Wesley?

Mary-Jane's face tightened and she blurted, "I wish this magic spell stuff could fix this! What good is it, if we can't use it to make our lives better? For you, Shannon and you, Libby?"

"Uh-uh. Don't go down that road, MJ." Libby rolled her eyes, before continuing, "We've seen how magic can go off the rails. Remember, use it with caution and for goodness' sake, do no harm!"

I nodded. "I get your point, MJ. I tried the protection spell this morning. And look what happens? Right after, I get this news about the tax bill. So much for protection. But I agree with Libby. Casting a spell on Devon or that Jolene would end up hurting us more when the powers that be, right themselves. Remember when I wished for Ass-hat to become impotent? No more spells or wishes like that!"

Mary-Jane's arms folded over her chest as she fixed me with a cold look. "Speaking of spells going awry, you need to remove that spell you put on me. It's causing problems between Ray and me. Not all of the spell, but that part that makes me like a cat in heat when I work out. That's got to go."

My jaw dropped. "Are you serious?" She nodded back with an expression on her face that told me she was waaay more than serious; she was peeved at me. I took her hand. "Oh, man, MJ! I had no idea that this was becoming a problem for you. I'm so, so sorry about that. You look fantastic, by the way." My gaze drifted to the side, trying to recall what I'd read in the magic book. Could I reverse that spell?

When I was silent for a few beats, MJ sat back, snapping her mouth shut. "You can't do it, can you? I don't even need to touch your hand to know that look on your face, Shannon.

You 'wished' that spell on me but you have *no idea* how to remove it!"

"No!" Libby gawked at me in horror. "Maybe if we all work on removing it? You know, the power of three and all that?"

Shit! I could barely cast a spell, let alone reverse one! I got up to start clearing the table, forcing a smile. "We'll make that the focus of our ceremony tonight—reversing that spell I wished on MJ. In addition, we can also ask for help for me finding a decent job and for Libby to land that promotion."

This magic stuff had to be good for something, aside from causing problems.

SEVEN

Libby

"Hurry up, Libby!"

At Shannon's voice, I turned from peering into the darkness of the forest. I couldn't help but think of that wild bobcat. It felt like something was watching the three of us as we walked along the side of Shannon's house, heading for the backyard. I was really glad that we weren't going to go traipsing off into the woods, to do this at the Witching Well, not with that wild bobcat hanging around.

I picked up the pace, huffing a reply, "If that bobcat attacks us…so help me, Shannon!" When I rounded the corner, Shannon was bent over, lighting the papers in the fire pit while Mary-Jane held the lantern-covered, white candle.

I shuddered, pulling the sides of my wool cape closer, when a gust of wind swept over my shoulders. The sky was dark except for the myriad of stars peeking through the clouds scuttling across the sky. Again, I cast a glance over at the trees, half expecting that cat to come bounding out.

Mary-Jane stepped closer to the fire, holding her hand out to warm it. "Of all the animals to have as a 'familiar'—a bobcat? That's what your aunt thinks it is, a familiar? I wonder if I'll get one? But with my luck it would be just an ordinary cat, and, of course, you know, Ray is allergic to cats."

As I stepped close to the fire, I sized up the branches that had caught the flame. If that cat came out of those woods, I would grab the nearest burning stick and chase it away!

Mary-Jane reached for my hand. "I think we're getting better at this ritual. Every time we do this, that magical part of me feels stronger somehow, like I'm part of something so much larger than me."

Shannon nodded. "Yeah, we're somehow bonding more with the universe."

MJ made a smirk. "I don't know about bonding with the universe, but my sex life's sure picked up!"

I let out a sigh. Yep, MJ's feeling randy. "Anything else, sweetie?" I asked. "Besides your excursions to pound town?"

My sarcasm didn't even register with her. "Yeah!" she replied. "Y'know how spells work better when they rhyme? I find myself thinking of rhymes and verses to use when I'm at work, cutting vegetables, or cooking."

When Shannon took my other hand, she looked over at MJ. "The Grimoire is starting to make sense. I'm even able to read Alice Johnston's entries, which were just chicken scratches at first. It's like poetry, the words and incantations she wrote about. And I totally get what you mean by empowerment. But with me, it's more a peaceful state after we do the Esbat."

It was like I was the odd woman out here with the two of them gushing over their growth and progress with the craft. As for my own Grimoire, I hadn't written anything in it since before Christmas. I needed to make more time for it.

With her free hand, Shannon picked a bundle of dry sage from the satchel at her side and held it high, looking up at the dark sky.

"We offer sweet sage to purify our way, Divine Mother." She tossed it onto the fire, where it caught immediately, flaring up and filling the air with a pungent smell.

Mary-Jane and I murmured, "So mote it be." That word,

"mote" had jarred me at first, but now it rolled off my tongue easily. At least that was something that I'd learned and mastered from my limited reading.

Next up was a small mason jar of water. After removing the lid, Shannon held it before us. "Water, a pure and clear element. Our intentions are sent. Clear and focused, flowing and merging together. In that spirit and by the freshness of the new moon, we ask the Mother's help. From Mary-Jane, lift the spell. Abundant blessings and good fortune to me and Libby in our pursuits of employment. Safeguard this sacred property."

As she spoke, my mind zeroed in on my own magical abilities. *Shower your gift upon me to serve you and help others,* I thought to myself.

It was a mantra that I silently intoned in my mind. I hadn't told MJ and Shannon of my growing frustration that the gifts bestowed by the Witching Well had somehow passed me by while flourishing in both of them.

Shannon's hand tipped, and water poured slowly out, hissing when it hit the edge of the flames and sending out a ribbon of steam.

"So mote it be."

I reached in my pocket and withdrew the satchel of soil, holding it high. "Divine Mother of us all, we offer you earth, a symbol of our connection to your bounty and protection. We ask for your blessings for us and our families." With that, I emptied the bag into the flames.

I turned to Mary-Jane and saw her smile as she held the candle aloft and began her own incantation. "As bright as this flame, as hot with purpose and desire, we give thanks for your blessings. For my psychic gift in 'reading' objects and people. For Shannon's gift of communing with the dead and for…" She peered at me.

"Uh…for my…" My shoulders dropped before I continued. "It's coming, okay? I've been able to make small objects move slightly with my mind. It's a start at telekinesis."

Her eyebrows rose. "For Libby's power, such that it is. May it grow stronger and expand in ways that serve you."

We finished with silence, each of us gazing up at the sky. Finally, Shannon bent to toss armfuls of snow onto the fire pit. A cloud of smoke and vapor swirled around us and we stepped back.

Mary-Jane giggled. "Now for my second favorite part—hot toddies in front of Shannon's fireplace." When Shannon shot her a dirty look, she quickly added, "It's the sisterhood, our bonding, and the development of our spirits. Admit it, you enjoy that part too."

I followed behind Mary-Jane as she stepped away, going back to the front of the house. When a sharp snap, like a branch breaking, sounded in the trees twenty feet away, my heart leaped into my mouth. I wasted no time catching up to MJ.

We hurried inside, but Shannon had paused, standing next to the door outside. She bent to pick something up before joining us. In her hand was a rolled-up newspaper.

Mary-Jane swept her cloak off and smiled over at Shannon. "That's the newspaper I was telling you about! I didn't think they delivered it out this far and—"

"At night." Shannon's mouth fell open. "This is the first time it's ever been left at the house." She stepped over to the door and opened it a crack, peering at the yard. When she came back inside, she shook her head as she slipped the rubber band from the rolled-up newspaper.

When the paper spread open, I noticed smudges and small punctures in the sheet of text. It looked like it had come from a dumpster. "Are those bite marks?"

Shannon's eyes flew to meet mine. "I think Bob left this. It's a sign, I think. I'm going to get a job at the newspaper office!"

EIGHT

Libby

My eyes narrowed, peering at Shannon. "Hang on! Do you seriously think that bobcat left the newspaper here for you? While we were outside at the fire?" Shit! I'd been right that the cat had been lurking in the trees watching us! But seriously! Delivering a newspaper? Was Shannon reading too much into this?

Shannon practically gushed, "Of course! He left me pine cones, so why wouldn't he leave this? According to Aunt Maeve, his job is to protect me. I can't think of a better sign that my problems will be soon solved."

Mary-Jane plucked the newspaper from Shannon's hands. "That's so cool! If you're right about this, maybe the lewd aspect of your spell will be lifted from me too!" A big grin spread on her face. "Esbat ceremony calls the powers of the universe to help us. Plus, we're getting so much better at all this! I can't wait till tomorrow morning to test this out. Maybe I'll be able to do the run without wanting to jump my husband. I'll get my life back to normal."

My mind was still on that bobcat out there, slinking around. "Shannon, promise me you won't go anywhere close to that cat! I know you think it's magical—a familiar—but to me, it's a wild animal! I've seen the damage done to people who get too close to bears and raccoons and—even squirrels can give you a nasty bite!"

"You worry too much!" Shannon took her cape off and hung it on the hook by the door. "It's not like I'm going to let it in the house and curl up next to it!" She led the way to the kitchen. "Let's have a drink by the fire. Tell me what's going on with your telekinesis. MJ and I will help you with that."

I held my tongue as I watched her pour the whiskey and add lemon, cinnamon, and hot water. There'd been just a little too much condescension in her attitude about my magical abilities, feeble as they were.

To make matters worse, Mary-Jane started in, "It's all in having pure intention, Libby. You need to calm your mind so you're open to the power all around you—the earth, air, and water. Your problem is that *you* can't slow down. If you aren't at work, you're racing around the house, hovering over your kids and trying to control everything."

I took the warm drink from Shannon. "That's easy for you to say, MJ. You've got Ray looking after things at work and there's only Zoe at home. I'm the only bread-winner, and the sole parent of three teenagers, one of who constantly tries to test my last nerve."

I glanced at Shannon. "Even you, Shannon. I know this tax thing is throwing you off your game but… there's *only* you. Your kids are at school, and you're basically free to learn more and more about magic."

Shannon's voice was gentle when she replied, "Which is why we want to help you, Libby. I didn't mean to belittle you or your efforts." She led the way down the hall to the living room.

Mary-Jane murmured an apology as she followed me. "We're in this together. A sisterhood. That's all I meant, Libby."

Shannon took a spot in front of the fireplace. "I read something last night about power being magnified when we come together and act with one purpose. Let's try this on you, Libby." She beckoned MJ, and the two of them stood on either side of me.

"We'll touch your back, Libby, while you focus on my drink on the coffee table. You're going to move it across the surface, using only your mind. Mary-Jane, envision your energy flowing into Libby to help her."

I felt the warmth of their palms under the skin of my shoulders and my eyes closed, trying to think of nothing but that glass. I could feel the smoothness of the glass, smell the warm, spicy scent fill my nostrils, and see the bright lemon slice in the amber liquid.

It started as a low hum, vibrating in my head. My hand rose when a zap of energy sizzled through my shoulder and down my arm. My face tightened as I pictured it sliding to the edge of the table. My eyes opened wider, and I felt a wave of energy tickling and sparking in my fingers.

At first, the tumbler shook, sending ripples through the whiskey. It seemed to wobble a long time before the glass shot across the table, stopping just short of the edge!

I blinked a few times, hardly believing my eyes! I'd done it! This was the first time that my efforts had produced anything like that!

Mary-Jane squealed, "Yay! I knew you could!" She rubbed my back before pulling me closer into a hug. "How'd it feel?"

I grinned. "Like getting an electrical shock but not painful. Just the buzzing in my arm and fingers." My hand rose, and I gaped at it, noticing the slight tremor in my fingers. "My fingertips are kind of numb, yet so alive at the same time!"

It was an intoxicating feeling...of *power*! Pointing at the glass once more, I repeated the process, focusing on drawing the glass closer. This time, it responded immediately, sweeping over the wooden surface to rest in its original spot.

Shannon reached for the glass and held it high. "To Libby! We knew you just needed a nudge. There's no stopping you now, lady!"

I stared at the glass and said in a whisper, "Did that just

happen?"

"Yes!" squealed MJ, jumping up and down, clapping her hands.

"No. Way!" I said. I stepped back from the coffee table. "No. Freaking. Way."

Shannon nudged me. "Way." She gestured at the glass. "Do it again, but move it to the left."

"Center yourself, Libs," Mary-Jane said in a tone of voice I hadn't heard her use before. "Try to fold your mind back into the state it was when you moved it," she continued. Her voice was comforting, like she was reading a bedtime story or settling down a skittish colt. "Close your eyes for a moment, and see the glass in your mind's eye…then open your eyes, and move it to the left…" Her voice trailed off. It was like listening to one of those meditation apps online.

I closed my eyes. Immediately, I saw the tumbler in my mind. Right down to the drop of condensation running down the side, and the tiny chip on the rim. I opened my eyes like a window, and gestured at the glass, gently pointing to it.

When I felt that zappy pulse in my arm again, I flicked my finger to the left, telling the glass—oddly becoming one with it somehow—to just move two inches to the left.

This time I felt a teeny pulse *back*, and the glass slid over.

"Whoa," I breathed. "I think…I'm not sure, but I *think* that glass told me 'okay' or something." When I felt MJ and Shannon stir, I hushed them with a wave of my other hand. They stilled.

I pointed again at the glass. '*Okay, my friend,*' I thought, '*One more time, all right?*' I gestured to the right.

You ever launch a rubber band from your fingertip? You pull back and stretch it, and just when you let it fly, you feel the rubber band sort of "kick" itself off your finger? The connection between me and that glass was something like that. I'm not saying the glass was "conscious" or anything, okay? I'm not crazy. I'm not saying it responded to me.

But…I'm also *not* saying it didn't.

It slid to the right. I let out a small laugh of delight. Like a child who was able to tie her shoes for the first time all by herself! I gestured to the left, and the glass zipped over. I laughed again.

There *was* some kind of connection! I felt a sense of joy between me and that glass as I played with it. It was wonderful. I slid it back and forth, then up and down the table a bunch more times.

Finally, I lowered my hand.

"Can we talk now?" Mary Jane asked. When I nodded dumbly, she let out another squeal. "Omigod! Omigod! That's sooo cool!" She was clapping her hands, then patting me, all the time hopping up and down.

I rolled my eyes at her and then got kind of wobbly on my feet.

Shannon was at my side in a flash. "Let's sit down, Libs," she said. "The first time you pull something off like this is pretty overwhelming."

"Yes!" gushed MJ. "It's awesome! Like the first time 'doing it' when we were kids, right? The whole world is totally different now!"

I lowered myself to the seat, chuckling. Leave it to the group nympho to make that comparison.

But she wasn't completely wrong.

"I'll be honest." Shannon looked at me and then MJ. "This afternoon when I got that news about the tax bill, I was discouraged. The first morning I try the protection ritual, and then that bill shows up."

"That was a serious bummer, all right." Mary-Jane's face lit up. "But this? This was amazing, Shannon. To see Libby—"

"I know. Our intention—Libby's intention—was strong. That's why she was able to do this. But we can't control everything, ladies. Other people have their own intentions. They also have free will. That is always going to play a part, sometimes   foiling   us."

I huffed. "And then there's the universe after we've 'wished' a spell. It can create havoc; offshoots with crazy consequences, when it bends to accommodate us. Look at what happened with you and your ex, Shannon."

She nodded. "For sure. But I think that kind of thing will happen less frequently as we ground ourselves in ritual and knowledge. I guess what I'm trying to say is sometimes shit happens and that's just life. Magic isn't going to make our lives perfect."

"But it certainly makes it interesting." Mary-Jane's eyes twinkled as she gazed at us over the rim of her glass.

I raised mine in a silent toast. Tonight had certainly proved that.

NINE

Shannon

The next day (Tuesday)

"Hey, Shannon!"

A tap on the window followed, yanking me back to reality. When I turned my head, Devon Booker smiled back at me as his hand signaled for me to roll the window down.

A knot twisted in my belly when I looked at him. I couldn't help thinking it was because of him that I'd gotten that stupid tax bill. And now I had to interrupt everything I wanted to achieve and get a job.

But as quick as that thought went through my head, I remembered how he'd punched out Ass-hat the night he'd crashed my Halloween party. And Devon had even plowed my driveway out a few times. He wasn't all bad, despite MJ's and Libby's opinion. Still, it wouldn't hurt to be careful in any dealings I had with him.

I pressed the button to lower the car window. "Hi, Devon. How are you doing?" His smile widened, deepening the dimple in his cheek while his blue eyes crinkled in the corners. He certainly looked to be in a good mood this fine morning!

"Great! What brings you to town? Did you need a break from all your renos?" He shoved his hands in his pockets and bent lower, his face only inches from mine. "I haven't seen you since before Christmas. I meant to call you this week, now that the holidays are over."

A smirk twitched. "Hoping I changed my mind about selling my place to you?"

His head bobbed back. "No. I mean, yes, I'd still love to buy your property, of course. But since that's not going to happen, I'd like to be friends. I thought we could have dinner or even a coffee sometime."

I paused and peered at him. He looked sincere enough. He was older than Steve, more my age, give or take. And like Steve, he was in really good shape. "Sure, why not? I've got to talk to Wayne Silver at the newspaper right now, but I'm free afterward. We could have lunch if you want."

"That works. I've got a meeting soon, but I'll be done in an hour." He turned and glanced at the window with the words *Wesley Weekly* etched in the glass." Why are you seeing Wayne? Putting up a classified ad or something?"

"Nothing that simple, I'm afraid. I hoping he'll hire me as a reporter or even a stringer. I need to get a job at least until the weather turns and I can get back to fixing the cabins." That's as much as he needed to know. I wasn't getting into the nine-thousand-dollar tax reassessment.

"I didn't know you were interested in working in news—if you can call the *Wesley Weekly* news, that is. More like a journal of events in town than anything groundbreaking. But if it will help, I could put in a good word. I'm one of the main advertisers in Wayne's rag."

"I won't tell him you called his paper a rag. But sure, I'll take any help to land me this gig." I grabbed my purse, and Devon stepped aside as I opened the car door.

His eyebrows rose, and his head bobbed back taking in my dress coat and the thigh-high boots. "Whoa! This isn't the Big Apple or *The New York Times*, Shannon. You clean up nice!

How about I meet you at MJ's restaurant when you're through here?"

"That works. I want to chat with Mary-Jane anyway, so I'll meet you there when your meeting is finished." My eyes narrowed, but I smiled to let him know I was kidding when I asked, "So, meeting with people to acquire more property? Pretty soon you'll own all the utilities, too, just like in Monopoly."

"Yeah, but you'll still own Boardwalk and Park Place." He held his hand up like a traffic cop. "But I'm not going down that road again. Still, my meeting should prove to be lucrative."

Walking over to the sidewalk, I smiled up at him. "So lunch is on you, then? Remind me to order the most expensive item. And dessert!"

"How about we flip for it?" At the look of shock on my face, he laughed. "I'd be happy to buy you lunch, either way. Bread and water?"

I poked his arm. "Steak with all the works! Now, wish me luck! I really want to nail this interview." I looked over at the large window with the words *Wesley Weekly* etched on the glass. It was a hole-in-the-wall outfit tucked between the dry cleaner on one side and an optometrist shop on the other. Small-town, USA.

"You've got this, Shannon. You don't need luck." His hand rose and he crossed his fingers. "But just in case. I'll see you in an hour, and you can tell me how you smoked old Wayne with your résumé and talent."

"Bullshit baffles brains?" When he mocked me with a frown, I added, "Your BS, my brains. Not Wayne Silver's." I stepped over to the door of the newspaper and hesitated, smiling back at Devon. "See you later."

***

When I arrived at MJ's restaurant twenty minutes later, I stopped at the bar before even taking a table. Ray looked up from behind the large oak bar, pausing in his task of polishing glasses.

"Can I get you a drink, Shannon? MJ didn't tell me you'd be here today." The smile on his lips never reached his eyes. Shit. It looked like he was in a mood. Were he and MJ still arguing? That didn't bode well for the spell being reversed for MJ as I'd hoped.

"Hi, Ray. I'll have a Jack Daniels with ice. Is MJ here? She came into work today, didn't she?" I slipped my coat off and looped it over my arm, watching his face.

He turned away to grab the bottle of Jack but not before I noticed the roll of his eyes. "Yeah. She's in the kitchen, working for a change. I'll let her know you're here and send her out."

When he set the drink on the bar, I smiled sweetly at him. "That's okay, you're busy. I'm supposed to be meeting Devon Booker for lunch. I'll just pop into the kitchen to see MJ before he gets here. Will you let me know when Devon arrives, Ray?"

When he nodded, I grabbed the glass and made my way, threading through the rows of tables until I came to the kitchen entry. When I stepped through, the smell of onions, grilling meat and a radio blasting out old hits from the eighties met me. Mary-Jane, in her kitchen whites, with a chef's hat perched on her head, was gyrating to the music as she stirred the contents of a large pot.

"Hey, Chef Boyardee! How's it shaking?" I laughed as I walked over to her, bending to sniff the contents of the pot. "Mmmm. I'll have me some of that!"

She turned the music down, and her eyes were like saucers. "How'd it go? Did he hire you?"

I shrugged. "He said he wants to hire full-time help, but he agreed to give me a shot part-time. I'm supposed to write a piece about the Feb Festival. He thinks an outsider's perspective might be interesting."

"So you going to keep looking? A part-time job's not going to cut it with the taxes."

"I think I have to. I'm going to visit the town office after lunch." I leaned in closer and looked over my shoulder at the door before asking in a low voice, "How'd you make out this morning with the run? You're here, so that's a good sign."

She sighed. "Good news and bad news. When I woke up I didn't feel the urgency to get dressed and go running. But I did anyway. I *had* to find out if exercising still made me horny as hell. I only made it a block before it happened again. The lust kicked in and I gave up."

"Damn it. Well, at least you're not obsessed with running like you were, right?" She nodded, and I added, "Maybe we needed to repeat what we'd done last night to remove the hedonistic side effect."

"I went home and had a cold shower…a long, cold shower. But it helped. I'm here, aren't I? At least Ray is off my back about that." She sampled the broth she was simmering and set the spoon aside. "After all the weight I've lost, it kills me to think I have to give up exercising, Shannon. I feel so good and I'm finally a size *twelve*."

"You won't put on weight! We'll keep trying. In the meantime, don't go running…or go to the gym. We'll figure this out." When I saw the look of doubt cloud her eyes, I added, "We helped Libby, didn't we? We will fix this for you, MJ."

"I hope so. Have you had lunch yet?"

"I'm having lunch with Devon Booker. I ran into him earlier. I know you and Libby aren't that fond of him but he's been okay to me. It's just lunch."

"Okay to you? Come on! He tried to have your house condemned last fall!"

"I'm not sure that was his idea, MJ. I think that the plumber guy ratted me out to the township because he was pissed off I didn't give him that forty-thousand-dollar contract to replace my septic system."

"Oh yeah? You sure about that?" When I stayed silent, she continued. "Be careful around that guy, Shannon. I know we sound like a broken record but we know Devon better than you do. I get that he's gorgeous and all that but so are poinsettias. But eat one and you'll get sick as a dog." She sliced a wedge from the apple pie on the shelf next to her and popped it in her mouth.

Oh shit. For months nothing but fat-free, nutritious food, and she was snacking on sweets?

The door behind me swung open and Ray stuck his head in. "Devon's here now, Shannon." With that, he left, never saying a word to MJ or even looking at her. My gaze shot to Mary-Jane. Things were still strained between the two of them.

She nodded. "He's still being pissy. But part of it is worrying about the business. I guess I'll have to balance my time better, show up to work more. That should make him happy."

Shaking her head, she sighed. "Sometimes I wonder if it's worth it, y'know. It's almost like he resents how much weight I've lost, after years of teasing me about being chubby. I don't think he knows what he wants. Does he even love me anymore?"

My heart wrenched seeing her like this, so discouraged. "I'm sure he does, MJ. We'll get this all sorted out, and things will be better between the two of you." I leaned in and gave her a quick hug. "I'd better get out there. I'll call you later, okay?"

She nodded and turned back to stirring the pot. As I walked across the room, heading for the window seat where Devon was seated, I looked over at Ray. This was causing problems between the two of them. There had to be some way to reverse that spell.

When Devon saw me coming, he jumped up from his chair and darted around the table to hold my seat out for me. He smiled. "Well, if it isn't Lois Lane. How'd you do? But before you say anything, this is off the record, okay? I don't want to be reading about myself in the *Wesley Weekly,* with some hit piece."

I smirked at him. "Too late for that. That was the sample piece that sold him on my talent. You should expect protestors outside your office tomorrow." When his mouth fell open, I grinned. "Kidding. That's for the 'Lois Lane' remark." When I was seated, I leaned over the table. "What the heck is the Feb Festival? I'm supposed to write a piece about it."

He laughed as he took a seat. "It's just the most talked about smorgasbord of fun you'll see this side of Vegas. It's a combo of Valentine's Day and Ground Hog Day all rolled into one syrupy package. I was going to ask you to go with me."

I took a long sip of my drink, smiling at him over the rim. "I'm working, I'm afraid."

"Your loss. By the time that rolls around, I'm going to be even more wealthy. My meeting went well, thanks for asking."

The server, an attractive woman in her mid-thirties appeared at our table, sidling close to Devon when she asked, "Are you ready to order? The special today is brown butter, hollandaise-fried chicken."

Devon's eyebrows rose, questioning me with a look. "Sounds good to me. Or are you holding out for steak?"

I looked over at the waitress. "I'll have a garden salad with soup de jour, please." I'd never seen this woman working here before. I couldn't help wondering when they'd hired her. Too bad I missed *that* job opportunity.

She nodded and asked, "Another round of drinks, Mr. Booker?"

"Not for me, thanks." As I spoke I couldn't help but notice the smile she flashed at Devon. Well, why not, I suppose. He was eligible and usually looked like he'd stepped off the cover of *GQ* magazine. Broad shoulders, full head of dirty blonde hair, with a delightful bit of muss, and not a hint of a potbelly; not bad for a guy in his forties.

I took a deep breath and forced a smile, turning to him again. "So the Feb Festival, huh? I'd better get researching this gala. Wayne asked if I could submit a piece by the end of the month. I'm kind of excited to get back into writing. Although I might still try to find another job. I was hoping for more than what Wayne can pay me."

Devon stared at me silently for a few moments before he spoke, "Do you do office work? Any bookkeeping? I could use some help." He leaned closer, folding his arms on the table. "It would only be a few days a week. I detest doing correspondence and filing."

"Seriously? You're not just saying this to help me out, are you? Creating some make-work project?" This was too good to be true. I watched his face closely. There was no way I was taking his charity, even if he tried to cloak it in some made-up job.

He rolled his eyes and chuckled. "Come over to my office after lunch and see for yourself. That's why I usually make a point of meeting clients in restaurants or at their place. You can't find the chairs in my office buried under the stacks of files."

My eyes opened wider as I stared at him. It sure sounded like he could use some help. "I have one stop to make after lunch and then I can pop by. There's only one thing left to ask. How much will you pay me?"

"How much do you want? The last person who worked for me charged me fifteen dollars per hour. I could go as high as twenty if that works for you." He sat back when the waitress appeared with our lunches.

It gave me time to calculate. If I worked thirty hours a week, I would have the tax bill covered in a few months. And maybe sooner if the newspaper gig panned out.

It was hard to keep the excitement from my voice when I answered him, "Twenty works. But this will only be for a few months, Devon. I want to get back to the renos by the end of March."

He extended his hand across the table to shake mine. "Deal. Let's shake on it before you see my office. You might want to charge me forty an hour after seeing that rat's nest."

I hesitated in taking his hand, even pulling mine back an inch. "Hang on. Forty?" But his hand arced out to close over mine. "Okay, you've got a deal, Devon."

TEN

An hour later, I walked into the town office to arrange a payment schedule for the taxes I apparently now owed. I followed the sign directing me to the area where everything from fishing licenses to property taxes was handled. There, standing before the high counter, I could see a series of desks where people from different departments worked alongside each other. As I waited for the clerk to finish with the person she was serving, I spotted Cynthia Granger when she turned from a small bank of filing cabinets.

I smiled. She sure looked a lot different from when I'd last seen her in her Wonder Woman costume at my Halloween party. Today, except for her striking blue eyes and perfect porcelain skin, she looked like any other thirtysomething office drone in a white blouse and skirt. Despite only meeting me that evening of the party, she'd showed kindness to me when the other partygoers had deserted like rats fleeing a sinking ship. I'd thought of her a few times after that and had intended to call her to have coffee or lunch sometime.

She must have sensed me looking at her because her head turned and our eyes met. I waved, about to beckon her over, but she looked away and returned to her desk. My cheeks heated up as my hand drifted slowly down. She'd snubbed me!

But not only that, from the hard glint in her eye and the way her mouth had snapped shut, she acted like she was angry or something. What the hell?

When the clerk finished with the old man she'd been serving, I spent the next ten minutes giving her the first check and arranging payment on the balance. But all the while, I couldn't help but wonder what was up with Cynthia. I was a pretty good judge of character, or so I thought! Before I left, I looked over at Cynthia once more. Nope. She kept her head down, busy with whatever, never giving me a look. It was more disappointing than anything as I knew she was the granddaughter of one of my aunt's best friends. I had thought *we* could be friends as well.

Devon's office wasn't far away so I decided to walk. It would give me time and fresh air to clear my head. I'd have to ask Libby about Cynthia. Maybe she knew why the young woman was acting as if someone had pissed in her cornflakes.

As I walked down the block, I looked up at the building where Devon worked. It was basically a three-story brick box, with a few windows on each floor, overlooking the street below. But rather than blinds, curtains were edging the sides of the windows. So it looked like his office didn't encompass those floors.

As I pushed open the door that said Booker Real Estate and Development, I must have set off a buzzer because he was right out. "Good! I'm glad you didn't change your mind, Shannon. Come in out of the cold."

"Gladly!" I squeezed by him and looked around the spacious room. My mouth fell open seeing the big leather sofa, the chair, and the coffee table, with magazines stacked neatly, all sitting on a plush burgundy carpet. What the hell was he talking about? The place was as immaculate as a dentist's office!

As if he'd read my mind, he chuckled. "Follow me. Stay close as I don't want to lose you in the jungle, okay?"

"Lead on, Macduff, or should I say, Bwana?" I shook my head before stepping through the door he'd just opened.

Words escaped me as my gaze took in his desk piled high with files and papers, the laptop perched precariously close to the edge, and the binders and books on a side table. Even the top of a large metal file cabinet was littered with what looked to be surveys and site plans.

When I spun around to look at him, he cleared his throat, trying hard not to meet my eyes. I'd seen that look before! Only it was on my son's face when I'd read him the riot act about the disaster zone that was his bedroom; yeah, he looked like a sheepish teenager.

"I'm afraid this isn't the worst of it, Shannon." He crooked a finger and turned to lead the way back to the reception area to another door off to the side. He opened it with a flourish. "The boardroom."

This time I was more prepared. Of course, you couldn't see any of the surface of the long wooden table for the stacks of papers and site maps. What I wasn't prepared for was the wavery, shimmering figure of an elderly woman who stepped right out of the wall at the side of the room. As I stared, her form became clearer, revealing a prim lace collar topping a simple black dress that ended mid-calf. With her gray hair swept up in a severe bun, I was reminded of the grim Victorian-era women in sepia photos. But what set me back on my heels were the narrow, dark eyes glaring at Devon. Not me, just Devon.

This was the third ghost I'd seen since my visit to the well. Of course, there was my regular visitor, Aunt Maeve, who was anything but scary. Even the old guy in one of the cabins watching me work at painting had only managed to startle me. But this one, this angry specter sent an icy chill up my spine and froze me in my spot.

"Shannon? Do you still want the job, or am I hopeless?"

I jerked at the sound of Devon's voice behind me. Spinning around to face him, I blurted, "Of course! It's just, it's just overwhelming." I turned to see if the old crone was still there. But only the gray walls and the disaster that was his table met my eyes.

Devon fell into place beside me, peering at me. "Are you okay? You look a bit pale, Shannon. Would you like a glass of water or a pop?"

"I'm fine. But maybe some water?" I couldn't keep my gaze from the spot on the wall where the ghost had stepped through. Who was she? The building wasn't that old, maybe only fifty years or so. And it didn't look like it had ever been any sort of residence, aside from what were probably apartments on the two top floors.

"I'll be right back with your water. I'll print a spreadsheet of my projects. I think this looks worse than it is. Have a seat, and when I return we can go through it together." Devon lifted some books from one of the chairs and then left me on my own.

As soon as the door closed, I stared at where she had been and whispered, "I saw you. I can see spirits. Who are you?" I suppressed a shiver and clutched the collar of my coat to my neck. This room wasn't nearly as warm as the others had been, or was it *her* influence?

The air beside me wavered, and her slender form once more materialized. She stood directly in front of me, peering at me as if *I* were the oddity, instead of her. Her mouth opened and closed a few times before faint words emerged.

"Who am *I*? The real question is who are *you*? Only one person has ever seen me and that was my brother before he passed on." Her eyes were so dark as to appear like black orbs as she drifted closer. Her hand rose, coming closer to my face.

I pulled back, avoiding her touch. "I'm Shannon Burke. Maeve Burke's niece."

Her head fell back and her face softened into a smile. "Of course. That explains it."

At the sound of Devon's footsteps outside, her face grew hard before she shimmered and faded. When the door opened, I blinked, staring at Devon. Whoever that spirit was, she sure hated Devon.

ELEVEN

Mary-Jane

Later that day...

W hat is it, Mary-Jane? Do you need something?" Ray sighed as he looked up from his laptop, exasperation etched in every line on his forehead. The stacks of invoices and receipts on the wooden desk in front of him were a wall of defense, that lately he'd spent longer and longer retreating behind.

The muscles in my neck tightened at his condescending tone. But I took a deep breath and forced a smile. This tension between us had to stop. Not only did we have a daughter to consider, but there was also a lot of history and good times that we had to get back to. Back when things were fun and we laughed more.

"I've got the kitchen closed for the night. I'm heading home soon, but I thought the two of us could have a nightcap together first."

He dry-scrubbed his face in his hands for a moment, and when he looked over at me, there was sadness in his eyes. "You go ahead and get yourself one if you want. I have to finish the books…" His voice trailed off and he stood up. "You know what? I *will* have a drink with you. This can wait."

I could hardly believe my eyes when he walked over and placed his hands on my arms, gazing at me gently.

"I'm sorry for blowing a gasket yesterday at you. You didn't deserve that. It's this place. I worry about surviving this winter lull. I'm glad you came in today, MJ."

The regret and love radiating from his hands on me melted the anger I'd felt all day. "I'm sorry, too, Ray. I hate arguing with you." My hand rose to cup his cheek, "We'll be okay though. Next month is the Feb Festival which always helps our business. Worst case, we take a loan out to float us till spring."

He put his arm over my shoulder as we walked from the office. My gaze lingered on the dining room, the chairs sitting upside down on linen-covered tables, the low booths next to plate-glass windows, and the amber light reflected in the mirror above the bar. The two of us had put our blood, sweat, and tears into making this successful. We'd been through worse times.

As Ray poured our drinks, he glanced over at me. "Old Man Cousins isn't doing very well, from what I heard today. The cancer is back."

I took a seat on the barstool and sighed. "That's a shame. He fought so hard, I hoped he would beat it." Not only was Ed Cousins the owner of the building, but he was also a pillar of the community, his family being some of the town's founders. But more importantly, he was a true gentleman, with always a kind word or a corny joke.

Ray handed me the glass of Jack Daniels. "As sad as that is, I can't help but wonder what's going to happen to this building when he passes. His two kids are settled in Albany. Will they keep the building as it is or will they sell it?"

My hand holding the glass paused midway to my lips. Shit. I hadn't thought of that. I'd always assumed things would just go on the way they had for the last twenty years. If they sold it…

A picture of Devon Booker, standing outside the building with a man and woman that morning, popped into my head.

They'd been talking and looking up at the top floors of the building, which were currently apartments rented to two young families. Of course I knew Ed's kids, Barry and Laurie, although they were years ahead of me in high school. They'd left Wesley right after graduating college. Could those two people bundled up in parkas and scarves have been them?

"Now we're on the same page, MJ. If the heirs sell the building, who knows what's going to happen to the rent? We're fine in the summer. However, if they increase it, there's no way we can survive." Ray shrugged before draining his glass. "But maybe I'm worrying over nothing."

"Maybe. Let's try to stay positive. I'll work harder, but in the meantime, we might consider putting some more ads in the paper. Anything to muster up some more business." There was no way I was going to tell him about seeing Devon Booker with those two people. First of all, I might be wrong, and second, why shoulder Ray with more worry?

"We'll think of something to bring people out. Maybe expand the daily specials and reduce the price. We make more on the bar, anyway. The important thing is to bring people in." He let out a chuckle. "If every weekend held the same sense of fun and community as Feb Festival, we'd be laughing."

I sipped my drink, pondering his words. Sure, the food was good and the atmosphere was as elegant as Wesley could support, but there had to be something that would entice people from the comfort of their homes in the dead of winter.

"We need something fun, like dancing or dinner theater." I slapped the bar with my hand and grinned at Ray. "Zoe's in the school play, *The Mousetrap*! Why couldn't they do it here? It would sure beat sitting in a crowded gym on hard seats, trying to hear anything from a squeaky sound system."

Ray's forehead furrowed as he listened. "You're onto something, MJ. A small stage can't be that hard to construct. We'd lose the use of about four tables at the end of the room, but if we packed the place, who cares? I'll go see the school tomorrow to see if they're interested in performing here."

"I know Zoe will be thrilled if they agree! She'll be a big

help in getting this off the ground. And then there's Shannon! Maybe she'll write a piece about it in the paper. She got a job there today."

"Perfect." Ray came around the bar and hugged me. "This is like when we were first starting out. Remember those times? It was fun back then." He nuzzled into my neck "So, is that offer you made yesterday still on the table, or better yet, in the shower, still open?"

I felt a thrill shudder through me. It had been a long time since I'd wanted sex without first running my ass off in my morning jog. Maybe the magic ritual at the fire was working. *Something* was working to bring us closer! Whatever! I'd take it.

***

The next morning I joined Ray as he outlined for Zoe our plans to host the school play with a dinner theater.

As I listened, standing at the stove flipping an omelet, the thought of running only entered my mind a few times. Sure, I was skipping the exercise, but reconnecting to Ray was way more important. There was no way I wanted to push my luck, getting my hormones raging and putting pressure on him.

Zoe gushed as I set her plate in front of her. "That could be so cool! Would you pay us?" She tucked a lock of long, blonde hair behind her ear and started eating.

"All the ice cream and desserts you swarm of locusts can eat. How's that?" Ray looked over at me and winked.

"Sounds like child labor, exploitation even." She scowled at her father before nodding. "Okay, but this means I get out of helping in the kitchen. You can't expect a production manager to be a dishwasher too!"

My eyebrows rose as I looked at my sassy, young daughter. "Production manager! Maybe your drama teacher will have something to say about that. Your father's going to see him this morning. You can catch a ride with him instead of taking the bus."

"No, that's okay. I'm getting a lift with Jack. I can't wait to tell him about this. He's also in the play, y'know." She went back to eating, concentrating on picking the onions out of it first.

There was something she wasn't saying. I could tell the way she avoided my eyes. I casually rested my hand on her shoulder. Much as I hated invading her privacy, as a mother, I needed to know more about her relationship with Libby's son Jack. They'd always been close, but how close?

I felt my cheeks warm as a flash of them snuggled on the sofa watching a movie popped in my head. But they were clothed and his sister, Dahlia, was in the chair next to them. That was good! Zoe was sixteen, and sooner or later I'd have to deal with her having sex, but hopefully not for a good long while.

As I smiled at her, I couldn't help thinking I was a TOTAL hypocrite. But my *obsession* with sex had only really happened after Shannon put that spell on me. And I wasn't going to focus on the problems that she'd caused in my marriage with that!

Ray stood up and kissed my cheek. "Well, I'd better get going if I'm going to see this Mr. Tremont before his classes begin. I'll see you at work. Don't forget to call Shannon."

A car horn sounded from outside, and Zoe jumped to her feet. "That's Jack! See you later, Mom."

As quick as breakfast started, it ended, with both of them heading for the door, leaving me standing alone. But it was a much better morning than the previous ones. I picked up my phone to ring Shannon. It was early, but she would be up— hopefully.

She answered on the third ring, sounding hoarse and groggy. "This better be good, MJ. I was having the most amazing dream and you interrupted it."

"It *is* good! Ray and I are, well, we're getting along again!"

"Whoopee. That couldn't wait? You had to wake me up—"

"Shush! We came up with an idea to pump new life into the restaurant. We're going to have a dinner theater! It's just the kids from school putting on *The Mousetrap,* but if it catches on, we'll try more; maybe hire professionals or alternate theater with live local music. Ray is meeting with the drama teacher this morning."

"Huh. That sounds pretty good. I'd love to have dinner while watching live theater. So you and Ray patched things up? Did he come around to your sexercise schedule or—"

"No. I'm laying off exercising for a while. If that spell reversal is working, it's as slow as molasses getting there. But that's not why I called. I want you to write a piece about our dinner theater. It'll give you a subject while giving us some free publicity." The last part came out as kind of a squee, I was so excited.

"Sure. I could do that. But I've got some news of my own! I'm working for Devon a few days a week helping him organize his office. The guy's a total slob. And guess what? There's an old lady ghost who showed up when I was there yesterday. She's got it in for Devon, let me tell you."

A knot of anger twisted my stomach as I listened. "You're working for Devon Booker? This is the same guy who had tried to manipulate you into selling your property to him. The same guy who'll do anything to get ahead. I wouldn't trust that guy farther than I can throw him."

"Hang on, MJ! It's a job! It's not like I'm marrying the guy! Besides, it worked out in the end. I proved that I can handle Devon. You sound like Steve right now, trying to tell me what to do."

"Maybe because we know Devon better than you, Shannon? We've seen him take advantage of desperate people buying their homes for a song and then building god-awful gated subdivisions for wealthy snobs. He's ruthless." Even though Devon was a regular customer at the restaurant entertaining clients, it didn't mean I had to like him. Shannon was making a mistake going anywhere near Devon Booker.

"Well, I'm not desperate, and I'm certainly not going to be manipulated by Devon." There was a pause before she added, "You didn't even ask me about the ghost woman. Instead of being excited for me, you go off on a tangent about Devon."

My eyes opened wider, hearing the subtle criticism that I

wasn't interested in her ghostly encounter. "Maybe when you reverse the spell on me, you know, the one that caused a big fight between Ray and I, maybe then I'll be interested in your ghost woman. Until then, cry me a river, Shannon."

"You didn't complain when you lost all the weight. And as I recall, you loved all the sex, another side benefit of the spell. You just need to be patient, MJ. Look, I've got things to do, like getting ready to go work for Devon. Don't worry, I'll write your puff piece about the dinner theater. I'll call you later."

With that, the connection was severed. I held my phone out, glaring at it. She'd hung up on me! And to minimize my financial problems… she'd even had the nerve to call it a "puff piece"! My jaw clenched tight. For two cents I'd give her a dose of her own medicine! See how she liked having someone disrupt HER life with some crazy spell.

Her words had really stung. And getting a serious case of the "hornies" when I exercised was…well, it was kind of embarrassing. I hadn't been to the gym in weeks. There was no way I wanted to be around ripped, handsome guys when I was in that state.

Huh! I'd like to see her get a taste of that embarrassment. See how she liked it, then! If she did, maybe she'd try harder to fix the spell she'd cast on me. My eyes narrowed as words danced in my mind:

'This day, let Shannon learn
A lesson she's rightly earned.
Embarrassment I hex
Her words that hide sex'

There. All those times I'd practiced spells, making the words rhyme as I worked in the kitchen had paid off. I'd come up with something to teach Shannon a lesson. But unlike Shannon, I'll remember the exact words I'd used and be able to reverse it. AFTER she reversed the spell she'd cast on me.

TWELVE

Libby

That same day...

"Wait up, Libby!"

I turned and saw Dr. Hawkins wave to me from where he'd parked his jeep in the hospital lot. He trod carefully, stepping wide over iced-over potholes, trying to catch up to where I waited.

"Take your time, Dr. Hawkins!" Considering he was pushing seventy, there was no way I wanted him to slip and break a leg.

When he stood next to me, his gloved hand closed over the sleeve of my coat. "I wanted to talk to you about the head nurse spot. We're scheduling interviews in two weeks, and I wanted to give you a heads-up."

Any morning cobwebs I had got blasted out with his words. "In two weeks?" It came out as a high squeak, so I took a deep breath, adding, "That's fast."

His jowls rippled when he nodded. "Edie is pushing her retirement date up. She wants to spend the rest of the winter in Florida with her son and his family." He scowled at the icy patch in front of us. "Can't blame her. Your only real competition is Jolene Barrymore. She's a strong candidate even if she doesn't have your years of experience."

My shoulders fell. I knew it would come down to this. And hearing Dr. Hawkins say that she was a strong candidate didn't help bolster my confidence. "Can you tell me who is on the hiring board; I mean, aside from yourself?"

Letting out a slow breath, he said, "Edie, of course. She's worked with all of the candidates and she's objective." His voice dropped lower, "Lance Struthers will be the third, deciding vote."

"What? The bean counter in admin? What would he know about it?" Shit. Lance was a penny-pinching accountant who would have us reusing needles if it wasn't against the law. What was worse was the fact we'd butted heads on more than a few occasions. I was pretty sure he'd favor Jolene, especially since she went out of her way to gush and compliment the jerk. She'd even baked cookies and distributed them to the office staff.

"The head nurse attends quarterly budget meetings with the hospital admin. So it's important to have Lance's input in hiring." He turned, his steel-blue eyes crinkling in the corners when he added, "You didn't hear any of this from me, Libby. The formal notice letting all the candidates know will be out at the end of the week."

"Thanks, Dr. Hawkins." My fingers slid along my lips, mimicking a zipper closing. But now that I knew, I'd have to hit the books I'd downloaded on hospital administration. The nursing part, even supervising and hiring, I knew I would breeze through. It was creating reports, schedules, and the administrative aspects where I was vulnerable.

Our paths diverged once we entered the building. He went to the second floor where administration and his office were located, while I went straight ahead to the locker room to hang up my coat. When I stepped in, Jolene was already there. She sat on a bench tying her sneakers, never acknowledging my presence till I murmured a hello.

She stood up, scooping streaked blonde hair into a ponytail as she looked at me. "Hello, Libby. I see they've scheduled us together again. I hope your kids don't need you at home again, and you'll actually finish the shift this time."

The muscles in my neck were a tight cable but I kept my voice even: "It was one shift, Jolene. And I only missed the last half hour. My kids—"

She cut me off with a wave of her hand. "Don't wanna know and I certainly don't care." She walked over to the door and paused, smiling sweetly. "I made sure Edie knew I had to take up the slack."

When she left, I rolled my eyes. *I'm sure you did, biotch! Anything to make me look bad before that interview for head nurse.* When I hung my coat on the hook, my gaze lingered on my hand for a moment. Now that I knew I could move objects with just my mind, there was probably a tray full of cotton swabs that could plug up her nasty cakehole. With just a thought...

Shit. I knew I wouldn't do that. But it was fun to dream. I sighed. Only twelve hours of putting up with Jolene's bullshit. Patience, Libby.

THIRTEEN

Shannon

That same day...

One good thing about working for Devon was that I could set my own hours; as long as I got five hours in, he didn't care when I showed up. I'd tried to return to sleep after my phone call with MJ, but she'd grated on my last nerve with her scolding that I was working for Devon. What did she take me for? I knew he could be devious, but it looked like he was trying to make amends, buying me lunch, and offering me a job.

Had MJ thought of me before they hired that new server in her restaurant? Nope. And yet she hadn't hesitated in asking me to write this puff piece about her dinner theater.

I turned off the coffeepot and then went to the door for my coat and boots. When I was bundled, I opened the front door and peeked out. No sign of Bob, so that was good. When I stepped out, my eye caught a brown envelope laying on the welcome mat. That was weird. My mail was usually delivered to the box at the end of the driveway.

I picked it up and noticed the smear of the return address

and the small puncture marks next to it. The letter looked official, from Amtrak? It was addressed to Mrs. Jane Thornley, 33 Muskrat Lane, Wesley. I held it up so the rays of the sun would give me some kind of clue as to the contents. Just a sliver of a five could be seen. A check? This was a pension check for Jane Thornley.

What the hell? Again, I stared at the puncture marks and how beat up the envelope was.

My mouth fell open.

Bob.

He'd left this for me. The punctures were suspiciously like teeth marks, and the smudged return address was from Bob's slobber. It hit me like a hammer. Bob had delivered an envelope containing a check because he was trying to help me. He knew I was under the gun with that tax bill.

A smile crept on my lips as I held my present. Aunt Maeve had said a familiar's job was to protect. Good old Bob had tried his best to do that. Too bad Bob didn't know anything about identity or even identity theft. I looked over at the woods beside my house.

"Can you rob a bank? Nice try, but this isn't going to cut it, Bob. Maybe next time bring me something I can actually use, okay?"

I tucked the envelope in my purse and proceeded to my car. That was one more thing now I'd have to do: deliver this envelope to Jane Thornley's house without her seeing me.

***

It was almost eleven by the time I walked into Devon's business. After hanging my coat up, as I was removing my boots, Devon called out from his office.

"Is that you, Shannon? I just made a pot of coffee, so help yourself."

"Thanks! Do you need a top-up?" I snickered, thinking of MJ's warning that Devon was devious and to be careful around him. Nothing sinister about his greeting or the offer of coffee. I stopped at the door to his office and peeked my head inside.

He looked up from his laptop and smiled. Just the way the light from the window hit him; his eyes were the deepest shade of blue I'd ever seen. A lock of hair curled on his forehead while the shadow of scruffy beard highlighted sculpted cheekbones.

"You are a sight for sore eyes, Devon. How can a guy as smokin' hot as you still be single?" My hand flew up to cover my mouth. *Shit*. Had I just said that? *Oh my God*.

He blinked a few times and his head tipped forward. "Uh…thanks. I think. Maybe I will have another coffee." He rose, still looking at me like I'd dropped out of the sky, as he walked over.

Even though my cheeks felt like someone had taken a flamethrower to them, I dug myself in even deeper. "Is that a new cologne? I really like it! It's musky with a hint of cedar, or, I don't know, warm and woodsy. It's so strong and masculine… like you."

Oh for shit's sake! My mouth was on a roll and I couldn't stop. What the hell was wrong with me? This was Devon Booker for Gawd's sake!

His eyebrows drew together as he peered at me. "You're being pretty friendly today, Shannon. It's a side of you I've never seen; not that you're rude or anything, but…"

"Why wouldn't I be friendly? You're handsome as hell, and I've always been attracted to you." *Kill me now! Did I just say that?*

His hand rose to tuck a lock of hair behind my ear, still gazing at me suspiciously. "You don't have to say that, Shannon. I mean, you already got the job."

What was happening? My heart was a racehorse galloping to the edge of a cliff. I clamped my lips shut, and nodding, I took a step back from him. I had to get away. Turning, I raced to the small kitchenette at the back of the office space.

I could hear Devon's footsteps behind before he spoke, "I'm sorry, I didn't mean to embarrass you, Shannon. This is just so… surprising, is all."

My hand shook as I poured my coffee, spilling a few drops

on the counter. I froze when I felt his hand on my back. *Oh shit. Please keep my trap shut so I won't fill it with both feet again.*

I could feel the warmth of his breath when he leaned in. "I confess, I've been attracted to you from the minute I saw you in September. It's wonderful to hear you feel that connection too. I'm flattered."

Yikes! He thought I was hitting on him! Well, who would blame him from what I'd said? Devon was—

"This isn't flattery, Devon. It's the God's honest truth. You're one of the most flaming-hot guys I've ever met." My face felt like a furnace. For a moment I felt dizzy, almost missing the burner on the coffee machine when I set the pot back. What made this even more embarrassing was the fact that I wasn't lying! Devon *was* all the things I'd said, but why in the world did I say it out loud?

I wished he'd take his hand off my back and step away. It was hard to breathe, let alone think. Think! I pictured the faces of my children, my house, trying to fill my head with anything but Devon. Who knew what would come out of my yap next?

"Thank you, Shannon. Coming from you, that's high praise. Maybe after we finish here today, you'll join me for dinner… at my place." His hand drifted lower to linger on my waist, his breath hot on my ear.

There was no way I was going to his house after all this! But my mouth went on autopilot. "Dinner in bed?"

THAT was too much! I hurried to the boardroom, calling over my shoulder, "We'll talk later, Devon." I shut the door and leaned my back against it, panting for air. After a few moments, I was composed enough to push away, but not before flipping the lock on the door handle. There was no way I could trust myself around him! My mouth was like a jack-in-the-box, with God knows what popping out next!

I'd just totally shocked the shit outta not only Devon but myself. OKAY! So everything I said was true, but that wasn't a reason to blare it like a foghorn. I had NEVER been so forward… coming on to a guy like that. To make matters worse, I still didn't really trust the guy! He might be gorgeous as hell, but he'd tried to trick me into selling my property to him. I had to keep my guard up, but my mouth had other plans.

I picked up the spreadsheet listing all the projects Devon was involved in. *Focus, Shannon! You're here to do a job.* A job that I wasn't entirely convinced was necessary because of Devon's influence with the town council. He may have said something to trip the reassessment resulting in a huge tax bill.

I made myself read the list.

> *64 Brookside*
> *Lot 4, Lakeshore*
> *Comm. Building 7*
> *Eastview Development*
> *C. Estate*
> *Merry Market*

Peering at the mess of papers and files on the table, I picked up the one nearest. It was a letter on Devon's stationery but addressed to a Ms. Collin who resided in Pennsylvania. The subject line was Lakeshore. Probably the best way to tackle this was arranging correspondence by property and then I could arrange them in chronological order.

Before I got a chance to pick up the next letter, the air next to me shimmered. My breath formed a vapor, even before the sudden drop in temperature registered in my shoulders.

A bony, pale finger materialized pointing at C. Estate on the list in my hand. I jerked back, staring as the old woman's form grew stronger, showing once more the lace collar and a silver brooch above the flowing, dark dress. Her eyes were like chips of coal in white, creped skin, staring at me.

"You're back." A small smile revealed the tips of yellowed teeth, before she continued, "You are going to help me."

I practically fell into the chair beside me. As if my day wasn't wacky enough with the outrageous things I'd said to Devon, the resident ghost had shown up to inform me I was working for her too? I felt like I'd just fallen down a rabbit hole along with Alice.

"You never told me your name when I asked yesterday. You know mine, so it's only fair I know who wants my help before I'll agree to anything." At least my mouth was under control again, talking to the old lady's spirit.

She hovered closer, once more pointing to C. Estate on the page. "That's who I am… or rather was when I lived."

"Okay, Mrs. Estate. That's cleared up. So what is it—"

Her hand swept the listing from the table. "Not Mrs. Estate! Who would have such a ridiculous name? I am Estelle Cousins, of course. You must have heard your aunt speak of me, even though she was very young at the time she knew me."

Just the way she spoke and her imperious attitude, like she was royalty or something, was downright annoying. After making a fool out of myself earlier, I was in no mood to be treated as an inferior. "Sorry. I guess she didn't think you were that important to sing your praises to me. You'll need to elaborate if you expect my help with… what is it you want?"

But even as I asked it, I knew it had something to do with Devon. She was certainly no fan of Devon Booker.

At the light tap on the door, Estelle's gaze shot over there, her face once more becoming hard with deep, angry furrows. She turned to me again. "You must stop him."

There was a clicking sound and the door burst open, with Devon standing there holding a set of keys. "I heard you talking to someone, Shannon. Are you okay?"

"I'm not sure, Devon." Keeping my eyes averted from him, I stood up. "I'm not sure I can work for you… even if you are an Adonis. Although I'll miss seeing that dimple in your cheek and those shoulders that would make a linebacker green with envy." I grabbed my purse and walked over to the door. This was CRAZY! Even trying to avoid looking at him wasn't keeping my motormouth shut.

He stepped to the side, blocking my way out. "You can't leave me like this, Shannon. It's not just that I need your help, I feel like we've reached a new level in our friendship."

"I can't, Devon!" My hand once more flew to my mouth

pinching my lips to keep them from flapping, gushing out more things better left unsaid.

His mouth pulled to the side as his gaze probed my eyes. "I'll pay you forty dollars an hour if you'll stay. And if you find my being here is too big of a distraction, I promise to stay in my office and leave you alone… until you're ready to leave with me."

My hand drifted slowly from my mouth as I gaped at him. "Forty dollars an hour? You'll pay me forty dollars an hour to clean up this hot mess? What are you, crazy? I mean in addition to being totally *GQ* gorgeous."

Laughing, he shook his head from side to side. "You're not only pretty, but you're also funny, Shannon. As for being crazy? Yeah, I guess I am. But I'm also serious. Forty an hour, and I will give you free rein, although it's hard to resist spending more time with you." He winked and then as he walked back through the door opening, he added, "But knowing I have this evening with you, I'll manage."

With that, he closed the door and left.

I practically stumbled as I went back over to the table. Forty dollars! That would mean I'd have that tax bill paid in no time. There was no way I could pass this job up. There was also no way I was going home with Devon Booker that night… or any night, for that matter.

My gaze scanned the room for any sign of my new ghost friend, but it was only me and those files. I'd wait till late this afternoon when Devon was on the phone or in the bathroom and sneak out of here. I'd text him that I had felt ill and had to leave. It would actually be true. My mouth sputtering gushing flattery was enough to make me cringe with shame.

FOURTEEN

Mary-Jane's day

G ood news, MJ!" Ray rushed through the swinging kitchen door and hugged me, lifting me off my feet. "The high school will run the play here!"

When he set me down, my arms pulled his head closer to plant a big smackeroo on his lips. "Fantastic! When? How soon?" This was the answer to our problems. I just knew it!

Ray beamed as he explained the details. "In two weeks' time! I had to assure them that we'd have the stage, lighting, and sound set up the week before so they can inspect it and ensure we're capable. Which, of course, we are! And it will add to the hype when our regular customers see the setup. They're going to help spread the word, I'm sure."

I felt ready to burst; this was such good news. I clutched his arms, mentally seeing him selling this idea to Mr. Tremont and succeeding! "What do we need, equipment-wise?"

"You leave all that to me. I'm going to see Steve at the hardware store for the stage. I had a look at the school's facilities, and I'm sure we can replicate it and then some! As for sound and lighting, I'll drive to Albany if I have to get what we need. You just plan the menu and I'll do the rest."

"You did great, Ray! I can't wait to tell Zoe… or Shannon! I'll have to let her know it's all settled and to get writing. For a moment my high spirits fell, remembering her slur, calling it a "puff piece." But still, she'd probably write a good piece.

When Debbie, the sous-chef, entered the kitchen carrying a tray of vegetables from the walk-in cooler, a big grin flashed on her face when she looked over at me. "Did you win the lottery? Holy Hannah! What's up?"

After I'd finished telling her our plan for the play, she grabbed her cell phone from her purse. "This is so cool! My niece is in that play. The whole family, all twenty of us cousins and aunts and uncles will be here with bells on. This is like Broadway or something. A real live dinner theater. Imagine."

I thought of something else to get the word out: a poster or flyer in the front window! Zoe was artistic and a whizz with the computer! She'd make an attractive, eye-catching notice. I rushed out of the kitchen to find Ray to tell him. But I stopped short seeing him standing close to Sylvie, the new server. He was laughing as he spoke to her, his hand on her shoulder. But when she threw her arms around his neck and hugged him, my gut felt like an icicle had stabbed me.

Not only was Sylvie years younger than me, but I'd noticed her flirting with some of the male customers. It looked like she wasn't stopping there but had moved on to my husband. And Ray didn't look like he minded the blonde floozy's arms around his body.

I turned and went back into the kitchen. This was the first time I'd ever felt jealousy when it came to Ray. I didn't like it ONE BIT.

FIFTEEN

Libby, that evening

"Mom, do you know where the X-Acto knife is?"

I'd barely stepped in the door before my middle child Jack pounced on me. No "Hello, how are you doing?" Nothing. After putting up with a shift working alongside Jolene, listening to her snipes, this didn't help my mood.

Jack held a sheet of poster paper as he stood in the archway leading to the kitchen. "Wait till you hear the news! I'm making frames for the flyer Zoe designed."

I hung up my coat and toed my boots off. "What news? Something for school?" As I walked toward him I couldn't help noticing the brightness in his eyes or the wide grin. This couldn't be anything for school; he'd never be that excited.

"The school play is going to be at Zoe's parents' *restaurant!*" His chin rose and he mimicked a British accent: "Dinnah theee-a-tah. Brilliant, whot?"

He was so silly looking, in his ripped jeans and sloppy, oversized sweatshirt that I had to smile as I hugged him. "Smashing. That's the play you scored the lead in, right? Sergeant Trotsky?"

Pulling back, he snorted, "Sergeant *Trotter,* Mom! Zoe is Molly, the owner of Monkswell Manor."

My other son drifted over carrying an empty bowl with a few popcorn kernels still rattling against the surface. Kevin's hand rose to cuff the back of Jack's head, playfully.

"You're more like Inspector Clouseau, dude." He flashed a smile when he looked over at me. "How was work, Mom? We saved you some lasagna." He brushed by us as he went into the kitchen, smirking now. "Don't go out in the garage, Mom. You don't want to know what Dahlia brought home this time."

"What did she do this time?"

He flashed me a cheesy grin. "I ain't sayin' nuthin'. She's your youngest child."

Oh no. Dahlia was the worst for bringing home stray animals. I decided to take Kevin's advice and leave it, at least until I had something to eat. I went to the junk drawer and rummaged until I had the X-Acto knife. Handing it to Jack, I cautioned, "Don't cut your fingers off, 'cause this nurse is officially off duty, okay?"

When he darted off with the knife, I opened the fridge to grab the plate of cold lasagna. As it heated in the microwave, I leaned against the counter, looking at Kevin scroll through his phone. "How was school today?"

He glanced up, and in that moment I saw Hank's face looking back at me. It sent a bittersweet warmth through my chest that I had Kevin, a living reminder of my deceased husband. Of the three kids, he was the one who most resembled Hank, in looks and actions.

"Okay, I guess. The same." His gaze once more was riveted on the small screen in his hand. "Will you be able to get the night off to see the play? Maybe we should reserve a table for the three of us."

"I'll juggle my shifts if I have to. There's no way I'm going to miss it. Now tell me what your sister dragged home this time." I sniffed the air. "Not a skunk, thank goodness."

He chuckled. "I didn't tell you this, but…it's a raccoon."

"What? How the heck did she end up with a raccoon? She

can't keep a raccoon as a pet!" Good Lord! I thought the miniature goat she'd found wandering alongside the highway was bad enough! Thank goodness the owners put up a poster and we could return it.

"You know Dahlia. She heard it chattering from a low branch. It's pretty small, maybe wandered away from its nest or something. She's keeping it in a box with old towels lining the bottom."

When the microwave beeped, I grabbed the plate and wandered over to the table to join Kevin. "We'll see about that. You know how I feel about keeping wild animals as pets. It's bad enough that there are feral cats hanging around the back shed."

My cell phone rang, and I plucked it out of my purse. Hmm. Shannon. When I answered it, Kevin got up and went back to the living room.

Shannon hardly waited for my greeting before launching into a tirade. "I had the *worst* day ever, Libby! I was at Devon's office… He gave me a job filing and getting his mess of an office cleaned up."

I closed my eyes and sighed. "No. Don't tell me you're that desperate that you asked HIM for a job."

"Stop! It's bad enough to have MJ lecture me without you piling on too. Devon offered me the job. Which is good because being a part-time stringer for the newspaper isn't going to cut it."

"I'm glad about the newspaper job. But what happened that's got you so wired?" I picked at my lasagna, waiting for her.

"Aside from seeing a ghost there, it was what happened every time I spoke to Devon! I don't know why, but I couldn't stop my mouth. I was saying outrageous things like how great looking he is, so totally ripped. Shit, I even complimented him on his aftershave!"

I started coughing, nearly choking on the bit of pasta. Finally, I was able to speak. "Shannon! That's insane! What the hell were you thinking?" If this had happened with anyone else besides Devon, it might even be funny.

"That's the problem, I wasn't…except I was! Everything, every impression Devon made on me blurted out nonstop! I'm so embarrassed. He thinks I'm so attracted to him that he asked me back to his place! Needless to say, I gave him the slip. But what about tomorrow?"

"Hang on." I got up and poured myself a glass of wine. The day wasn't crazy enough but Shannon was hitting on Devon? When I was settled again, I continued, "Just quit. If you're that embarrassed, and you really didn't mean to come on to him, then don't go back."

"I CAN'T! He's paying me forty dollars an hour! Look, I need the money, okay? I'm just going to have to come up with some way to wire my mouth shut!"

"That wouldn't be safe. Maybe pretend you have laryngitis? Let me think about it. In the meantime, what's with the ghost you saw?" Trust Shannon to get herself into a stupid mess like this, but the ghost was interesting.

"It's some old lady from the Victorian era or something. Estelle Cousins. She hates Devon, let me tell you. She said she knew my aunt and that I have to help her. But don't ask me why, because she vanished when Devon entered the room."

When Shannon said the name of the ghost, my ears perked up. "Estelle Cousins? I've heard the name. She has to be related to Ed Cousins. Why would she be in Devon's building and not haunting her family's estate? And why would she want your help?"

Shannon's words, answering me, went in one ear and out the other. This whole thing was odd. First Shannon's behavior with Devon and then that ghost. Were they related? I interrupted her diatribe. "Could that ghost have caused you to say all those things to Devon, do you suppose? But you said she hates him."

"I have no idea if she was the cause of all the stupid things I said. I can't imagine that being the case." She was silent for a few beats before she asked, "How are you doing, Libby? Did you manage to get through your shift without murdering that bitch you work with?"

The door leading to the garage opened, and Dahlia stepped into the kitchen. I waved to her before answering Shannon. "It was awful but I managed. Look, I've got to go. Can I call you tomorrow? Maybe take a sick day until we can figure out this thing with Devon, okay?"

"I might have to. I'm going to look in my books of spells and witchcraft to see if there's anything I can do. Talk to you later."

When she hung up I turned to look at Dahlia, scrubbing her hands at the kitchen sink. "What were you doing in the garage? Is there something you want to tell me, Dahlia?"

She grabbed a paper towel and dried her hands, avoiding my eyes. "I know I can't keep it, Mom, but I rescued a raccoon." Her mouth pulled to the side as she walked over to hug me. "He's so little and so cute though. Come and see him!"

The excitement in her eyes was hard to resist. "Sure. But remember you promised you won't try to wheedle me into keeping it as a pet." I stood up and let her pull me toward the door.

When I stepped into the garage, I saw the plastic bin draped under a pink towel at the foot of the stairs. I shuddered from the chilly air as I stepped closer. Dahlia lifted the corner of the towel and when I leaned over, two black eyes, rimmed in a dark mask stared back at me. It started chattering, hunched in a ball in the corner of the bin. It wasn't a baby, but it wasn't yet an adult, judging by its size.

Dahlia looked over at me. "See? I told you he was cute. He was wandering around a big tree at the side of the road when I walked home from school. He looked so lonely and cold."

Something about the poor animal, shivering with fear, touched a chord in my chest. It missed its mother and the nest, snuggling with littermates. Dahlia had put a carrot and an apple in the far corner of the bin. The small animal opened its mouth still making that chattery sound.

"Water."

My head jerked back and I stared at the raccoon's white snout and the twitching whiskers. Oh my God. Had I just heard that thing say "water"?

"Water."

I sank down onto the step, backing away from the box. My heart had kick-started into overdrive. I must be losing my mind because I could swear that creature said "water."

"Mom? What's wrong? Dahlia reached for my shoulder, leaning close. Her brown eyes were filled with worry as she peered at me.

I took a deep breath. "I'm fine. Just a bit tired, I think. You need to get a dish of water for it, Dahlia."

She nodded and took off up the stairs. When the door closed behind her, I edged closer to the bin and peeked in again.

"Water."

I jerked back. Shit! What the hell was happening to me? That thing had definitely said "water."

SIXTEEN

Shannon

The next morning...

I t's some kind of spell, Shannon!" My Aunt Maeve's form had never been clearer than it was the next morning. She floated close to me and pointed at the objects that were set before me on the floor: the candle, pentagram, spices, and my magic book.

"You saw it yourself! The candle kept going out, and your offering of spices spilled onto the floor. It practically flew out of your hand!"

My shoulders fell as I looked up at her. "You think so? You think that someone hexed me or something?" But nothing about the protection spell had gone right. I'd done it a couple of times before and I knew the difference. It didn't *feel* right either.

My aunt's hands flew up and she cursed, "Damn right, you've been hexed! I can practically smell the stink of a hex." She fixed a hard look at me. "But who would do that? What have you been up to, Shannon? You've made an enemy. A powerful enemy from the looks of this."

I proceeded to tell her everything that had happened the day before at Devon's place, ending with my text to him, that I'd felt ill and had to rush home.

Aunt Maeve shook her head. "Okay, so you couldn't control your speech with that man. The ghost of Estelle Cousins interests me, but I'll circle back to that after we figure out your behavior."

Shit! Just when I thought I was progressing with magic, of course, it would go totally off the rails. Was there any reason at all in dealing with magic? Must it always swing around and bite me?

"I don't have any enemies, Aunt Maeve. The only one who comes close to being an enemy is Devon, and he's being pretty decent right now. If it weren't for this damned tax bill..." My eyes opened wider as a picture of my visit to the tax office flooded into my mind.

Cynthia! She'd acted like she hated me, snubbing me even when I was at the office. I looked up at my aunt. "Is there any chance that Cynthia Granger is a witch? I mean her grandmother Ruth was! You and Ruth were friends. Could she have taught her granddaughter the craft?"

My aunt hovered above the sofa before flopping down onto the surface. "That's it. Ruth was always putting Cynthia forward, trying to get her into our coven. Cynthia was a quiet child, kind of a loner, if the truth be told. I let Ruth bring her to one Esbat at the well, but the child didn't seem interested. Or maybe she was just shy and intimidated by the three of us."

My eyes narrowed, picturing the woman who'd acted so cold with me. It was like I'd done something to offend her. Now with what Maeve had said, it made sense that Cynthia might be a practicing witch. Her grandmother had probably schooled her in secret. It HAD to be Cynthia who hexed me!

"So what can I do to remove her hex, Aunt Maeve? It's got to be Cynthia's doing. How powerful a witch is she?" I couldn't figure out how to remove the spell from Mary-Jane, let alone remove this hex from myself. How was I going to manage with this thing? That tax bill wasn't going away!

"This will mean a special trip to the Witching Well, Shannon. You'll need your friends with you. Hell! I'll go along too. Call them and assemble the coven, the sooner the better. In the meantime, you'd better stay put. At least you won't further embarrass yourself with Devon Booker. And for it to be HIM, of all people."

"I'm not going anywhere, don't worry. But what is it that you've got against Devon? And why does Estelle Cousins detest him?" I got up from the floor and took a seat next to my aunt.

She sniffed and her chin rose high. "Devon put a lot of pressure on me to sell my land to him. He made trouble for me with the town council, trying to shut my resort down. There were all kinds of jigs and reels that I had to maneuver to carry on. But I did. He's money-hungry, Shannon. He won't stop until he owns the whole town."

I nodded. This was pretty much what I'd heard from Libby and MJ. "But why would Estelle Cousins hate him? Why would she ask for my help?"

Aunt Maeve smiled. "Estelle was a lovely person when she lived here back in the fifties. I bought this place in 1954 when the Catskill Mountains was the place to be for vacationing New Yorkers. It was booming but petered off in the seventies. People were using airplanes to go to more exotic vacation spots. That is, for the ones who could afford air travel. The ones who stayed home had air-conditioning so they could stand the summer heat."

Okay, this was becoming a bit of the history lesson that I'd heard before. Still, it might help in research for the article I promised the newspaper. "Okay. Getting back to Estelle…"

"Yes. Yes." Maeve nodded. "Estelle always presided over town celebrations, ribbon cutting, and fundraising for the church and the poor. The Cousins are one of the founding families of Wesley, you know. She was not only gracious, but she was generous. Many a struggling family were fed from her kitchen." Maeve's eyebrows rose high. "God forbid that a child would go hungry. Not on her watch!"

She fixed me with a steely-eyed stare. "If Estelle asked you for help, then you can count on the fact that it's important. Devon must be up to no good again for her to appear there."

I sighed. "If that's the case, I need to help her. I have to find out what's going on to stop him." Shit. But how could I do that with that damned Cynthia working bad magic on me?

***

After spending time on the computer researching the Feb Festival and the history of the town, for context, I stood up from the kitchen table and stretched. I'd made some good notes and now had a rough idea of where I was going with my piece. But first I had to get outside for a break-even if it was just a walk to the mailbox at the end of my drive.

Looking out the window, the sun broke through the bank of clouds, spreading sparkles over the pristine blanket of snow. I glanced to the side where huge trees with thick branches laden with snow swayed in the slight breeze. More importantly, no sign of Bob.

My cell phone went off with a text message and I scooped it from the table. My mouth snapped shut seeing Devon's name on the small screen.

> Sorry to hear you aren't feeling well. I just finished a meeting with clients but if you'd like I can bring you lunch or dinner? You've only been working here one day and I already miss you! TTYL Devon

I rolled my eyes before my fingers flew over the tiny keyboard.

> Thanks but I'm horrible company right now.
> Every bone aches and my head is pounding.
> I'll call you with an update tomorrow.

I hit send and then scrolled through my messages. Nothing back from Libby or MJ about meeting tonight, although I would have heard it ding. Still, I could hope.

When I was bundled up in my coat, boots, and a scarf, I

ventured out, inhaling deeply the cedar-scented air. My gaze lowered to the pie pan I'd left out for Bobcat Bob. All the leftover pork chops and canned tuna were now gone but, next to the pan was a worn, brown leather wallet.

I picked it up and opened it. My mouth fell open seeing the wad of money tucked in the flap. A glance at the driver's license showed the owner as Stan Jones. Stan Jones. The fireman who was hot after Libby.

I looked over at the forest and gritted my teeth. "Bob! You can't just go stealing people's wallets! I know you mean well and you're trying to help, but this is just wrong." Nothing but silence answered me.

I shook my head before going back inside to grab my purse, cell phone, and car keys. So much for staying put to get some research and writing in. Now I had to drive to the fire station and somehow get this wallet back to Stan.

When I started the truck, I sat there for a few moments letting it warm up to get the frost from the windshield. When a small patch cleared in the glass, I peered over at the forest again. This time a pair of yellow eyes ringed in white stared back at me peeking out from behind the big maple. He stepped out and planted himself down in the snow, casually watching me.

That cat! According to Aunt Maeve, he was supposed to be helping me! I'd be lucky if he didn't land me in jail for theft!

SEVENTEEN

Mary-Jane

That same day

H ere's the first of the lunch orders, Mary-Jane! Ray had just seated another table of six." Sylvie set the order slip on the ticket wheel.

I snatched it up, making a pretense of reading it but sneaking glances at Sylvie.

She was pretty in a blowsy way; the eye makeup was a little overdone, with brilliant blue eye shadow. Hmph. More like a tropical fish than anything attractive. And that hair! Could it BE more teased and puffy, piled high on a head that looked too big for her scrawny body? How could Ray be attracted to her? She was nothing but a young floozy, flirting with anything in pants.

I pointed to an entry on the order. "Does this say 'Special' or 'Steak'? Your handwriting is worse than my doctor's."

She leaned closer, sending a waft of dollar store perfume up my nostrils. "It's *'Special.'* Two orders of today's special." She pointed at the rest of her slip. Then there's one order for pecan chicken and an order of salmon." Peering closely at me, she asked, "Do you think you maybe need glasses, MJ? Your eyes change as you age. It happened to my mother."

I stiffened, glaring at her. She was comparing me to her *mother*! I wasn't that old, and considering she was only ten years younger than me, it was insulting! "My eyes are fine. I've seen more legible scrawl from my kid when she was in kindergarten."

"Whatever you say, MJ." With that, she turned and flounced out of the kitchen.

My eyes narrowed and I shook my head. Beside me, Debbie, my sous-chef, was busy chopping chives to be used as a garnish. I thrust the order slip under her nose. "Can you read this? It's not me, it's her lousy writing, right?"

Debbie's hand paused while she stared at the note. "Two specials, chicken and salmon. It looks okay to me, MJ."

I gritted my teeth. "That's only because you *heard* her say it. Never mind." I picked up a salmon steak and set it on the gas-fired range. All the while, that picture of Sylvie's arms around Ray the night before was a throbbing pain in my head. No doubt she was sidling up to my husband right this minute as she waited at the bar for her drink order.

Ray probably didn't mind that. My teeth gritted. He pushes me away but is fine with being fawned over by that floozy!

Debbie sidled over to me. "I've got to get the sauce and more vegetables from the walk-in."

Her words barely registered. The green-eyed monster of jealousy was riding roughshod through my head, envisioning Sylvie flirting with Ray and him eating it up. I had second thoughts about hiring her over another candidate but Ray had been the deciding vote. It was clear *now* why he'd picked her. My eyes narrowed thinking of that stupid job interview: she was all jiggly and floozy, practically ignoring me, but hanging on every word Ray said! Shit.

I was on autopilot going to the fridge to get the chicken to place in the oven. When I pulled the tray out, it slipped from my grasp and landed on the floor. Chicken thighs and breasts glistening in the oily marinade spilled into the area around my feet. Damn!

Thankfully, I managed to salvage half of it from falling but the rest was ruined. I plucked up the chicken from the floor and tossed it into the garbage at the far end of the room. Grabbing a roll of paper towels, I proceeded to clean up the puddles of marinade from the tile. This was all because of that skanky Sylvie flirting with my husband and making me crazy.

"Mary-Jane!" Debbie yelled. Her eyes were big as golf balls gaping at the stove. The vegetable tray slipped from her grasp, crashing onto the floor.

What the hell? My gaze darted to where she was staring. I gasped! Orange tongues of fire leapt high from the salmon broiling on the range! It spread to engulf the grates of the stove. In a flash, the fire grew, coating the counter and cabinet next to it.

I scrambled to my feet, racing for the fire extinguisher. My foot landed on a head of romaine lettuce and I pitched to the side. A sharp pain jarred my arm as I stumbled onto the garbage container. SHIT!

Now, a wave of fire rolled over the counter igniting the marinade and dried herbs. The whole cooking area exploded in a ball of fire as the smoke alarms began blaring.

Oh my God! I tried once more to get to the fire extinguisher but Debbie was ahead of me. She yanked it from the bracket and aimed the nozzle at the flames. But nothing happened.

"I can't get this damned thing to work, MJ! Help!" She beat at the handle with her fist. "Come on, you bastard!"

My chest tightened, watching in horror as the fire spread. The door to the kitchen burst open and Ray was there. "Mary-Jane!" He rounded the serving counter and grabbed the extinguisher from Debbie. "Get back! Both of you! Get out of here! Call 9-1-1!"

Debbie hurried to my side. "Let's go, MJ!" She grabbed my arm, pulling me to the back door.

"No! I've got to help Ray!" But her grip was an iron band. Smoke filled the area around us. Coughing, I lurched out the door into the fresh air. It wasn't five seconds before Ray flew out the door behind us, his face contorted as he gasped for air.

After a few deep breaths, he managed to speak, "Oh shit! The customers! I gotta get them out!" He'd barely finished saying it before racing around to the front of the building.

In the distance, the wail of a fire truck pierced the air. Debbie pulled at me, and we followed Ray to the front of the building.

This couldn't be happening! My life's work—our dream—engulfed in flames. But when we rounded the corner and I could see the front of the restaurant, it looked the same. No flames or smoke billowing out the front door.

Across the street were a group of people gaping at the building. Our customers. Thank God they'd gotten out okay. Even Sylvie was there.

But then that scene became blocked from sight when the red fire truck pulled up in front of the restaurant. It was hardly parked when firefighters flew out, grabbing hoses before they raced inside.

Ray put his arm over my shoulder when I stepped next to him. "What happened, MJ? You're always so careful."

I grabbed his free hand, looking over at him. "I don't know! I left it for only a minute or so. There must have been oil on the burner that flamed up. God, it happened so fast!" My throat stung from the smoke and I started coughing again.

Ray squeezed my hand. "Thank God everyone got out okay. But this… this is bad, MJ."

Shit! This was all my fault. If I hadn't been so caught up in foolish jealousy, I would have been paying more attention. Now it looked like we might lose everything.

EIGHTEEN

Shannon

I'd just turned into the fire station's parking lot to return Stan's wallet when the wail of the siren shrieked. The enormous garage door shot up, and a fire truck emerged from the building. Holy shit! There was a fire somewhere? I watched it drive by me and onto the street.

I needed to follow that truck and get the story. This would be my first article to submit to the paper! I wheeled my truck close to the still open garage door and lowered the window. There was no sign of anyone. I tossed Stan's wallet into the garage and steered the car to the street. Tough luck for the person whose house was on fire but good that I could return the wallet with no one ever knowing.

In no time flat, I was right behind the big red truck. It slowed and then swung around a corner up ahead onto a side street. Luckily there weren't many cars around, especially police cars, as I was driving well past the speed limit. When I turned the corner, my mouth fell open.

Shit! A billow of dark smoke hovered in the air… above *Mary-Jane's restaurant*! Oh no! When I was half a block away, I parked and took off running. The firefighters raced into the building while a huddle of people stood gawking at the action from the safety of across the street. And then I saw Ray and Mary-Jane.

"MJ! Ray!" I bounded to them and pulled MJ into my arms. "Are you okay?"

There were tears in Mary-Jane's eyes when she eased back. "Everyone got out. But this… this is going to ruin us, Shannon."

My heart broke seeing despair lining her face. "I'm so sorry, MJ. But no one was hurt, so that's…" I couldn't even say the trite platitude. This was their life, their livelihood devastated in the blink of an eye.

Ray left us when Stan, the fire chief, emerged from the building. Had they gotten the fire out already? It was hard to tell what was happening from the look on his face, all professional and calm.

Mary-Jane clutched my arm, leaning in closer. "I started it, Shannon. My mind…" She sucked in a breath of air and looked up at the sky, with tears freely flowing. "I saw my server hugging Ray last night and I got so jealous! I was still ruminating on that and I got distracted. I'm to blame for this catastrophe."

"The blonde one? She was hugging Ray?" I peered at Ray and then across the street where Sylvie was gesturing wildly, talking to people staring at the building. First of all, Ray wasn't exactly God's gift to women with his beach-ball belly and receding hairline. And as for Sylvie… I'd seen her flirt with Devon. She was nothing to write home about either, totally overdone.

But whatever. Mary-Jane's feelings had been hurt, and that was what was important.

Stan and Ray walked over to join Mary-Jane and me. My gaze took in Stan's face. Now, if Sylvie had flirted with him, I could totally get that! He could be in any hot-firemen calendar and put waaay younger guys to shame, with the dark bedroom eyes and weathered, but totally attractive face. And he was tall… filling out that firefighter gear and making it sexy. Why the hell hadn't Libby ever gone out with him? He'd certainly asked her enough times. He was a catch.

Stan looked at Mary-Jane. "The real damage was confined to the kitchen, MJ. There's some smoke damage in the dining area, but that's all. What happened? And, more importantly, where was your extinguisher?"

Mary Jane answered, her voice still shaking. "We had the extinguisher, Stan. But the handle, it was stuck or something. But the smoke detector worked fine."

"How did it start?"

"I spilled a pan of chicken. When I was cleaning it up, the flame from the broiling salmon flared up. Debbie…" She looked around and rolled her eyes, seeing Debbie across the street with Sylvie. "Debbie had gone into the walk-in. What happened was Murphy's law, I'm afraid."

As I listened, it occurred to me that MJ was omitting the part about being distracted with jealousy. Which was probably a good thing to do considering they probably wouldn't want to mention that in any insurance claim. What she'd told me earlier would be off the record in my article.

Turning to Stan, I sighed. "Accidents happen. That's why we have big, strong, guys like you around, Stan. Hot firemen to the rescue." The breath froze in my chest, hearing these words fly out of my mouth. *Shit!*

What was worse was the shocked expressions on Stan's, MJ's, and Ray's faces, looking at me! I'd gushed like a simpering teenage girl talking to a rock star. Stan was hot but he was no Axl Rose.

Stan's eyebrows rose high before he turned once more to MJ. "The extinguisher wasn't working? Much as I hate to do it, I'm going to cite you for defective equipment. That's not going to play well with your insurance company, I'm afraid."

My hand rose to rest on Stan's arm. "The extinguisher is probably fine, Stan. In the heat of the moment, MJ couldn't get it to work. But I'm sure if a guy like you tested it, you'd see that it's fine. I mean, look at you. You must bench press at least two hundred pounds."

Stan's eyebrows knitted together as he peered at me. "Are you okay, Shannon? You weren't in there inhaling smoke, were you?"

I sucked my lips in, locking my jaw from opening. I shook my head no.

"Of course, I'll test it, Shannon. I'll be going over the whole area of the fire closely. Now, if you'll excuse us, I want to go back inside with Mary-Jane and Ray."

"I'm doing a story on this, Stan. For the newspaper. I'm not just MJ's friend, I'm the press. You can't ditch me so easily. I need to be here, close to you to find out what happened. Lucky me! I'll try not to drool on you."

Stan's eyes flashed wide, and he gave his head a shake. "Fine. But I will be focusing my investigation with MJ and Ray. Just don't get in the way, okay?" He took a step away, gesturing for Ray to follow.

Mary-Jane scowled at me. "What is *wrong* with you? Openly flirting with the fire chief when my whole world is collapsing? And *Stan*, of all people! You know he's the perfect guy for Libby. And for the record, he thinks you've lost your marbles, too, in case you haven't noticed."

She started to follow the two guys but I grabbed her arm. "I can't HELP it, MJ! Cynthia Granger hexed me! Now when I'm around smokin' hot guys, there's no *filter*! What I think just pops out of my mouth."

Her eyebrows arched to her hairline. "So Ray's not hot? I noticed you focused all your attention on Stan." She plucked my hand off her arm. "Go home, Shannon. I've got more important things to worry about than some so-called hex."

She left me standing there on the sidewalk. What could I say? She was right.

NINETEEN

Libby's day

Right from the moment I walked onto the floor, Jolene was on me with the sweetly snide remarks about how I'd been late answering a call signal, which SHE had to rush to. My patient notes weren't complete. My bedside manner was cool and not supportive. Was I wearing perfume in a fragrance-free facility? On and on.

When it was time for my lunch break, I put on my coat and boots to get out of there for a half-hour of freedom. I stepped outside the main door of the hospital, and the scent of smoke pinched my nostrils. My gaze swept the skyline, to the west side of town where a cloud of dark smoke hovered. Please let no one be hurt or badly burned; burn cases were the worst.

I trudged through the snow until I came to the picnic table set up for people visiting patients in the summer. After I swept the snow from the seat, I flopped down, my thoughts once more free to ponder the evening before when I'd heard that raccoon say, "water." I know it had happened even though I spent hours afterward trying to rationalize it away.

But as soon as my eyes popped open that morning, I knew that I wasn't going crazy. Somehow I had heard that raccoon, Rascal—the name Chloe pinned on him—communicate the word "water." I couldn't say he *said* it. He was an animal after all. But he'd managed to get the message across.

I opened my lunch container and took my sandwich out, still reliving that scene with Rascal. This was all connected to magic; there was no other way this could have happened. It was the only thing that made sense. Had a floodgate opened when I made that glass fly across the table with my mind? The fact that I had heard that raccoon made that theory more plausible.

No doubt about it, I understood what that raccoon was conveying.

Movement to my left caught my attention. A black squirrel sat on its haunches munching an acorn or something, sheltering under the boughs of a big pine tree. It stopped for a moment and twitched, turning its head to stare straight at me.

The poor thing was probably hungry, foraging in the snow. I picked off a chunk of my spiced salami and cheese sandwich and tossed it close to him.

He hunched lower, still staring at me, but then his eyes darted to the piece of food. He leaped up and hopped through the blanket of snow until he was at the bread. I sat still as a statue watching and even listening for anything to break through my consciousness. The squirrel picked up the bread and began eating. His paw plucked the meat off and dropped it.

"Not good."

My eyes opened wider, hearing that message in my head. Oh my God. I'd wanted to see if it could happen and it did! The squirrel demolished the bread and cheese but turned his back on the salami, gazing at me once more. His nose trembled, and those dark eyes flashed, edging even closer to me. He was only about six feet away.

As I watched him, I wondered. Focusing my mind on him, a question formed. *Hey, Mr. Squirrel! Come closer if you want some more.* Would he be able to understand me?

The squirrel stretched higher, its head cocked, looking at me. In a flash, it turned and hopped a few feet away before hunkering lower.

The trembling creature looked like it was afraid now. I whispered, "Sorry. I didn't mean to scare you. Guess you're more frightened than hungry, huh?"

Its ears flattened before it took a few steps closer.

"Food. Hungry!"

I jerked back, hearing the words in my head. It had been more insistent and louder! The squirrel took a couple of steps closer. My fingers shook a little, tearing off another hunk of the sandwich.

Still whispering, "Okay, we'll try this again. Don't worry. I won't hurt you. I'm as amazed by this as you are!" I tossed a quarter of my sandwich over to him.

Again his paws closed around the piece of my lunch, and he flicked the meat away. *"Stinks, nasty."* He quickly demolished the bread and cheese though.

I leaned closer, peering at it. "So not a fan of processed meat. I get it." It was hard to keep my body calm and still. I fought the urge to jump up and down, yelling to the world, *I can talk to animals! Call me Nurse Doolittle!*

At the sound· above me, and flakes of snow falling from a pine bough, I looked up. Perched on a branch was a brown cowbird, fluttering its wings before it turned to stare at me. I grinned. Would this work with birds? I let out a soft whistle before whispering, "You want some of my lunch, too, little bird?"

It stared at me for a couple of moments and then took off, swooping to a tree in the distance. Hmm, so maybe this new talent I had didn't work with birds? Whatever. I turned my attention back to the squirrel. "Hey, little buddy. I wish I'd brought some peanuts or sunflower seeds."

The squirrel sprung up and took off through the snow, disappearing into the branches of the tree. For a few minutes, I could only sit there staring after it. My world had tipped on its axis since last night. I was actually able to communicate with animals! I'd heard that squirrel in my mind as clearly as if one of my kids had spoken to me. Weird, but totally rocking cool. I jumped to my feet, looking around at the lawn and trees for any other animal to try this with!

My cell phone chirped with the tone I'd chosen for Shannon. Oh no, not now! I sighed. Shannon had texted me earlier, but I hadn't had a chance to get back to her—something about an emergency meeting? I'd better get back to her, and besides, I had amazing news! I pulled it from my pocket.

Before I could finish saying hi, Shannon blurted, "MJ's restaurant caught fire! It was limited mostly to the kitchen but…she's freaking—"

I gasped. "Oh my God! Is she okay? Did anyone get hurt?" A quick look to the west showed only tendrils in the sky now. They'd gotten it out, thank God.

"Everyone is okay. Well, not really okay. This is devastating for MJ and Ray."

"Shit. They sure don't need this. So, you were there, with MJ and Ray? You decided to stay away from Devon?" But if that was the case, why was she in town? Wasn't she worried about running into him?

"I had to come in to return Stan Jones's wallet. Bob brought it—"

"Slow DOWN, Shannon! What the hell were you doing with Stan's wallet? Was he at your place? Did he leave it?" My jaw clenched tight thinking of Stan visiting Shannon! She had Steve Murphy on a string as well as Devon Booker. Was she making a move on Stan Jones as well? Stan who had asked ME out, I don't know how many times.

"The bobcat has been bringing me stuff, Libby. Yesterday it was some old lady's pension check, and this morning it was Stan's wallet. I came into town to return it and saw him heading to MJ's fire."

Her voice held an edge when she continued. "Aunt Maeve and I figured who put this hex on me—you know, making horribly flirty things fly out of my yap? Cynthia Granger! She did this! She acted real nasty when I saw her the other day!"

In all this time, I hadn't been able to get a word in, hardly at all. I glanced at my watch. My lunch break was almost over with no time to get into my new thing talking to animals. Besides, Shannon was wound for sound, talking crazy shit, a lot to untangle that I definitely didn't have time to tackle now.

"Shannon, I have to go back to work, but we need to talk about all this. Plus, I've got some news of my own! I'll call you when I finish here, okay?"

"So, you're not coming to my place? I really need your help, as well as MJ's."

I rolled my eyes. Sometimes Shannon could be so self-absorbed. MJ just had a fire and I was able to communicate with animals, but EVERYTHING had to revolve around Shannon. Still, maybe we could help MJ with her catastrophe. The magic was getting stronger, and MJ needed our help more than Shannon did.

"I'll see what I can do. I want to call MJ when I get my afternoon break. Poor MJ having a fire. No promises, but I'll try to get her to go to your place with me. If she's not up for it, we'll try for tomorrow."

"Really try, Libby! I have to get Cynthia's spell removed! It's making me crazy and I can't work—"

"I'LL TRY!" It was so hard to keep my temper with her, right now. Plus, I was going to be late getting back to the ward. Jolene would pounce on that! It would be hard enough to stay focused knowing that I could talk to animals without giving her more ammunition.

"Promise you'll come?"

"Shannon! I'll do my best, but I can't promise, okay?"

"Okay." Shannon sounded like she lost her best friend. With that, she hung up.

I tossed the rest of my lunch into the snow for the squirrel. So much for peace and quiet on my break. Everything was going to hell in a handbasket. I looked over at the tree where the squirrel had been. Well, not everything. I mean… *I can freaking talk to animals!*

TWENTY

Mary-Jane

Late that afternoon...

Mary-Jane! Shannon told me the news about your fire! How are you doing?"

When I heard the concern in Libby's voice, I had to swallow the lump up in my throat, fighting tears. "Terrible. But at least no one was hurt." I looked around at the charred wall joists in the kitchen, the gas range that was ruined, the stump of the sooty counter, and dirty water on the floor.

"Thank goodness for that! But your restaurant... how bad is it, MJ? It wasn't the whole building, right?"

I sighed. "No, the dining room got hit with smoke, but the kitchen is a disaster. Ray is on the phone with the insurance adjuster right now. The only saving grace is the fact that our smoke detector worked, and Stan was able to confirm the extinguisher was okay. Although it didn't want to work when Ray tried it."

"I guess that's good news. Will your insurance cover this?"

"We're sure as hell going to try for that! But you know what they're like. They don't make money paying claims. I'm sure it's going to be a battle." It made my blood boil to think of all the premiums we'd paid over the years and never once put in a claim. But I'd heard enough horror stories about others who had.

"I am so sorry this happened, MJ. Getting everything up and running again is going to take a lot of time, right?"

"No kidding. We were supposed to have the dinner theater. How the hell is that going to happen now? We'll be lucky to be running by Feb Festival." We'd have to take out a loan at the bank to get through this. If they'd even loan us money. And the house was already mortgaged.

"Listen, I know this may sound like terrible timing but... maybe we should meet at Shannon's. Tonight, if you can manage that. You need luck or magic or whatever to help you through this. Hell, even a few stiff drinks with us will help. Shannon's got some crazy problem with what pops out of her mouth, but I'm more concerned about *you*, MJ."

My eyes narrowed, thinking of Shannon. Guess she wouldn't have to write a *"puff piece"* about the dinner theater now.

"You wouldn't believe the ridiculous crap she said to Stan, Libby. I was *embarrassed* for her." Immediately after I said it, I regretted it. I shouldn't be dumping that on Libby... but misery loves company, I guess.

"She said something about that. And some crap about Cynthia Granger putting a hex on her." Libby was quiet for a moment before adding, "You know, I'm having some pretty awesome things happen to me, MJ. I think the coven should meet tonight. And if not tonight, then tomorrow for sure."

I glanced over at Ray hearing his voice raise as he talked to the insurance people. That didn't look like it was going so well.

Magic. If anything could help me out, it might be magic. My intentions in asking for help were good and that was important.

Intention!

Oh my God! What I'd wished was for Shannon to experience a taste of her own medicine, getting as embarrassed as me. I'd wished for that! After that exercise spell, specifically the galloping-hormones side effect, she deserved that. Well, it sure as hell was working, judging by the ludicrous things she'd said to Stan, hitting on him!

Guilt shot an icy arrow through my chest at the next thought. What you send out will come back to you, *threefold*. I'd wished that rotten spell on Shannon, and now it was ricocheting back to me.

The fire! But not only that but WHAT had caused it. If I hadn't been so distracted with jealousy over Sylvie hugging Ray, that wouldn't have happened. The universe was sending punishment back to me. But it happened in threes. The fire counted as one, and maybe that jealousy thing was another, but what was the third?

Oh shit. What would happen next?

"Mary-Jane? Are you still there?" Libby's voice yanked me from the cold dread.

"Yes. I think you're right, Libby. We all need as much magic and luck as we can muster. Pick me up at eight-thirty. We're going to our coven meeting." I had to come clean about this spell I had cast on Shannon. Reversing it might be the only way to dodge that third shoe dropping.

TWENTY ONE

Shannon

I had barely finished setting my candles on the pentagram when Libby's ringtone sounded from my purse. I grabbed it and read:

> MJ and I will be at your place at nine tonight. I just talked to her on my break. I've got to get back to work or Jolene will use it against me. TTYL

A wave of relief washed through me. We'd get all this mess sorted out, remove Cynthia's spell, and wish for a bit of luck to help Mary-Jane and Ray with their restaurant. I sank back on my haunches looking at the items around me. I still needed to do this protection spell. When MJ and Libby got here, it would just add to what we needed to do—remove that blasted spell and help MJ.

Even though I'd already cast the circle, I repeated it after the interruption of Libby's message. I lit the tea lights and concentrated on the white candle set in the center of the pentagram. It took more than a few deep breaths to reach the calmness I wanted.

"Okay, Aunt Maeve, I've done more studying on 'magik witchery' in these books than I've done since college," I said aloud. No response. "I'm doing the work you said I need to. Hope I'm on the right track, no thanks to you!" Still no response. I went back to casting my spell.

I took the pouch of anise and pinched a few grains in my fingers. As I let it fall into the dish holding the candle, I spoke with confidence,

"Anise to banish dark energy. Only peace and love will preside."

I closed my eyes, envisioning shadows fleeing from my sacred space, leaving only pure white energy.

Next, I took a little allspice, dropping it into the dish.

"Allspice to protect me from my enemies."

I pictured Cynthia's face when she snubbed me at the tax office. From what Aunt Maeve had said, she would be a formidable enemy.

Taking the cinnamon, I dropped the powder into the bowl

"Cinnamon for added protection."

I watched the candle's flame dart to the side, almost extinguishing. What did *that* mean? Was it working? I held my breath in case I was causing that.

Tap. Tap. Tap.

I practically jumped out of my skin at the series of taps! It sounded like they were coming from my front door.

When they repeated, I gritted my teeth. Who the hell was *that*?

I heard the click of the door handle and then, "Shannon? You here?"

My mouth fell open hearing Steve Murphy's voice! What was *he* doing here?

"Hang on!" I leaned over and blew the candles out, silently praying that I hadn't screwed everything up by doing that! From what I'd read, you were supposed to let them burn out on their own.

By the time I was up and storming down the hallway, Steve had stepped inside, brushing some flakes of snow from his collar. His smile was sheepish when he looked at me.

"Sorry to disturb you, Shannon." He sniffed. "Is that cinnamon? Are you baking?"

"No. Is something wrong? Did you need something?" My voice was cold. Maybe he was here about the bobcat again. Had he seen Bob on his own property and stopped by to complain about it?

"I'm here about Mary-Jane. Did you hear that she had a fire in her restaurant? Being such good friends I thought you should know." Steve's mouth became a thin line, peering at me. "But if I'm disturbing you—"

"No. I mean I was doing some reading and stuff, that's all. Yeah, I know about the fire. When I went to town, I got there shortly after the fire truck. Poor MJ." I folded my arms across my chest, looking up at him. It *was* kind of nice of him to stop to let me know about MJ.

Nice. My brain kicked into gear. I was having a conversation with a guy I'd come close to sleeping with because he was so *attractive.* Yet I hadn't said any of those crazy, flirty things to him. And if I could say those things to Devon and then STAN, why not Steve? He was every bit as hot as either of those guys.

Holy shit! That protection spell! It had already worked! That had to be it! Otherwise, I'd be flirting like some hooker in a bar trying to drum up business.

"You okay, Shannon? It's a terrible thing, I know. I delivered wood and supplies for their stage just this morning. Now they're going to need the kitchen overhauled. I'd like to help them out if I can."

It felt like a giant rock had been lifted from my shoulders! I was FREE! No more idiot gushing and flirting! The spell was reversed! I'd done it!

And talk about timing! If Steve had stopped by even an hour earlier, it could have gotten QUITE embarrassing. He read so much more into it than I ever wanted. Not to mention that I still didn't appreciate his attitude being so bossy about Bob.

"Me too! I want to help MJ and Ray." And I had it all

planned out how that was going to happen: the trip to the Witching Well later.

"Hopefully the insurance will cover everything, but the contractors need to work fast. Maybe even overnight. I thought of helping with the cleanup in the dining room. What do you think? Would you like to pitch in?"

Holding his hat with both hands, he leaned closer. "I'm sorry about what happened the other day between us."

Something in my chest loosened at the sadness in his eyes. Steve meant well even if sometimes he came off as bossy.

"Apology accepted, Steve. Would you like to try another coffee? Maybe this time, we'll finish it." I took his hat from him and hung it on the hook.

"Sure, I'd like that." He took his coat and boots off before following me into the kitchen. "No baked bread or pie? This place sure smells good."

There was no way I was going to get into why it smelled good. It really was none of Steve's business. I decided to change the subject. "I picked up a stringer job as a journalist at the *Wesley Weekly*. I was going to write a piece about MJ's dinner theater. Now I guess I'll write something about the fire. That sucks."

Steve took a seat at the table. "The dinner theater was a dynamite idea. It would help the restaurant and also be good for the town. It'd be nice to see people getting together for a little *culture* rather than heading to the church basement for bingo."

I chuckled as I went about making the coffee. "People really do that? Isn't there an age restriction, like you have to show your Medicare card to get in?"

"Hardly. My ex and her wife are regulars, when Byron's not at their place." He was quiet for a moment before he spoke, "But getting back to helping Ray and MJ. If a bunch of us worked together cleaning the place, it might get them up and running sooner. What do you say?"

I took a deep breath. Shit. I had hoped to avoid this subject with him. "I don't think I can, Steve. I'm working for Devon

Booker, helping him organize his office. It pays pretty well, and frankly, even though I'd like to help with the restaurant, I could use the extra cash." I looked over at him, not surprised to see the scowl on his face.

"You know how I feel about Booker, Shannon. But far be it from me to tell you what to do. It's your life. Just be careful around him."

I was getting so tired of hearing the same thing from all my friends. But I decided to let that go. At least Steve and I were talking again. That protection spell had worked better than I'd hoped.

Note to self: make sure I write about this in my Grimoire. It had to be the allspice that did the trick.

TWENTY TWO

Libby

That night...

L ibby! Are you serious?" Mary-Jane gaped at me. Her head bobbed forward, with a mouth wide enough to catch flies. If it were summer, that is.

My grin was a mile wide when I turned from staring at the road ahead. FINALLY, I got to tell someone about my gift! To be fair, MJ was understandably wired tight when I'd picked her up to drive to Shannon's, but after she'd vented, the news just burst out of me!

"YES! Believe me, I was as shocked as you when it happened. The raccoon said 'water'. Not out loud but...in my head! And then the squirrel... he told me he was hungry and that salami is nasty. And when I whispered to it, I think it understood me." My head was still buzzing with how amazing that had been. It had taken an act of supreme willpower, trying to concentrate on work, to get through my shift with that bitch, Jolene.

Mary-Jane's eyes narrowed and she was quiet for a moment. "Sounds like how I pick up other people's thoughts, their emotions, and memories with a touch of my hand. All of a sudden it's there"—she tapped her temple—" it's there in my head, playing like a movie."

"YEAH! That's it! It's there in my head!" I did a drum roll on the steering wheel with my hands. Mary-Jane totally GOT it! "Amazing, huh?"

She leaned over and squeezed my thigh. "I'm so happy for you, Libby! I was worried when this stuff, this magic stuff, wasn't happening for you. I mean, Shannon sees spirits and can wish a spell…" Her voice trailed off.

"Don't forget I made that glass move! And I've been practicing on light stuff at home with some success. But THIS? This is amazing!" Seeing Shannon's driveway up ahead, I flipped the turn signal. I couldn't wait to tell Shannon this. She'd probably be as smoked as MJ! Once we got past her diatribe about Cynthia's spell.

When I parked the car next to Shannon's truck, MJ reached over and stopped me from opening my door.

"Libby? I did something really bad. That fire happened because I screwed up." She sank back into the seat, clutching her hands together.

I sighed. "You can't blame yourself for the kitchen fire, MJ. It was an accident. You're not infallible, you know. We all make mistakes." It was a little exasperating for her to drag us back to *her* problem after I'd just shared incredible news!

She had her head down, murmuring something to her lap.

"Pardon? You need to speak up if you want me to hear you." It was difficult to keep the sharpness from my voice.

She looked over at me. "I wished that spell on Shannon. She made me so *mad*, Libby! It wasn't bad enough that I couldn't exercise anymore without getting a case of the hornies, but she mocked my idea of the dinner theater. She hurt my feelings."

All the air got sucked out of the car as I looked at her. Oh. My. God. SHE did that? After all, she'd learned about wishing bad on someone else, she went ahead and did it anyway, breaking the most important rule in witchcraft. Shit! I hadn't dared do that to Jolene, although I'd been seriously tempted.

"What am I going to do, Libby? Shannon's gonna kill me."

What could I say? She'd already been punished having that fire happen. She didn't need me piling on. I sighed. "You have to be honest, MJ. You've got to tell her."

MJ's eyes narrowed. "Well, she did it to me first!"

I threw my hands up. "What are you, a six-year-old? Besides, Shannon had only good wishes for you when she cast that spell. The raging hormones were a weird side effect, totally unplanned. You don't need to lose more weight, so don't work out. Problem solved."

MJ turned, and her hand slowly lifted to the door handle. "Okay. Let's get this over with."

Much as this was exasperating, I also felt sorry for MJ. She'd been paid back in spades for what she'd done. Now, if we could just reverse that spell and help both of them.

When I stepped out of the vehicle, I scanned Shannon's yard for any sign of the bobcat. But this time, I wasn't nearly as frightened of encountering it. Shit. I could talk to it, so why not? But there was only the stillness before Shannon's voice shattered the frosty night air.

"What's keeping you? Hurry up! I've got amazing news!"

I looked over at MJ. Whatever "amazing" news Shannon had would soon get blown out of the water by MJ's confession. And so much for my *own* "amazing" news.

TWENTY THREE

Shannon

S o what's your amazing news, Shannon?" Libby stepped into the house and then seeing MJ linger in the doorway, she tugged her into the warmth. "C'mon, MJ."

My gaze pinged between Libby and MJ. MJ looked like hell, with worry casting a pallor on her usual perky features. After the fire, that was understandable. But Libby... her face was drawn and she looked *miffed?* Considering she'd just worked a twelve-hour shift, she was probably tired.

Well, my news would cheer them up! Now we had only MJ to focus on tonight. "I blasted Cynthia's spell right out of the water. That's my news! I did a protection rite, and this time I used allspice! I think it did the trick. When Steve stopped by earlier—"

"Shannon! Slow down. We've hardly taken our boots off and you're going a mile a minute." Libby slipped her coat off and looked over at MJ.

Oh shit. I'd been so excited about the spell reversal that I wasn't thinking of MJ. The poor thing, with that fire today. I pulled MJ into a warm hug. "I'm sorry about your restaurant, MJ." I held her arms when I pulled back. "That's just so *awful*. We're going to do whatever we can tonight to get you back up and running."

"Speaking of running…" Libby fixed MJ with a flinty look. "MJ? Don't you have something to tell Shannon?" She hung her coat on the hook and sighed.

My face tightened, peering at the two of them. What the hell was going on? They were sure acting odd, even considering the circumstances. I looked at MJ. "What is it, honey? You can tell me." Oh God, not more bad news, I hoped.

Her chin dipped lower, and she looked up at me through her long lashes. "*I* cast the spell on you, Shannon. Not Cynthia—me. I'm really, really sorry."

My gut felt like someone had hit me with a sledgehammer. Mary-Jane? My forehead tightened as I peered at her. "*You* cast that spell on me so that every stupid sexual thought in my head came pouring out? Embarrassing me so much that I felt like crawling under a rock? *You* did that?"

I could hardly believe my eyes when she sheepishly nodded.

"Why? Why would you do that to me? I've only ever wanted the best for you. You're my friend." At least I thought she was my friend.

Right after the shock and bewilderment settled, a white-hot ball of anger rolled in. "ANSWER ME!"

She stamped her foot. "You started it! You and your stupid spell!"

"Back to kindergarten again," Libby murmured, looking down at the floor.

But MJ wasn't finished. "I had to quit the gym, and then I had to even quit running outdoors because of your stupid spell! It was too uncomfortable, and poor Ray was going to have a stroke. But when you looked down your nose at my idea of a dinner theater, calling your article a 'puff piece,' that was… that was mean."

All the while MJ justified her stupid spell, my blood boiled. Finally, she finished. "MEAN? I only said the truth! If you knew anything about journalism, you'd know the term is accurate. Ever hear the terms, hit piece, profile piece, or obit piece? Puff piece wasn't meant to demean you." My jaw clenched. "How could you do this to me?"

Libby lifted her hand, separating Mary-Jane and me. "Stop it. Let's have a seat and figure out how we're going to help MJ." She led the way to the kitchen and took a seat at the table. "The way I see it, your problem is solved, Shannon. MJ made a mistake and she's paying for that mistake. She also said she was sorry."

Mary-Jane nodded, looking over at me. "I really, really am, Shannon. And not just because it's coming back at ME now. I did something stupid and bad."

Although I was still fuming, I could tell her apology was sincere. "Don't you EVER cast a spell on me again, MJ!" When her eyes welled up with tears, the ball of ice in my gut started to melt. "Okay. So where do we go from here? We still need to ask for help for Mary-Jane and Ray, right?"

"Please." MJ stepped over to me and opened her arms inviting me to hug her. "I promise I'll never do anything like this again, Shannon. Forgive me?"

I sighed and stepped into her, hugging her. "Of course! You made a mistake; who hasn't?" I rubbed MJ's back with my hand. "It was so awkward—all those crazy things I said to Devon and Stan. Thank God the filter between my brain and mouth is back."

"I heard that you sounded like a schoolgirl, gushing over Stan." Libby snorted. "I can't wait to run into him at the coffee shop to hear what he has to say. That should be rich."

A soft thud sounded right outside the kitchen window. Libby jumped to her feet, peering out before I could get there. Immediately, she turned with a wide grin.

"It's the bobcat! I just saw him take off across your yard! I've got to talk to him." Libby bolted for the front door like her ass was on fire.

"Talk to him?" I looked over at Mary-Jane. She had a big grin as well. What the hell was going on with these two?

TWENTY FOUR

Mary-Jane

"Mary-Jane! Wait!" Shannon looked at me like I had two heads as I slipped my feet into my boots. Outside, Libby's voice was faint, calling to the bobcat.

"I can't! Libby can talk to animals now! I've GOT to see this. C'mon, Shannon!" I scrambled into my jacket and headed out the door. Libby was perched on the end of the verandah, staring into the black stand of trees at the side of Shannon's yard.

"I know you're out there. Come back. Please come back. I can talk to you, cat." Libby tried to step off the wooden platform, but when her leg disappeared into a foot of snow, she jerked back.

"What's going on, Libby? Is this true? You can communicate with animals now?" Shannon joined us, standing on Libby's other side. "When did this start? Why didn't you tell me?"

Libby's hair swished over her face when she turned to Shannon. "I can't get a word in edgewise with you two!" She glanced over at me. "I didn't mean you, MJ. Not with the shit that happened at your restaurant today."

But her voice was sharp again when she looked back at Shannon. "All you could talk about was your problem with that spell! Meanwhile, I had just communicated with a raccoon and a squirrel! Did you ever think to ask how my day was going? No. It was all about you!"

I touched her arm, trying to calm her. Libby didn't get angry very often but when she did... look out. "Maybe we'll see him again when we go to the Witching Well. Then you can show us."

Shannon folded her arms in front of her chest. "Sheesh, Libby. You need to just speak up, especially when it's something this awesome! You literally spoke to a squirrel and a raccoon? I can't wait to hear what Bob will say to you! Maybe you can tell him to bring me something I can actually use instead of stealing a wallet." She started to rub her upper arms with her hands. "I should have grabbed my coat. I'm going to get it now."

Seeing Libby straining to see the animal but failing, I placed my arm around her waist. "Everyone's on edge, Libby. The whole day has been shit from start to finish. I'm sorry we've been so caught up in our drama that we've kind of left you in the cold."

"Hey! Bob left me another present. Come see."

I turned at Shannon's excited voice. She held a cardboard box in her hands, peering at the label. "Let's go in and see what my familiar left me now. Then we can get ready to go to the well."

Libby sighed. "I guess he's not coming out. We might as well see what treasure he left for Shannon."

I followed behind her as we went back inside the house. Now that I could see the box, the damage that the big cat had done to it was plain to see. One corner was missing, the packaging label had streaks of dirt on what little remained of it.

Shannon snickered. "Bob will never get a job with UPS. He's pretty rough on the stuff he brings me." She nodded her head to the side, signaling for us to follow her into the kitchen. "I'll get the X-Acto knife and we'll see what treasures he's stolen this time."

As she worked at it, Libby and I huddled close, watching the flaps of the box open from her incisions. Shannon plucked the packing bubbles out, revealing a rectangular, shiny, pink box.

"What the hell?" Shannon lifted the smaller box out and broke the seal on its lid.

When it opened, and I could see what was nestled inside, my hands flew to my mouth! "A *vibrator*! Your bobcat brought you a VIBRATOR?"

"No. What the…" Libby's hand shot out, trying to take the hot-pink, curved shaft from Shannon's fist. "Let me see that!" Shannon yanked it back before she could touch it. But Libby didn't stop there, grabbing the small, pink box and turning away, quickly.

I looked over at Shannon and saw my own confusion mirrored in her eyes. What the hell was with Libby? This was hysterical! The porch-pirate bobcat had stolen some poor woman's package and not any package—but a *sex toy*!

My hand rose to rest on Libby's shoulder. Immediately, my face flamed when I read into her, picking up her thoughts. That wasn't just some random women's sex toy. It was Libby's!

LIBBY'S? The woman who had teased *me* about being obsessed with sex! Well, it seemed like she had a few obsessions of her own. My hand dropped from her shoulder. This was too out-there for words!

Shannon flicked a switch. The hum of the object sounded as the extension rabbit ears whirred, the movements so fast it was a blur. "Well, look at that. Bob didn't damage *this* little puppy. It's ready for action."

Libby turned around. Her face could not have gotten any redder unless she was bleeding. "Turn it off! This isn't right! Why would that stupid cat bring you that?"

Shannon smirked. "He knew I was frustrated when he brought me Stan's wallet. Not only is he a lousy delivery cat, but he's not that bright, mistaking normal frustration for… you know… the sexual kind." She laughed. "He should have brought it to you, MJ! You could probably make use of this until we remove my spell." Her eyes flashed wide. "It's yours, isn't it! Oh my God, MJ!"

"It's not *mine*, Shannon, although I might take it home with me if you don't remove that damned spell, you witch!" I looked over at Libby. Well, it was now her turn to fess up, wasn't it? "Do you have something to say, Libby?"

"Just shut up, MJ! You know it's mine! Why don't you just take out an ad in the newspaper? Better yet, Shannon can write a *puff piece* about it!" Libby grabbed the buzzing vibrator from Shannon and shoved it in the box. Then she picked it up to turn it off before once more slamming it in there.

"This is YOURS, Libby?" Shannon's mouth dropped almost to the floor. "Oh my God, this is too funny."

"It is NOT funny! This is *personal*, and absolutely none of your business!" Libby's eyes were narrow, spittle flying from her mouth when she barked at me, "I don't have a husband anymore, MJ! Not like you!"

Libby turned to glare at Shannon. "As for you…Steve wasn't enough for you? No, you came onto Devon Booker and then Stan! You have the nerve to make fun of MJ! Ha! You're worse! At least she's got the spell to blame."

I barely breathed, staring at Libby: Miss High and Mighty! She was wound tighter than a spool of thread! I spoke up, "Maybe if you weren't such a prig, you'd finally go out on a *date* with Stan. He's only asked you a million times. Maybe then you wouldn't need to buy *sex toys*!"

Shannon's head dipped, gawking at Libby. "You had this delivered to your HOME? What if one of your kids had opened—"

"They wouldn't DO that! I raised my kids to respect privacy. A lesson that neither of YOU ever learned!" Her nose lifted higher. "I was being discreet. That's not easy in a small town and especially with friends like you two! I've got my family to consider, which is why I've never accepted Stan's offers."

"Maybe it's time you did, Libby." Shannon reached for the

bottle of Jack Daniels in the cabinet next to her. "I don't know about you, but I need a drink. This night has been a rollercoaster."

My eyebrows rose and I took a deep breath. "Make mine a double."

Libby shook her head. "I'm driving, so—"

"Pour her a stiff one too!" The corners of my mouth twitched—*a stiff one*? That was apropos. "Just make sure it doesn't vibrate." I couldn't help it. It just popped out.

I smiled at Libby, speaking in a gentle tone this time. "We just want you to be happy, Libby. Your kids are pretty much self-sufficient, in high school. It's been years since Hank passed. It's time to start living again. Hank would want that for you."

Shannon murmured, "Yes. It's been what…six years since Hank passed?"

"Seven!" Libby took the drink that Shannon handed her, draining half of it in one swallow. "You two don't know what you're talking about."

Shannon shot a look at me before she nodded. "Yeah, I think as your best friends, we DO know what we're talking about. We know YOU, Libby. I get that this is a small town and you're a nurse and some pillar of the community, but…you're a woman who's been on her own a long time. Too long, if you ask me. No one's saying you should marry Stan or anything like that. But it's obvious you need to get laid, girlfriend."

Libby rolled her eyes. "Exactly why I bought that stupid toy. It's a biological need. I will not disrupt the kids' lives by dating Stan. End of story."

Lights flickered and then beamed in the kitchen window. I stepped over to check it out. "Someone is driving down your lane, Shannon. Who would be coming out here at almost ten o'clock?"

Shannon joined me at the window. When the lights extinguished and the car door opened, I couldn't believe who got out. "What the hell?"

TWENTY FIVE

Libby

Despite the humiliation deflating every cell in my body, the surprise in MJ's voice caught my attention. "Who is it? Should we lock the door?" I glanced at my watch. This couldn't be good for someone to show up at Shannon's house this late.

When Shannon turned, her face was a knot of worry. "It's Cynthia Granger! Why would she visit me at this time of night?" She stepped back, then walked across the room to open the front door.

MJ swore, "Shit! Are we ever going to get to that Witching Well tonight? This is like that play, *Waiting for Godot,* where he never shows up! I need some magic from that well, Libby."

"Don't we all." I joined Shannon in the foyer, waiting with the door open, peering at Cynthia's approach. From the quick strides across the verandah, and the stern look on her face, this couldn't be good.

Cynthia came to a halt, her red hair whipping across her cheek in the breeze. But it was her eyes, hard emeralds glaring at Shannon, then me, and behind me to MJ, which made me edge back a little.

"Cynthia! What in the world are you doing here?" Shannon stepped back, bumping into me and almost sending poor MJ onto her ass.

"That's astute. What in the *world*, indeed!" With hands thrust deep in the pockets of her white sheepskin jacket, she stepped inside and closed the door.

"Is something wrong?" From the thin line of her lips, and glaring at each of us, I had to ask.

"What the FUCK are the three of you doing? WRONG is a serious understatement, Libby! I know what you're up to— casting spells and hexes and generally creating a shitstorm in the universe!" She loosened her wool scarf and threw it at Shannon. Her fingers flew, unbuttoning her coat and hanging it on the hook.

Shannon raised her hand about to toss the scarf back at the younger woman, but Cynthia's voice stopped her cold.

"I wouldn't do that if I were you! You're in enough hot water as it is."

Her voice was soft, deadly soft, sending a chill down my spine. But it wasn't just the anger flowing in waves from her eyes, it was the cold and confident way she'd cowed Shannon. This was a side of Cynthia that I'd never experienced. She's always been assured… but at least she'd been *friendly*?

The heels of her leather boots clattered on the hardwood floor as she stomped into the kitchen. My heart raced faster as I watched her go to the counter and pour herself a tumbler of whiskey. It was as if *she'd* lived here for years and Shannon was the guest.

When she turned, she downed a few swallows of the amber liquid, leaning her backside against the edge of the sink. Mary-Jane took a seat at the table while Shannon stood her ground with her arms crossed over her chest.

It was high noon at the OK Corral.

"What's gotten into you, Cynthia? You snubbed me at the tax office, and now you barge in here…practically threatening us, acting so arrogant. And you're welcome for the drink, by the way." Shannon took a step closer, edging into the space that Cynthia had staked out for herself.

Cynthia ignored her, tipping her head up, smiling at the ceiling above. "*Neophytes!* Divine Mother, spare me having to deal with neophytes."

Her gaze then fixed on Shannon. "Your Aunt Maeve and my grandmother were friends, Shannon. Good friends, as in sisters in their coven. And now, you and these two…" She huffed, sending a filthy look at MJ and me. "Let's just say, the coven you are trying to create is interfering. With ME!"

Shannon's head turned, looking at a spot across the room. "You were right, Aunt Maeve! She IS a practicing witch!"

For a moment I felt dizzy, trying to follow the conversation where one of the participants was invisible—a ghost.

I ventured a question to Cynthia, "How exactly are we interfering with you? We're new to this but our magic is growing. How are we a threat to you?" I couldn't imagine how. The young woman exuded power from her pores, while we were still bumbling along.

"That's just it! You ARE bumbling along."

Holy shit! She read my mind! She WAS powerful. I backed up until I was at the table, taking a seat next to MJ.

But Shannon wasn't backing down one bit. "No. We're learning—protection spells, wishing spells, telekinesis, and psychometry."

"Don't forget I can talk to animals!" I was sick of being ignored! It was time my new talent got some recognition.

Shannon continued, "Yes. I don't know the name for it, but apparently Libby can now communicate with animals. What's any of this got to do with you, Cynthia? You aren't explaining yourself very well."

"For the last few days, whenever I cast a spell or ask for the Mother's assistance, things go haywire. A simple spell, like asking for guidance for a problem I'm having with my landlord, and the situation goes off the rails! Instead of him fixing the jets in my hot tub, he's spending his days in it— nude! It ain't pretty. There's no way I'll ever go in there again with all the hair he sheds."

Mary-Jane leaned forward gaping at Cynthia. "You can do a spell for that? Why not just contract it out?"

Cynthia shook her head in exasperation like she was talking to a toddler. "I'm not supposed to even HAVE a hot tub! How do you think I got it in the first place? I spelled Zach into installing it, and then I put a glamour on it. Only he and I can see the thing. So, if he doesn't fix it, I'm screwed. Or at least that's what the old fart wants to do with me in that tub! Yuck!"

Mary Jane squeaked, "What's a glamour? I don't think you're talking about the magazine?" Her voice was so small, like a kindergartener.

Cynthia did an eye roll. "It means that only people *I* choose can see it." She took another slug of her drink. "Neophytes!"

"Cry me a river!" Shannon stepped over to retrieve her drink, purposely bumping into Cynthia. "It's a free world! Who says you're the only one who can practice magic? The fact that you're losing your touch isn't our fault, *dear.*"

Cynthia's hand rose, and she flicked her finger at Shannon. Immediately, Shannon jolted back, arms swinging until her hand gripped the microwave stand to prevent her from falling over.

"It seems I still have it, *dear.*" Cynthia's hand rose to her lips, and she blew on her fingertips, smirking at Shannon.

And then like a chameleon, her face became hard once more. "My cat used to snuggle but now he *bites* me. The pimply-faced dork who doesn't know a spreadsheet from a piece of toilet paper got the promotion that was supposed to go to *me*! And now I catch whatever cold or flu bug is lurking around, no doubt carried by my coworker's children! The last few guys I dated were impotent. Need any more?"

Her hands rose to fist her wavy hair. "THIS SUCKS! You three have got to get your freaking act together! You're screwing with the universe and me!"

Mary-Jane snickered and grabbed the pink box from the table. "This might help with the impotence problem."

I snatched it out of her hand and set it next to my purse, purposely ignoring her snide remark. "Shannon has a Bob as in bobcat, and this is Libby's B.O.B." She snickered. "As in Battery Operated Boyfriend!"

Cynthia turned to Shannon. "YOU got the bobcat? He picked YOU?" Her mouth fell open as she gaped at Shannon. "Next, you're going to tell me you've visited the Witching Well."

Shannon grinned. "Yes, Bob chose me! And as for the well, how do you think this all started? Of course, I've been to the well; it's on my property." Her nose went up, looking down at Cynthia. "You've been to the well?"

Cynthia nodded. "Just once. I know it's powerful, but I never wanted to get involved in a coven. I'm not only gifted, but I've learned a lot all on my own."

Watching the exchange, the two of them stubborn, each powerful in their own right, I offered my opinion. "We need to help Mary-Jane. Once we're back on track, abiding by the rules, we shouldn't cause any more problems for you, Cynthia. But MJ really made a mess, and to reverse this, we might need your help."

I looked at Shannon. "I think you should ask Cynthia to go to the well with us tonight."

Shannon looked over at Cynthia, staying silent for a few moments."Considering that you'd benefit as well as us, would you like to go with us? Tonight. But you're only coming as my guest. Got it?"

Cynthia's eyes narrowed. "Agreed. On one condition. You have to listen to me. You're straying from your path"—she looked over at Mary-Jane and me—" all of you. You need a course correction for this coven. This isn't junior high, but lately, you three have been acting like classical 'mean girls.' Time to put your big-girl panties on, ladies."

TWENTY SIX

Shannon

Ten minutes later we left the house, bundled in our winter jackets with wool capes topping them. The supplies, which I'd organized earlier—the lighter, lantern, white candle, soil, and a jar of water—were divided among the four of us. The only thing I'd added was the flask of Jack Daniels, tucked into the bottom of my satchel.

The whiskey was a tribute to my first trip, stumbling upon the well with only a thermos of Jack Daniels to offer. The well had appreciated it, almost making me soil myself when it belched a *"Thanks."*

When I saw Libby lingering, peering into the forest for any sign of Bob, I nudged her. "He's out there. I can't wait to see you do this, Libby. Sorry for how I was so self-absorbed today."

"It's okay." She looked behind her at Cynthia, who was walking next to MJ. "What do you think of her? I thought you two were going to get into a catfight."

"Believe it or not, I like her. She was abrasive at first, and she shocked the hell out of me when she flicked her finger. I think she means well though."

Right on time, Cynthia strode forward to catch up with us. "You'll have to lead, Shannon. It's been years, and I only visited the well once. Are you ready for some tough love, now?"

I chuckled. "Does it matter if we're ready? You're going to have your say anyway."

"Touché. I'll try not to lecture though." Cynthia cast a glance over her shoulder. "Mary-Jane! You know what you did wrong, and you're paying for it now. *Never, ever* cast a spell when you're angry. You were pissed with Shannon, and yes, she meddled in your life with good and bad results. Honesty, being forthright would have made your friendship bond stronger, and you wouldn't be in this mess."

My jaw muscles tightened hearing Cynthia. "I never meant harm to MJ! My intention was pure. I didn't know that she'd get raging hormones from exercising." The toe of my boot caught on a tree root hidden in the foot of snow, and I grabbed Cynthia's arm to steady myself.

"I know that." Cynthia patted my hand on her arm. "Magic can sometimes be perverse. It happens to the best of us."

She sighed. "Now for the bad news, Shannon. That spell that MJ cast on you, with sexual thoughts rocketing out of your mouth unfiltered, that's still on you."

Cynthia leaned forward and laughed as she looked over at Libby. "You didn't see a ball gag in your shopping online, did you? Shannon's going to need one if she's ever going to be around your guy or Devon."

"What's a ball gag?" MJ piped up. "I feel like I'm missing out on something."

I ignored MJ because Cynthia hit a nerve with Libby. "MY GUY?" Libby practically shrieked. "Stan Jones isn't *my guy*. We're friends. That's it."

My head was still reeling about the stupid spell. *It was still on me?* Ball gag? No way was I wearing some stupid ball gag! This wasn't *Fifty Shades of Grey*! She had to be wrong. But before I could tell her that, Cynthia turned to Libby again.

"There's a connection between you and Stan, Libby. You

don't have to be clairvoyant to see it. You're hiding behind your family, too afraid to put yourself out there again. Hank's death was a tragedy. But so is a life lived in fear. You deserve more intimacy and its concurrent fulfillment than what that sex toy will provide. Grab the brass ring, woman!"

I tapped Cynthia's arm to get her attention. "Hang on! You're wrong about that spell! I spent some time today with Steve Murphy and it went okay. I never once told him he was hot or had bedroom eyes I'd love to drown in. I was in control of my tongue, and considering it was *Steve*, well, you KNOW! You dated him for a few months!"

Her head tipped to the side as she peered at me. "I honestly don't know why it didn't affect you with Steve. That's odd. Magic. It can be fickle and unpredictable sometimes." She elbowed me. "Get the ball gag is all I'm saying."

We trudged on in silence for a few minutes. The moon was a silver cusp peeking through occasionally as we wound through the forest. I pulled the hood of my cape up to cover my head when a gust of wind whispered in the boughs overhead.

Cynthia cleared her throat. "Promise me you'll be kind with each other from now on. That will work wonders in making powerful magic. Shannon, there are other ways you can help Mary-Jane. I heard you got a job at the newspaper. There's power in words."

I rolled my eyes. "Don't forget I have that job with Devon too! What we do at the well should remove MJ's spell, so I won't need to wear a ball gag."

"What's a ball gag!" MJ piped up again.

Cynthia shook her head slowly. "You need to read more, hon; I'll fill you in later, okay?"

Which prompted my next question, about my encounter with the ghost at Devon's office. "What do you know about Estelle Cousins? She's the ghost haunting Devon's building. She asked me for my help."

Cynthia stopped dead in her tracks. "Estelle Cousins? Are you sure?"

"Yes. She detests Devon. Every time he shows up, she fades into the woodwork."

"That's not good. I don't mean Estelle. She had a reputation as being one of the sweetest women this town ever knew. My grandmother told me about her. But if she's asked for your help, there's something important going on. You need to listen to her."

Cynthia looked over her shoulder before she started walking again. "You okay back there, MJ?"

When I turned, MJ's coat was thrown back over her shoulders, and the sides of her jacket hung loose as she fanned her neck with her hand. "Is that supposed to be *funny*, Cynthia? My heart is pounding like a racehorse trudging through a foot of snow! This is EXERCISE, in case you didn't know. We all know what happens when I exert myself like this."

Libby let out a hoot of laughter. "Want me to go back to get that pink box? You need it more than me, from the look of your face!"

I had to laugh seeing Mary-Jane practically panting.

"Shove it up your—"

"That'll be enough!" But after she barked the order, Cynthia looked over at me, giggling softly. "Shines a whole new light on the perversity of magic, doesn't it?"

TWENTY SEVEN

Shannon

The Well

It looks so different from what I remember, Shannon." Cynthia lifted the hood from her head and stared around at the dark trees circling the snow-filled glade.

The moon shone down, casting a sheen of sparkles over the pristine white. The well was a sharp contrast, with shadowed wood above the stone base. I noticed snow-like white loaves of bread perched on the boughs of the trees surrounding us, but the well was completely clear. Even the bucket hanging from the crossbeam was bare of any snowfall.

I glanced over at Cynthia. "Can you feel it?" I said. "Every time I come here, it's like stepping into another realm. Peaceful yet alive with hidden power waiting for release." My toes which had ached from the cold, now were warm, sucking in the vibration from the earth below.

Mary-Jane sighed. "I feel it. The quiet, especially after the walk here. It's refreshing after the day I've had, like sinking into a cool lake on a hot summer day."

"Right now the only feeling that's drowning out everything else is that we're being watched." Libby turned in a circle probing the shadows, searching. "I know the bobcat's out there checking our every move. I've felt it for the last five minutes."

I smiled. "At least Bob's not stealing any more packages, then." I took a deep breath of the frosty air. "Shall we, sisters?" Without waiting for their reply, I stepped into the glade, walking with confident purpose to the well. With every step, a quiet certitude grew in my chest. The day had been a maelstrom of chaos and sniping, but being here brought order.

When the others took their spots around the well, my eyes opened wider, seeing the perfection! Across from me, Cynthia was standing in the most southerly point, while Mary-Jane was positioned at the east and Libby at the west. Unconsciously we had cast a compass circle!

I scooped the lighter from my jeans and set the lantern containing the candle on the lip of the well. Soon the glow of the flame sparked high, lighting the area around us.

Divine power, protector of life
We bring this fire, providing light
Strong intention, pure and strong
Our plea for you to right this wrong

I held the lantern aloft, arcing it in the four directions. When I finished, lowering it, I nodded to Mary-Jane.

She held the cloth bag containing soil over the chasm of the well.

We honor the earth, nourishing life
From our hearts, remove all strife
Casting in anger, my grave sin
Create order amidst the din

With that, Mary-Jane emptied the bag into the well and nodded to Libby.

Libby stepped closer to the well, holding the jar of water over the hole.

Blood of life my hands do hold
More precious than stores of gold

Wash away bad which caused pain
As gentle as the healing rain

She tipped the jar and let the water trickle out into the well. When it was empty, she looked over at Cynthia.

Cynthia's arms rose high, and clasping the sides of the cape in her fingers, she swirled in a counterclockwise direction, the cape ballooning around her.

The fourth element, the breath of air
Our hearts and bodies we lay bare
Open to guidance, power for good
As I dance with my sisters in these woods.

"So mote it be." The rest of us joined in the refrain.

We joined hands, and instead of raising them to the sky, honoring the moon, I stepped to the side, pulling Libby and nudging Mary-Jane until we were all walking around the well. Whether it was Cynthia's "dance" that inspired me or just the sheer joy of being there, it was the right ending to our ceremony.

Our footsteps became faster, our faces beaming with laughter. Mary-Jane was the first to cry out, "Blessed Be!" Soon all of us chanted it as we pranced in the snow circling the well.

"ENOUGH! WE RECOGNIZE YOUR PRESENCE!"

When her hands flew to her mouth, Cynthia was the first to break the chain! "IT SPEAKS? Divine holy shit! That thing yelled at us!" She took a few steps back, gaping at the well.

It was the first that I'd seen a chink in her air of confidence. She was cowed, her face blanched as white as the snow at her feet. I laughed, and then Mary-Jane and Libby joined in.

"That's Alice Johnston. I inherited her Grimoire, Cynthia. Come back to our circle because I don't think she's finished." I scooped the flask of Jack Daniels from my satchel. "Alice, I'm sure you'd like a little whiskey on such a cold winter night."

Flashing a warm smile at Cynthia when she joined us at the edge of the well, I poured half of the flask down the dark cavern. My hand cupped my ear as I leaned over the rim.

"THANKS!"

"See?" I practically beamed, grinning at the young woman who'd joined us for the first time.

"NOT SO FAST!"

This time it was me who jerked back! Shit! Did it want more? I'd hoped the four of us could have a swallow to warm ourselves on the way back to my place. I lifted the flask again about to empty the container into the well but Cynthia stopped me.

"I'm getting the message that she's referring to the spell."

Mary-Jane's fingers touched the cold stone of the well and she nodded. "That's what I'm picking up too. The spells aren't reversed, Shannon. The only way that will happen is through us."

"What does *that* mean?" Libby peeked over the lip of the well. "So we went through all this for nothing?"

"THE SPELLS YOU HAVE CAST
SHALL BE IN THE PAST
BY YOUR DEEDS BE PROVEN
WHEN YOU ACT AS A COVEN

There was a pause, and then it cried out:

YOU'VE BUT SPOKE WORDS
BUT TALK IS CHEAP
IT TAKES MONEY TO BUY WHISKEY
NOW DROP THE REST OF THAT FLASK OF
WHISKEY TO ME AND LEAVE."

A belch followed this thundering outburst.

My hand shook as I emptied the flask down the well. Even though I'd heard this well speak before, it had never said this much or with such force.

Mary-Jane started putting the lantern and empty jar into her satchel, mumbling. "'By your deeds be proven,' huh? So in order to remove these spells, we have to do something together, act as a coven."

As we walked across the clearing to the trees, Libby wondered aloud, "So I take that to mean, we have to help one another, support each other." She looked over at Cynthia. "Are you part of our coven now?"

Hearing Libby say what I was secretly afraid would happen, being upstaged by Cynthia, was an arrow in my chest. "Maybe just until we get the spells reversed, Cynthia will be part of our coven. It doesn't have to be forever."

"That's what *I'm* hoping." Cynthia's eyebrows shot up to her coppery hairline. "I don't play well with others. I'd rather be on my own practicing magic but… I want to get right with the universe again. That can't happen unless I join with you, at least temporarily."

I looked over at her. "Don't get me wrong. I like you, Cynthia, but the rest of us are kind of on the same level, magically speaking. Plus, aren't we supposed to honor the power of three? You'd literally be the fourth wheel."

Mary-Jane muttered, "The term is *fifth wheel*, Shannon, but we get what you mean."

Cynthia looked at each of us in turn as we retraced our footsteps in the snow. "The power of three doesn't refer to the size of a coven, you guys. The law of three means that what you send out into the world, comes back to you by an order of three." She gave a pointed look at MJ. "That's why we *never* cast in anger to hurt someone."

"You're telling me! My freaking kitchen caught fire. I'm hoping that our server flirting with Ray was the second thing. I'm worried about the third."

"Hush!" Libby took a few steps going off the path and deeper into the forest. "Bobcat? Is that you? Come out. We won't hurt you."

I stopped in my tracks along with MJ and Cynthia, watching Libby call to the bobcat. When a branch snapped, followed by what sounded like a crying baby, my mouth fell open.

Bob. I'd know that yowl anywhere.

TWENTY EIGHT

Libby

I locked eyes with the cat as its feet picked a path through the snow, edging around fallen branches. It was as graceful and theatrical as a ballet in slow motion. Tempting as it was to squat lower, I had to remind myself that this wasn't a squirrel I was dealing with. This was a big cat! And from the looks of its ear, it had been in a fight or two.

"Come closer. I can talk to you. Can you talk to me?" My breath hitched in my chest, unsure whether my gift only worked on very small animals. Maybe this guy would leap at me and I'd be in serious trouble.

When the cat was about six feet away from me, it sat down, flicking its good ear. *"What is it you want? I'm not for you."* He looked at something behind me.

I grinned! This was working! The bobcat—Shannon's familiar—was communicating with me! Holy shit! I gushed, "I know you serve Shannon. Don't worry, Bob. I get that. I was only—"

"ROBERT! If she has to label me with some fancy 'human' label, at the very least it should be more dignified. It's Robert." The cat's ear flattened against its head, letting me know he meant business.

"Is it working? Are you talking to Bob?" Shannon called as she scrambled through the snow, stopping a few feet behind me.

When I turned my head, I saw MJ and Cynthia huddled next to her, watching with wide eyes. "Yes! I'm talking to the bobcat! And his name is Robert, not Bob."

When I turned back to Robert, Shannon mumbled, "He'll always be Bob to me. He's *my* familiar, and I'd say shortening his name is pretty familiar."

I waved my hand behind me to get her to shut up so I could go back to my convo with Robert.

"Can you let her know that the food she leaves out for me is not acceptable? I manage to choke it down, but it gives me gas."

I thought of the squirrel picking the salami from my sandwich. "Kind of like salami? Too spicy? The squirrel didn't like—"

"I am infinitely greater than a squirrel! I probably shouldn't even bother talking to you if that's the company you keep. Next time, bring your squirrel with you. It would be a welcome treat compared to the scraps from her plate."

"What's he saying? You're talking about salami? You finally manage to talk to him and it's about FOOD?" Shannon snickered.

"See what I have to put up with? She's so coarse, absolutely no class. How did I get stuck with her? I should have chosen you. At least I could have a sensible conversation. You'd feed me wild salmon, not something shot full of chemicals. And her drool on the pieces of"—Robert shuddered— *"cooked, ruined carcass. But it's a life sentence with her, I'm afraid."*

I looked around at Shannon. "He doesn't like what you've been leaving out for him at night. Now, let me talk to him, okay?"

Shannon barked out a laugh. "He *eats* it! It can't be *that* bad. Can you tell Bob that he's got to stop being a porch pirate? Of all people, I would have thought that would be the first thing you'd tell him!"

I felt my cheeks get warmer thinking of Robert stealing my

"package." Turning back to him, I said, "She wants you to stop stealing packages, Robert." My forehead bunched as I peered at him. "How DO you manage that? Aren't you afraid of someone seeing you in town and maybe shooting you?"

"This from the witch who is standing in the forest, in the middle of the night, on her way back from the Witching Well? How do you think I manage it, Einstein?"

My cheeks went even hotter being chastised by the cat. "Okay. Stupid question. Magic, of course."

Cynthia stepped up beside me, casting a wide-eyed look at me before smiling at Robert. "This is really happening! You're talking to that cat!" She turned to him, extending a hand. "He's so beautiful! Do you think he'd mind if I petted his fur?"

I smiled at Robert. "She wants to pet you. Would that be okay?" I was as smoked by all this as Cynthia, but I also knew that Robert was prickly.

He rolled onto his back, wiggling in the snow, edging closer. *"Behind my right ear, or what's left of it. It gets itchy sometimes."*

"That must have been one hell of a fight."

He looked over at me and his eyes hooded. *"It's now in the past, and it's not the proper time to discuss that episode."* There was a look in his eyes that told me he meant it. He glanced over at MJ. *"My scratches, if you please."*

After I told her, Mary-Jane joined us. She shook her head in wonder, before joining Cynthia in giving Robert a few pets and scratches.

I looked back at Shannon. This was HER familiar. Wouldn't she want to join in? Even if he wasn't, who wouldn't be stunned by a talking bobcat, let alone being able to pet him? But she just watched us, arms folded across her chest.

"Shannon? Don't you want—?"

"Can we do this back at the house?" She shifted and crossed one leg over the other. "I have to pee, you guys. Bob can even come in the house if he wants, but I really have to go to the bathroom."

Mary-Jane and Cynthia stood up, leaving a dazed, sleepy-looking Robert laying there. His head jerked up, and the rumble in his throat, the purring, stopped.

"I'm afraid we have to head back, Robert. It's Shannon. A bio break, y'know? Come with us. I want to keep talking to you." I watched him stare at Shannon and slowly get to his feet.

"So SHE wants to go! The fun police! I guess that means we all have to go. Just when I was starting to enjoy myself, getting the attention I so rightly deserve."

He fell into step beside me, while MJ and Cynthia walked ahead. I looked down at him. "Robert? Is this normal for a familiar to resent his witch? Shannon's pretty nice once you get to know her."

Robert yowled before he looked up at me, *"I don't dislike my witch. In retrospect, I didn't make the best choice with her, but I've also made far worse choices. She's a little rough around the edges, but she's got real potential...with the correct training."*

I stared down at him, sauntering through the snow, his shoulders rolling while the stub of his tail twitched. "So, you're training *her*? I thought you were supposed to serve your witch."

"I AM! Right now I'm giving her a lesson in humility. Shannon doesn't have to urinate. I'd know! My olfactory senses are an encyclopedia of information. She's miffed that SHE can't communicate with me. But if she didn't belittle me, I'd make more of an effort to get my points across."

For the next few minutes, my head spun with everything that had happened that night. And to end it with a cat psychoanalyzing its witch.

Bizarre didn't even come close.

TWENTY NINE

Mary-Jane

The next day...

"Mary-Jane! We have to meet the insurance adjuster in half an hour and you're still in bed. What time did you get in from Shannon's last night?"

My eyes slowly opened, as if they had a mind of their own and wanted to stay shut. When the sand finally scraped away from the burning orbs in my face, I saw Ray standing there, hands on hips, tapping his foot impatiently.

"Can *you* do it? Why do *I* have to be there?" I tried pulling the covers over my head but Ray yanked them away.

"We BOTH have to meet with him, MJ! Especially you. You were in the kitchen when it caught fire. He'll want to hear it from you." He turned and walked to the bedroom door, pausing for a moment. "I'm leaving in twenty minutes! You'd better be ready."

I yawned and then swung my legs over the side of the bed. SHIT! Of all the times I needed to sleep in, *this* was the morning. I'd only had four hours sleep, for Pete's sake!

Trudging to the bathroom to shower and fix my face, I had to smile. If Ray only knew what had happened at Shannon's. As if the rite at the well wasn't weird and wonderful enough, we'd spent another couple of hours sitting by the fire, while Robert entertained us with tales of previous witches. That cat was hilarious, although Shannon didn't appreciate his humor. But Libby and I noticed she hadn't kicked him out when we left either.

Exactly a half-hour later, Ray and I unlocked the front door of the restaurant and went inside. The acrid smell of smoke clung to everything! I ran my finger along the oak bar and it came back black with soot.

"It looks like the insurance guy is here."

When I turned, a stout, dark-haired guy with a trim goatee and mustache stepped into the foyer. His dark eyes behind heavy frames took in the room in a glance, and walking over to us, he extended his hand.

"Mark Brown of Empire State Insurance. You must be Mr. and Mrs. Matthews."

When I took his hand, skepticism leaped into my head. If there was any way he could blame this fire on negligence, or use some loophole in the policy to deny our claim, he was going to find it. When did it happen? It used to be you felt relieved that you were insured. Nowadays, not so much; the presence of an insurance adjuster wasn't a comfort, it was another headache to contend with. Nowadays, they prided themselves on claims denied.

My smile faded. "Pleased to meet you. Let me show you around to the kitchen, where the fire started."

He nodded. "Yes. If you don't mind, I'm going to record this as well as take photos. We need to present as clear a picture as possible to my boss. Mr. Ambrose makes the final approval on claims."

"Yes. Yes. Of course," Ray murmured, leading the way through the dining room. The adjuster paused, taking photos with his cell phone, making it a slow procession.

At the sound of the door opening, I was about to tell any

prospective customer that we were closed when I saw it was Cynthia and Shannon! What a sight for *literally* sore eyes.

"What are you two doing here? I thought you'd still be in bed. That was a late night!"

Shannon handed me a paper cup of coffee. "We almost didn't come here. When I checked my phone messages this morning, Ray had left one. Apparently, he couldn't reach you, so he let me know about this meeting with the adjuster, so I'd get you to leave early. Fat chance of that!"

"I was on my way to work when Shannon kidnapped me." Cynthia looked around at the restaurant. "This sucks. We're here for moral support, MJ. I've dealt with insurance people. You're going to need some help."

I leaned in and lowered my voice, "When I shook his hand, I knew he had no intention of honoring the claim. Tried to spin us about having to get approval from his boss. Total bullshit."

Cynthia winked at me. "Watch and learn, MJ." When she took a few steps, heading for Ray and the adjuster, her hips swayed in the short, flirty skirt. She looked over her shoulder at me. "A pinch of witch, with a dollop of bitch."

Shannon grabbed my arm, pulling me closer. "That poor man doesn't know that a Mack truck is bearing down on him. He'll never know what hit him." She laughed. "She knows how to work it. I wish my ass was *half* that sexy."

I elbowed her. "You're every bit as attractive. You're just *seasoned* more." But even that wasn't true. Shannon was one of those rare women who just never aged. Aside from laugh lines around her eyes, her skin was smooth and clear of wrinkles.

She pinched the skin on my arm, and I jerked back. "That's for the 'seasoned' comment." Her head nodded to the side, indicating Cynthia and the others. "Let's ratchet this up a few notches to help Cynthia and get that insurance adjuster to approve your claim."

Shannon closed her eyes, murmuring, "You will approve MJ's claim for damages. You will *want* to do this more than anything."

I nodded and joined her, chanting this softly, all the while picturing that little toad writing a check to us. I could picture it very clearly—see the contractors restoring my kitchen and getting this restaurant up and running again.

I started when Shannon scooped my hand into hers. She smiled. "Okay, hold those thoughts while we see how it's going with Cynthia. C'mon." I let her lead me across the room to join the others.

The first thing that struck me was how Cynthia sidled up close to the adjuster, hovering over his shoulder as he held his camera out snapping photos. When my eyes met Ray's, I knew exactly what was going through his mind. *What the hell is she doing, flirting with this idiot?* Not magic this time, but over twenty years of marriage to credit for that insight.

"You're very talented, Mark. Your ability with that camera is, well, it's *magic*." Cynthia followed this saccharin comment with a sly wink at me. She continued, "You can even see the sooty shadows on the curtains in that shot. So much damage. This is like watching a maestro work, Mark."

His hand rose to push his glasses higher on his nose, before his Adam's apple bobbed, swallowing hard. "Uhhh, I've got some experience with this."

Her hand casually draped over his shoulder as she looked down at him. "I can tell. Experience always shows. I bet you have oodles and oodles of it. Your job must be so interesting!"

Even though the area above the goatee flashed pink, it was like watching a peacock fan his feathers as he rocked back and forth on his feet. "I could tell you some stories, Cynthia!"

Her hand slid down his arm and hooked his elbow, guiding him to the kitchen. She had to lean to the side, almost putting her head on his shoulder when she cooed. "I'd love that! I bet you've helped so many families with your generosity. I'm so glad that *you* are the expert your company sent to help my friends."

As we followed Mark and Cynthia through the swinging door to the kitchen, I looked over at Shannon and stuck my finger in my mouth, feigning a gag. Her eyebrows bobbed in acknowledgment.

Before I could step through, Ray grabbed my arm and leaned in. "What's going on, MJ? The way Cynthia's acting, that guy looks like he doesn't know whether to shit or wind his watch."

I chuckled. That was exactly the point. "As long as he writes us a check, who cares?"

He nodded and slipped through the door ahead of us. When we entered, my gut sank seeing the charred mess and water damage. So many happy hours spent in that room; now it was a disaster. Beside me, Shannon muttered.

"Wow! Payback from the universe is a bitch."

Which reminded me of the spell I had cast on her. She hadn't said anything outrageously flirty with Mark, not that Cynthia didn't have that covered like a weighted blanket! But a glance at Mark and the answer was clear. Shannon didn't need a filter on her mouth around that toad.

Mark stood in the center of the mess, with his arms extended taking photos, when he lurched to the side. Cynthia's hand whipped up to catch him at the last moment. He took a deep breath, staring at the floor. "I don't know what came over me… I guess just a dizzy spell."

Cynthia patted his arm. "It's probably your heart hurting, seeing the damage that this fire has done to an innocent family. You're such a good and kind man. I can tell these things about people, Mark."

He cleared his throat and looked down. "Yes." Sneaking a glance up at her, he added, "This is a strange morning. I'm glad you're here. I might have fallen."

Cynthia's glance at Shannon and me was just a glimmer, silently confirming the magic fog that Mark floundered in. She smiled down at him, practically purring. "I'm glad to be of service to someone like you."

We watched the show with Cynthia fawning over Mark and him eating it up like it was cordon bleu, for another half hour. Finally, preening in front of his gorgeous admirer, Mark pulled a tablet from his satchel and smiled.

"The damage is extensive, and as this is your first claim in all the years you've been with us, I trust that this was purely accidental. Your policy covers you for loss of income during the time your business is down. It would be in both parties' interests to expedite matters."

Cynthia gushed, "What an astute businessman! Not only handsome, but clever!"

He nodded, accepting the admiration before turning once more to Ray and me. "Based on my experience in settling claims, I am prepared to write you a check for sixty-eight thousand dollars. That will replace your equipment, the repairs to the structure, and the dining room clean up."

Ray's gaze darted to meet mine, his shock mirroring mine. We had talked about the cost but this estimate was easily 20 percent higher than we'd expected! Give us the pen and show us where to sign!

Cynthia tsked, stepping closer to Mark, running her finger over his collar. "You couldn't increase that to seventy-five? It would mean so much to the people in this town to have the restaurant running again. I'd consider it a… *personal* favor."

Mark's mouth opened a little before his hand rose to wipe a bead of sweat from his brow. The poor guy looked like he was about to stroke out. "Well…maybe I didn't factor in the loss of goodwill in the community. I could go that high. But that's it, Cynthia."

She actually threw her arms around him to hug him. Mark's face nestled into her neck, while she gave me and Ray a thumbs-up behind the adjuster's back.

Butterflies swooped in my stomach the whole time the adjuster's pen scribbled on the blank check: SEVENTY-FIVE THOUSAND! Oh my.

We'd be back in business in no time with that kind of money!

My eyes slowly opened, as if they had a mind of their own and wanted to stay shut. When the sand finally scraped away from the burning orbs in my face, I saw Ray standing there, hands on hips, tapping his foot impatiently.

"Can *you* do it? Why do *I* have to be there?" I tried pulling the covers over my head but Ray yanked them away.

"We BOTH have to meet with him, MJ! Especially you. You were in the kitchen when it caught fire. He'll want to hear it from you." He turned and walked to the bedroom door, pausing for a moment. "I'm leaving in twenty minutes! You'd better be ready."

I yawned and then swung my legs over the side of the bed. SHIT! Of all the times I needed to sleep in, *this* was the morning. I'd only had four hours sleep, for Pete's sake!

Trudging to the bathroom to shower and fix my face, I had to smile. If Ray only knew what had happened at Shannon's. As if the rite at the well wasn't weird and wonderful enough, we'd spent another couple of hours sitting by the fire, while Robert entertained us with tales of previous witches. That cat was hilarious, although Shannon didn't appreciate his humor. But Libby and I noticed she hadn't kicked him out when we left either.

Exactly a half-hour later, Ray and I unlocked the front door of the restaurant and went inside. The acrid smell of smoke clung to everything! I ran my finger along the oak bar and it came back black with soot.

"It looks like the insurance guy is here."

When I turned, a stout, dark-haired guy with a trim goatee and mustache stepped into the foyer. His dark eyes behind heavy frames took in the room in a glance, and walking over to us, he extended his hand.

"Mark Brown of Empire State Insurance. You must be Mr. and Mrs. Matthews."

When I took his hand, skepticism leaped into my head. If there was any way he could blame this fire on negligence, or use some loophole in the policy to deny our claim, he was going to find it. When did it happen? It used to be you felt relieved that you were insured. Nowadays, not so much; the presence of an insurance adjuster wasn't a comfort, it was another headache to contend with. Nowadays, they prided themselves on claims denied.

My smile faded. "Pleased to meet you. Let me show you around to the kitchen, where the fire started."

He nodded. "Yes. If you don't mind, I'm going to record this as well as take photos. We need to present as clear a picture as possible to my boss. Mr. Ambrose makes the final approval on claims."

"Yes. Yes. Of course," Ray murmured, leading the way through the dining room. The adjuster paused, taking photos with his cell phone, making it a slow procession.

At the sound of the door opening, I was about to tell any prospective customer that we were closed when I saw it was Cynthia and Shannon! What a sight for *literally* sore eyes.

"What are you two doing here? I thought you'd still be in bed. That was a late night!"

Shannon handed me a paper cup of coffee. "We almost didn't come here. When I checked my phone messages this morning, Ray had left one. Apparently, he couldn't reach you, so he let me know about this meeting with the adjuster, so I'd get you to leave early. Fat chance of that!"

"I was on my way to work when Shannon kidnapped me." Cynthia looked around at the restaurant. "This sucks. We're here for moral support, MJ. I've dealt with insurance people. You're going to need some help."

I leaned in and lowered my voice, "When I shook his hand, I knew he had no intention of honoring the claim. Tried to spin us about having to get approval from his boss. Total bullshit."

Cynthia winked at me. "Watch and learn, MJ." When she took a few steps, heading for Ray and the adjuster, her hips swayed in the short, flirty skirt. She looked over her shoulder at me. "A pinch of witch, with a dollop of bitch."

Shannon grabbed my arm, pulling me closer. "That poor man doesn't know that a Mack truck is bearing down on him. He'll never know what hit him." She laughed. "She knows how to work it. I wish my ass was *half* that sexy."

I elbowed her. "You're every bit as attractive. You're just *seasoned* more." But even that wasn't true. Shannon was one of those rare women who just never aged. Aside from laugh lines around her eyes, her skin was smooth and clear of wrinkles.

She pinched the skin on my arm, and I jerked back. "That's for the 'seasoned' comment." Her head nodded to the side, indicating Cynthia and the others. "Let's ratchet this up a few notches to help Cynthia and get that insurance adjuster to approve your claim."

Shannon closed her eyes, murmuring, "You will approve MJ's claim for damages. You will *want* to do this more than anything."

I nodded and joined her, chanting this softly, all the while picturing that little toad writing a check to us. I could picture it very clearly—see the contractors restoring my kitchen and getting this restaurant up and running again.

I started when Shannon scooped my hand into hers. She smiled. "Okay, hold those thoughts while we see how it's going with Cynthia. C'mon." I let her lead me across the room to join the others.

The first thing that struck me was how Cynthia sidled up close to the adjuster, hovering over his shoulder as he held his camera out snapping photos. When my eyes met Ray's, I knew exactly what was going through his mind. *What the hell is she doing, flirting with this idiot?* Not magic this time, but over twenty years of marriage to credit for that insight.

"You're very talented, Mark. Your ability with that camera is, well, it's *magic*." Cynthia followed this saccharin comment with a sly wink at me. She continued, "You can even see the sooty shadows on the curtains in that shot. So much damage. This is like watching a maestro work, Mark."

His hand rose to push his glasses higher on his nose, before his Adam's apple bobbed, swallowing hard. "Uhhh, I've got some experience with this."

Her hand casually draped over his shoulder as she looked down at him. "I can tell. Experience always shows. I bet you have oodles and oodles of it. Your job must be so interesting!"

Even though the area above the goatee flashed pink, it was like watching a peacock fan his feathers as he rocked back and forth on his feet. "I could tell you some stories, Cynthia!"

Her hand slid down his arm and hooked his elbow, guiding him to the kitchen. She had to lean to the side, almost putting her head on his shoulder when she cooed. "I'd love that! I bet you've helped so many families with your generosity. I'm so glad that *you* are the expert your company sent to help my friends."

As we followed Mark and Cynthia through the swinging door to the kitchen, I looked over at Shannon and stuck my finger in my mouth, feigning a gag. Her eyebrows bobbed in acknowledgment.

Before I could step through, Ray grabbed my arm and leaned in. "What's going on, MJ? The way Cynthia's acting, that guy looks like he doesn't know whether to shit or wind his watch."

I chuckled. That was exactly the point. "As long as he writes us a check, who cares?"

He nodded and slipped through the door ahead of us. When we entered, my gut sank seeing the charred mess and water damage. So many happy hours spent in that room; now it was a disaster. Beside me, Shannon muttered.

"Wow! Payback from the universe is a bitch."

Which reminded me of the spell I had cast on her. She hadn't said anything outrageously flirty with Mark, not that Cynthia didn't have that covered like a weighted blanket! But a glance at Mark and the answer was clear. Shannon didn't need a filter on her mouth around that toad.

Mark stood in the center of the mess, with his arms extended taking photos, when he lurched to the side. Cynthia's hand whipped up to catch him at the last moment. He took a deep breath, staring at the floor. "I don't know what came over me… I guess just a dizzy spell."

Cynthia patted his arm. "It's probably your heart hurting, seeing the damage that this fire has done to an innocent family. You're such a good and kind man. I can tell these things about people, Mark."

He cleared his throat and looked down. "Yes." Sneaking a

glance up at her, he added, "This is a strange morning. I'm glad you're here. I might have fallen."

Cynthia's glance at Shannon and me was just a glimmer, silently confirming the magic fog that Mark floundered in. She smiled down at him, practically purring. "I'm glad to be of service to someone like you."

We watched the show with Cynthia fawning over Mark and him eating it up like it was cordon bleu, for another half hour. Finally, preening in front of his gorgeous admirer, Mark pulled a tablet from his satchel and smiled.

"The damage is extensive, and as this is your first claim in all the years you've been with us, I trust that this was purely accidental. Your policy covers you for loss of income during the time your business is down. It would be in both parties' interests to expedite matters."

Cynthia gushed, "What an astute businessman! Not only handsome, but clever!"

He nodded, accepting the admiration before turning once more to Ray and me. "Based on my experience in settling claims, I am prepared to write you a check for sixty-eight thousand dollars. That will replace your equipment, the repairs to the structure, and the dining room clean up."

Ray's gaze darted to meet mine, his shock mirroring mine. We had talked about the cost but this estimate was easily 20 percent higher than we'd expected! Give us the pen and show us where to sign!

Cynthia tsked, stepping closer to Mark, running her finger over his collar. "You couldn't increase that to seventy-five? It would mean so much to the people in this town to have the restaurant running again. I'd consider it a… *personal* favor."

Mark's mouth opened a little before his hand rose to wipe a bead of sweat from his brow. The poor guy looked like he was about to stroke out. "Well…maybe I didn't factor in the loss of goodwill in the community. I could go that high. But that's it, Cynthia."

She actually threw her arms around him to hug him. Mark's face nestled into her neck, while she gave me and Ray a thumbs-up behind the adjuster's back.

Butterflies swooped in my stomach the whole time the adjuster's pen scribbled on the blank check: SEVENTY-FIVE THOUSAND! Oh my.

We'd be back in business in no time with that kind of money!

THIRTY

Shannon

H ey, Shannon! Hold up. I want to talk to you."
Crap! I'd practically run to reach my truck after finishing at MJ's restaurant. But trust my bad luck that Devon was nearby and had spotted me!

With my hand still on the door handle, I slowly turned, watching him stride across the street to where I was parked. Cynthia was long gone, fleeing after that check was in MJ's hand. I couldn't look to her for help. I lifted my hand and fluttered my fingers at him.

"Are you feeling better, Shannon? I was worried about you." Devon's hand rested on my arm, leaning closer to inspect my face. "You look okay. A little pale maybe but still pretty as a picture."

My hand rose to my throat and I whispered. "Laryngitis." Before he could respond, I blurted, managing the volume, but not the content. "You didn't shave today. I like the dark whiskers. It's an attractive look."

Oh Gawd! Shades of Cynthia with that adjuster! But she'd been right about the spell! I DID need a ball gag to shut my mouth the hell up!

A grin spread on his chiseled features, crinkling the corners of his icy-blue eyes. "Were you on your way to the office? Can

I get you a coffee? Maybe even spike it with a shot of bourbon for your throat?"

I shook my head. "Thanks, but no. I was…" I feigned a cough, wincing like I'd taken a bullet. When I straightened, I grabbed the door handle once more, hoping he'd take the hint.

But my stunt had the opposite effect when his hands gripped my arms, and he marched me to the passenger side of the truck. "This is crazy, Shannon. You're all by yourself out in the country with no one to take care of you. You're coming to the office. You can lie down on the sofa while I make you a hot drink. I'd take you to my place, but I've got to meet some clients in an hour."

"I'm fine. Don't trouble yourself." And then, of course, my mouth couldn't leave it just at that. "Although I'm not minding having your hand on me…not. At. All."

When he had me settled in the seat, even leaning over me to fasten the seatbelt, I sighed, watching him round the front of the truck. I was digging myself in deeper being around him with that damned spell on me!

Cynthia's words about Estelle Cousins sounded in my ear. At least with Devon busy with clients and out of the office, I'd get another chance to talk to Estelle. Cynthia had acted like it was really important to hear what the issue was which brought the woman's spirit back.

Devon got into the truck, and soon we were on our way to his office. He looked over at me. "Are you hungry? I can stop by the coffee shop and get you some soup?" His hand reached over to cup mine. "I kind of wish I could cancel this appointment but the people are from Albany. They were here to see a sick relative but are heading back this afternoon. I'd rather get you tucked into my bed so I can pamper you."

"I'd rather that you did too." SHIT! I'd said that out loud! Not even a whisper this time! It had been waaaay too long since I'd had sex! Being close to Devon was like inviting a starving woman to an all-you-can-eat buffet. A gourmet buffet!

His hand slid over to my thigh, rubbing it affectionately. His voice deepened to…well, dammit, a really nice tone—sue me. Almost a growl but still controlled. This guy would be a beast in the sack; I'd bet my life on it! "You don't mince words, do you, Shannon? I *like* that. My only question is why it's taken us so long to get together. You're hot. I'm hot." He tapped my thigh. "DAMN! I wish you weren't ill and I wasn't meeting with those Cousins heirs! We'd have *such* an awesome time!"

"Absolutely!" My hand flew up to cover my mouth, the other one grabbing a tissue from the box in the console. I'd shove my fist in my mouth to stop the lecherous monologue if I could.

Cousins. He said he was meeting with the Cousins heirs.

As I held the tissues to my mouth, my eyes grew wide. Cousins was Estelle's last name! The people Devon was meeting had to be descendants of the poor ghost. What was Devon up to? No wonder she was haunting his office!

I looked over at him, only to see his hooded eyes, probably picturing "tucking me into his bed." Tucking into bed? Ha! Tucking into ME! Now, that was a euphemism if ever there was one!

Ten minutes later, I was sprawled on the sofa in his office, with a pillow propping up my back and one tucked under my knees. Devon looked over at me as he adjusted the heat setting on the thermostat, making it warmer. "You're sure I can't get you some lunch?"

My teeth clamped down on the insides of my mouth as I shook my head. I tried not to make eye contact, hoping that might help.

"Okay. But I'm not taking no for an answer on the bourbon. I'm giving you a healthy dollop in your coffee. My old man always swore that as the best thing for a sore throat." He left the room, heading for the kitchen.

As I waited, I fished my cell phone from my purse and shot off a text message to Cynthia.

> Devon kidnapped me so I'm at his office. He's meeting with the Cousins heirs from Albany. Has to be related to Estelle Cousins.

Are there still Cousins in Wesley?

When Devon appeared, carrying a mug of steaming coffee, I slipped the phone under my thigh and smiled at him. "You're such a sweet guy to take care of me like this. It's another side of you that's so irresistible." Please gag me with a spoon even if it was true what I'd said.

"You make it easy to be nice, Shannon." He handed me the mug, along with a napkin. When he straightened, he winked at me. "Maybe this will make you better. Y'know, that dinner invitation at my house is a standing offer."

"I can't wait to take you up on that, Devon. The main course better be you." I groaned inwardly. Maybe in my next life, I could write the dialogue for some cheesy porn flick.

His eyes sparked wider above a big grin, letting out a low growl. "Yowza! I like the sound of that! You're my kind of woman, Shannon—nice, but deliciously *naughty*!"

My phone beeped with a text message, and the smile fell from Devon's lips.

I pulled the phone out and held it on my chest, signaling for privacy. "It's my kids. I've got to take this."

"Yeah. Of course." He pulled his phone out to check the time. "I'd better get going. It's a ten-minute drive to meet with these people. I'll be back in a couple of hours." He grabbed his overcoat and slipped out the door.

As soon as he was gone, I read the message from Cynthia.

> Ed Cousins still lives in Wesley. He's pretty sick with cancer. If his two children are in town, it's the hyenas circling for the inheritance. So why is Booker meeting with them? Let me do some digging and I'll get back to you. It's handy working at the Land Titles & Property department. TTYL
>
> P.S. That adjuster has texted me twelve times! As. If.

I got up and went to the boardroom where I'd seen Estelle before. "Estelle? Mrs. Cousins?" It didn't take long for the air to change, shimmering at the far wall. In just a few seconds, her dark dress with the lace collar showed under her stern features.

When she recognized me, the stern look on her face melted. She sighed. "You came back. I was worried that he fired you or that you got scared off. We must stop him. He's going to ruin everything." She floated toward the table, pointing at a paper lying on top of the scattered mess. "There. It's right there."

As I walked over to pick it up, I told her, "Right now, Devon is meeting with heirs to the Cousins estate. They're related to you, right?" I picked up the spreadsheet, zeroing in on Project "C," what she'd pointed to on the first visit.

"That would be my great-grandchildren, Barry and Laura. They were lovely children until they went off to college in Boston. They turned their back on the family and the town after they graduated. I think in the forty years since then, they've only been back a handful of times. Good riddance, I say."

I looked up at her. "Good riddance? That's an *awful* thing to say about your great-grandchildren. They must have been only babies when you were alive."

"Hmph!" She looked away for a moment. "Baby jackals are cute pups until they are grown. That would be those two. They've been in town for three days which is more time than they've ever visited before. And you know why? Because my poor Eddie, my grandson, is dying." She shimmered in sadness. "Their own father…"

My chest fell as I looked at her. How sad. To be dead and see someone you cared about to be treated so cruelly. It had to be heartbreaking even if she and Eddie would soon be reunited. "I'm so sorry about that. Cancer, I heard. I hope he isn't in a lot of pain."

"Not at this point; the medicine controls what's there." She looked at me with a small smile. "I used to read him bedtime stories. His favorite was *Velveteen Rabbit*. He loved it although it was terribly sad. I would never have credited that such a sensitive lad would be the class clown when he got to school. I don't know how many times that prankster set off the fire alarm in the school! Always when he had an exam that he hadn't studied for! The last time, they suspended him for three days. Three wonderful days we spent together, walking the trails in the forest."

My eyes stung and I swiped a tear away. Her sweet but painful memories tore my heart despite knowing they'd be together soon. I took a deep breath and sighed. "You said we must stop Devon. I'm not following. What's going on?"

My cell phone beeped and I pulled it out, peering at the screen.

"*Excuse me?* We were having a *conversation,* my dear! That's something I've noticed in these strange times. That wafer makes a sound and immediately captures the person's focus. I've seen teenagers walk into poles and trip on their feet while gazing at those things. Pay attention!"

I jerked back and quickly shoved the phone in my pocket, chastised like a grade-schooler. When I looked up into her eyes, she smiled, the flinty look fading.

"That's better. Now, where were we?" She hovered closer, sending off a waft of floral scent.

"I was asking you about Devon. How does he fit into this?" Unconsciously, my posture straightened, paying closer attention to her.

"You need to go through his files. He's obviously meeting with Barry and Laura to buy the property they stand to inherit. Knowing him, he's going to convert my home, the home my husband, Jacob, and I built, into some tacky hotel, or worse."

I nodded. "Condos. I think Devon likes the business potential of condos."

She shuddered. "I don't even know what that is, but it sounds *dreadful!* I'd always hoped that if the homestead passed out of the family, that the town would acquire it. Surely, there's a need for an orphanage or home for the poor."

I wasn't going to bring her up to date on current social programs. Were orphanages even a thing anymore? "Okay. I'll find out more about this Project C. And then we'll find out how to stop him from getting it."

"Fine." Her form started to dissipate, wavering and mingling like smoke. And then she was gone. When I looked at the mountain of papers and files, it was daunting, if not downright depressing. Before I tackled that morass, I'd see what Cynthia had to say. I pulled my phone out and sent a text:

Got anything?

Her reply came back immediately.

> Ed Cousins owns many properties in town, along with his home on Westmoreland Lane. One of those properties is the building where MJ's restaurant is. If the heirs sell it, then MJ and Ray could be facing increased rent or even be forced out.

I sank into the nearest chair. Oh my God. They were having a tough time making money as it was, in the winter. If the rent was increased, it would hurt them, maybe too much; it could even mean the end of their business.

But it was a free country. The heirs could do whatever they wanted with their inheritance. If they chose to sell everything, take the money and run, then that was their choice.

I shot off another text to Cynthia.

> We HAVE to let MJ know this. I'm going to stop by the restaurant when I leave here. I don't know how she's going to take this but she should know before she sinks that insurance money into the restaurant.

I got up and began sorting through the files and papers on the boardroom table. It was now clear what Project C was. The "C" had to stand for Cousins. I scooped up a black binder labeled "Project C," as well as any letter, note, or file that contained any mention of the project. I'd read them later when I was at home. For now, I needed to work fast and be gone before Devon returned with his amorous intentions.

THIRTY ONE

Libby

That same day...

When my cell phone dinged with a text, I turned from reading the test on the monitor. No matter how comfortable my sofa was at home, the book I was reading was hard as hell to get through. It was a copy of Leadership Roles and Management Functions in Nursing. As if the thoughts of last night, talking to Robert the bobcat wasn't distracting enough, the business book was dry as dust. But I had to get through it if I was going to do well in that job interview for the head nurse.

My head dipped back, seeing Stan Jones's name on the small screen. Well, speak of the devil after all that had been said the night before. Hmph. "My Guy." That was how Cynthia had referred to him.

> Hi Libby! After seeing Mary-Jane at the fire, I wondered if you'd talked to her. How are she and Ray doing? I'm about to take a hike up the Ole Pike logging road and wondered if you'd like to join me? That is, if you're free.

It's the first day that's held a hint of spring, just perfect for a hike.

I sat back and reread the message, picturing Stan's face, the quirky grin lifting more on one side, and his deep-blue eyes. But it wasn't just that he was great looking, he was funny in a dry way: Lord Of The Quips, for sure. And a sense of self-confidence that was almost magnetic. Not to mention persistent. How many times had I turned him down, yet he never gave up?

But I had to get this studying in. I got up and stretched my neck from side to side before I grabbed my empty glass. As I filled the glass with water, I thought of the raccoon sitting out in the garage. Dahlia had set up an old heating pad on the bottom of the crate with the heat on low for him, but he might need a drink.

I took my glass with me and went into the garage. As soon as my foot hit the stairs, the critter arched itself up on its back legs, twitching its nose, watching me. "Hey, Rascal. Want a drink?"

"Water."

I stifled a chuckle comparing Rascal with Robert. Rascal was a creature of few words, but he sure liked his water.

As I topped up his bowl, I mused, "What do you think, little fella? Should I play hooky and meet Stan for a hike? According to my friends, I'm not putting myself out there enough. What do *you* think? Do I need to live it up more?"

The raccoon looked up at me with droplets of water still clinging to his whiskers. *"Live."* Then as quick as that, he went back to the bowl, now concentrating on washing his paws.

My eyebrows shot up. *"Live."* It was the first thing he'd said other than "water." Had he really understood me? "You think I should meet Stan and go for a hike in the woods?"

Again he looked at me. *"Take a hike."*

My head dipped forward, staring at him. I couldn't help smiling at the silly creature. "Take a hike? Some people would say you're trying to get rid of me." I laughed. A raccoon not only talking to me, but he was also giving me the brush-off!

I squatted there for a few moments, looking at Rascal. Maybe he was right. He'd said to "live." Cynthia had also said there was nothing more tragic than a life lived in fear. Was that what I was doing? Living in fear? Fear of getting close to anyone again and experiencing loss, like I'd gone through when Hank died? There could be some truth to that even if it was on a subconscious level.

Mary-Jane's words echoed in my mind about my kids being grown and self-sufficient. Many times I'd felt like an observer watching them go about their daily routines, making dinner when I wasn't there and generally being independent. Which was every parent's goal in raising kids. Was I using my kids as an excuse to cover my own insecurity?

I watched Rascal finish cleaning his paws. Magic was the reason I was able to communicate with him. Would it be so crazy if his answer was also inspired by magic? And it wasn't just him, it was my friends encouraging me as well!

"Okay, Rascal! I think you have a point. I'm going on that hike with Stan! Hell! It's only a hike, not a marriage proposal."

"Mate."

My mouth snapped shut. And then it fell open. "Hang on, Rascal! Was that a noun or a verb? Did you mean 'a mate' or 'to mate'?" I shook my head. I was discussing semantics with this creature?

I got up and strode back into the kitchen to grab my cell phone before I changed my mind. The books could wait. The kids were at school. What harm would it do? My fingers flew across the tiny keyboard.

> Sure! I'm going cross-eyed studying and a walk in the fresh air sounds great. Meet you there?

I hit send and watched the phone. My breath was shallow, and there was a pleasant tingle in my stomach, waiting for his reply. My hand rose to cup my cheek, turning my head to the side. *Libby Walker! Look at you! Sitting by the phone like some silly schoolgirl.*

When the phone chirped, I grinned. That was fast!

I'm two minutes from your house. I'll swing by and pick you up.

Oh my God! I was actually doing this!

I looked down at the sweatpants and ripped plaid shirt, my sexy loungewear. Yikes! I raced up to my bedroom to change into a sweater and jeans. My fingers trembled with excitement as I slipped the pants on and zipped them up. Then a mad dash to the bathroom, applying mascara and lipstick, a brush through my mop of curls—and voila! I grimaced at the mirror, checking that there wasn't any pink on my teeth, and I was all set.

When the doorbell chimed, I looked up at the ceiling. "I'll always love you, Hank, but it's time to shed the widow's weeds. You always liked Stan, so I know you'd approve."

I took a deep breath to compose myself and walked down the stairs to greet Stan. When I opened the door, my stomach fluttered. He looked so ruggedly handsome in the tan sheepskin jacket and faded jeans.

"Hi, Stan. I'll just grab my jacket and I'm ready to go." I pulled the door wide, extending an arm to invite him in.

"No rush! It's great to see you, Libby. I can't believe my luck that you agreed to join me! There's a stream just off the trail that you're going to love. It's… well, you'll see." He held his ball cap in both hands, watching me slip my boots on.

"It's been years since I hiked out there, Stan." I threw my scarf on and grinned at him. "I'm glad you asked me. This is just what the doctor ordered." Well, not actual doctors, but my sisters in the coven sure as heck counted.

Not to mention the pithy encouragement from the raccoon in my garage.

He laughed, and the crinkles at the corners of his eyes showed, along with lines framing his mouth. "Well, in that case, tell that doc to send me his bill." He held the door for me, and soon we were in his truck heading out of town.

After we'd exhausted the conversation talking about MJ and the fire, there was a long pause. I clasped my hands in my lap, casually admiring the scenery out the window, but inside, my head was screaming. What do I say next? It'd been so long since I'd been on a date—hell, was this even a date? I was waaaay out of practice. Not that I'd had much practice. I'd married Hank straight out of college.

Stan cleared his throat. "I'm trying not to read too much into anything, Libby, but this feels so right, having you next to me in the truck." He looked over at me and a smile formed on his lips; he looked almost bashful when he added, "Or maybe I've dreamed of this so many times that it feels…it feels familiar."

My head spun to look at him. *Familiar?* As in Shannon's bobcat, Robert? Naw… that couldn't be it! But damned if this wasn't one hell of a coincidence!

"What's wrong? Did I say something wrong?" Stan shook his head. "I'm sorry if I—"

"No! That's not it, Stan. You're right, this is pleasant, even if I'm seriously out of practice talking to a guy when it's not about meds or catheters or—" My mouth shut tight. Why'd I mention catheters?

His eyebrows shot up and he laughed. "I'll pass on THAT procedure if it's all the same to you." He flipped the turn signal on and pulled over at the entrance to the old logging road. "We're here."

I got out of the truck, still mentally berating myself for the silly comment. When I joined him at the snowy track leading into the forest, I tried for something a little more normal: "Dahlia brought home a young raccoon a couple of days ago. She named it Rascal. We've got a heated crate set up in the garage for him."

He looked over at me and smiled. "That so? That's kind of cool. Even though they get into my garbage bins sometimes, I like watching them. The little bandits are pretty clever."

"Well, Rascal's clever!" On a whim, I added, "I wasn't sure if I should keep hitting the books or play hooky with you today, so I asked his opinion. He told me to take a hike! Can you believe that? The sassy critter!"

With his hands deep in his pockets, he stepped closer, nudging me with his elbow. "Sounds like a wise raccoon."

"*Wiseacre,* you mean! But yeah, he was right." I looked over at him, admiring the way the sun glinted on the hair on his temple, highlighting the bit of silver. He bent to toss a stray branch littering the path, and I couldn't help but notice the muscles in his thighs and his tight butt. My face became warm and I looked to the side. Oh God! I was starting to sound like Mary-Jane or…even Shannon, now that she'd been hexed!

But when my eyes gazed into the forest, I saw movement. Straining, I paused to look closer. Amber eyes below one good ear and one stump of an ear looked back at me.

"Grab that brass ring, my lady. Or in this case—"

I turned my head, shutting out the last part of Robert's comment.

When I faced Stan again, he remarked, "Spring is definitely in the air today, Shannon. And speaking of springs"—he pointed to a spot where the snow was beaten down, a path leading off to the side— "it's right over there. That spring I was telling you about. The water still bubbles along, even in winter."

"Lead the way, Stan." I looked over at Robert sitting in the stand of maples. He blended in pretty well, but *I* could see him. I mouthed the words, pointing my finger at him, "Behave yourself or I'll tell Shannon!"

I followed Stan, casting a glance over my shoulder a few times. But Robert had disappeared into the undergrowth.

THIRTY TWO

Mary-Jane

That afternoon...

I stretched higher, my fingernails scraping on the metal of the curtain rod, trying to remove it, when the door to the restaurant opened.

"Mary-Jane! What the heck are you doing up there?" Shannon rushed over to steady the chair under me. "Where's Ray? Shouldn't he be doing this? Or a contractor or—"

I handed her the curtain. "He went to the bank, and then he was going to visit a few contractors. You know me. Impatient. I'm anxious to get started on this mess. Plus, getting that check this morning gave me even more motivation. Wasn't that *something?* Getting that much money?"

Seeing the forlorn look on Shannon's face, my smile faded. "What's wrong? You look like—"

"I've got bad news, MJ." She reached for my hand, helping me down from the wooden chair. "You might want to hear what I've learned before you sink any money into this place."

For a moment I just looked at her. What the hell was she talking about? She'd been here helping us get the insurance adjuster on board with our claim. "I don't understand. We've GOT to get the business going again. It's not like we couldn't use the income, Shannon!"

As I was about to move the chair next to the window, her hand gripped my arm."When the owner of this building dies, Devon is going to purchase it from the heirs. He's meeting with them right now. Who knows what he'll do when he gets his hands on this property?"

My chest sank into my gut as I listened to her. Ed Cousins had never increased our rent by more than a couple of percentage points each year that we'd been here. But Ed was dying. If Devon Booker owned the property, we'd be lucky if he didn't give us our notice! I sank down into the chair watching Shannon pull another one up beside me.

"Shit. It's not just us, Shannon! We're just one tenant in this building. There's the flower shop, the dental office, and the antique store! Not to mention the two floors above! The apartments." This was a disaster! All of us would suffer if Devon got his hands on the building.

Shannon nodded. "I know. Devon will probably turn this into some kind of mall or luxury condos. And even if he doesn't do that, he'll want top dollar in rents, knowing him." Her head dipped to look down at the floor. "I just thought you should know before you sink that insurance money into the place."

I was numb with shock. A picture of Devon meeting those two people outside the restaurant, I'd seen a week ago, flashed in my mind. That HAD to have been Laura and Barry, Ed's kids. They lived in Albany, and in all the years we'd been in the restaurant, I'd only seen them a couple of times. Of course, they'd sell it to Devon!

Shannon's eyes welled with tears when she looked at me. "This all started with me, MJ. I cast that spell on you, then you got angry and hexed me, and—"

"The third thing!" My eyes closed and I sighed. "That thing seeing Sylvie flirting with Ray, the fire, and now *this*. This is the third payback the universe is hitting me with. It might be the end of us, Shannon."

Shannon wiped a tear and took a deep breath. "I don't see any way of stopping Devon. And there's no way we're using magic to wish this away. We've seen how wishing ill on someone turns out."

She was silent for a few moments while I felt all my energy vanish, leaving me deflated. Maybe I should call Ray, so he didn't put down any kind of deposit with the contractor. He needed to know this. We needed to talk and decide what to do.

"Estelle Cousins said we must stop Devon. She's more worried about her family home being sold, but I'm more worried about you and this building." Shannon's forehead furrowed. "Cynthia said I needed to pay attention to Estelle. But what can be done? Ed Cousins will leave all the properties to his kids and that's his right. And, of course, they can do whatever they want with the estate."

My head tipped to the side as I remembered how it had been back then for Ray and me—two fresh-faced, optimistic kids with the world at our feet. "You know, Ed and his wife, Judy, were our first regular customers in the restaurant, Shannon. We'd bought the business from the Spinelli family and changed things from Italian to traditional American. Ed and Judy would be here every Friday night, like clockwork. They'd linger on well after their meals, sipping Spanish coffees till closing. Even after Judy passed, he'd maintained that tradition, although without all the liqueurs. Now all that is just a memory. Everything will change once Devon gets his mitts on this place."

This time it was me who swiped a tear. I stood up. "I'd better call Ray. This is going to be hard, Shannon." I patted her hand before I went to get my purse. "Don't blame yourself. This is on me. I screwed up wishing that spell on you."

I'd ruined everything with that damned wish.

THIRTY THREE

Shannon

Later that afternoon...

W hen Ray arrived at the restaurant, I left to give them privacy to discuss the nightmare that I'd discovered. I let myself out.

I looked up at the sky as I crossed the street to get in my truck and drive home. "This is so unfair! Why are you doing this to MJ? The fire wasn't bad enough?" I didn't care who saw me yelling! And if that damned Devon drove by, I'd tear a double strip off him for the threat he was to my friends.

When I settled in my truck, with my finger on the start button, I paused for a moment. Were we jumping to conclusions? We couldn't be certain that even if Devon purchased the property, he'd screw over MJ and Ray. My thinking the worst was based on everyone else's negative opinion of Devon. There was only one way to know for sure.

I grabbed my cell phone from my purse, and after taking a deep breath, I made the call.

Devon answered on the first ring. "Shannon! Where are you? Are you feeling better?"

I crossed my fingers for luck that the spell wouldn't work

when I talked to him on the phone. Please let it be just when I was with him in person. "I'm outside Mary-Jane's restaurant."

My eyes opened wider! Holy shit! It had worked. Only "normal" came out of my mouth instead of the flirty crap.

"What are you doing *there*? I heard about the fire—"

"Are you planning on buying that building where the restaurant is? Is that why you were meeting with Laura and Barry Cousins? What's going on, Devon?"

There was a heavy silence that lasted for a few moments before he spoke. "I gather you read the correspondence. The Cousins heirs have no interest in coming back to Wesley. They approached *me* first, Shannon."

My face tightened. So that part was true. "What do you plan on doing with the building, Devon? Will MJ still have the lease on the restaurant space? Do you plan on jacking up her rent as well as the others, or are you going to do something altogether different to the property?" This was the real crux of the matter.

"What's gotten into you, Shannon? You sound so... so cold. We were getting along so well. Why don't you come back, and we'll have a nice dinner and some drinks? We'll discuss this over drinks. I'll answer your questions then." His voice had changed a bit, had become softer, slicker.

"No, Devon. I want to know the answer right now. No dinner and drinks." I decided two could play at that game. "Dinner can wait until I know what your intentions are for that building." Thinking of Estelle, I added. "Or any of the properties, like Ed Cousins' home."

I rolled my eyes, chastising myself. I should have dragged MJ to Devon's office and got her to touch his hand! She would have picked up on Devon's intention without any bullshit he might try to spin.

"You want to know my intentions for the Cousins' property?" His voice was flat. "Frankly, Shannon, that's none of your business. And furthermore, I don't appreciate you snooping and then blabbing my affairs all over town. I'm sure you gave Mary-Jane and Ray a bellyful of my business plans. That wasn't professional of you, Shannon."

His answer told me about as much as MJ could have read by touching him. If he didn't have some nefarious plan to evict or fleece MJ and Ray, he would have just said so. It looked like my friends were right about Devon.

"You know, even after you tried to trick me into selling my property to you in the fall, I was willing to give you a second chance. I was naïve, my bad. People are right about you, Devon. You're a heartless bastard."

"Hang on, Shannon! There's no call to start with the name-calling. You know, I don't get you. You were so much fun, so flirty. And, of course, I'm attracted to you." He paused before adding, "Was that all an act? Did you take this job so you could spy on me? Make trouble for me? I thought I was giving you a break, offering you this job."

I rolled my eyes. Yeah, I'd said some outrageous remarks, coming onto him. That damned spell! "It's not like that, Devon. I accepted the job in good faith, with no ulterior motives. But what I've seen in your files and even by your own admission, meeting with the Cousins' heirs, you're going to hurt MJ and Ray if you acquire their building."

His voice now blared in my ear. "You don't know what you're talking about! But...you make trouble for me and I'll sue your ass, Shannon. I'll bankrupt you, and I'll have your property as well. So you better think about that before you write some kind of *hit piece* on me!"

My breath froze in my chest! Hit piece! I heard Cynthia's words in my head:" Words are power, Shannon." And Devon had reminded me of that!

Laughing, I got my final dig in, "You're not as clever as you think, Devon. You never asked me to sign a nondisclosure agreement. I'm going to stop you from ruining my friends if it's the last thing I do." With that, I clicked the phone off.

I only hoped that my threat wasn't an empty one.

THIRTY FOUR

Mary-Jane

As soon as Shannon left the restaurant, Ray walked over to me, shaking his head. "I know how upset you are, MJ. This is terrible news about Devon Booker buying the building."

Again the waterworks started flowing. I grabbed a tissue from my purse and dabbed my eyes. "What are we going to do, Ray? We can't throw good money after bad to fix the kitchen! Maybe we could take that insurance money to build a place of our own! One that WE control! We could get a bank loan and—"

"No. We can't, MJ. We don't have a choice in this. We have to restore the kitchen and premises to what it was before."

I stared at him, not believing my ears. "Restore it so that that *bastard* can toss us out on our asses when the lease is up for renewal? That's *crazy*, Ray!" I looked around at the dining room and felt my heartache all over again.

"Mary-Jane, *listen* to me! It's a condition of the lease. We had a fire here, and according to the terms of the agreement, we HAVE to fix it! The lease mandates that we carry insurance for a reason, MJ. Ultimately, we don't own the property, so we can't decide NOT fix it."

Oh my God! This was worse than I'd thought. But he was right. Ray might lack my customer service skills, but he was no slouch when it came to legalese crap; junk that made my eyes cross!

I groaned. "Maybe we could skip town? You've always wanted to visit Tahiti? Now might be the right time."

"Mary-Jane! Don't talk nonsense! We wouldn't do that in a million years! This is our home. We grew up here, have friends and family in Wesley. We wouldn't do that to any of them."

Even though I'd only been half kidding, I knew he was right. We were trapped in a situation that was looking darker by the minute.

He put his arms around me and rubbed my back. "Whatever happens, we'll be together, with Zoe. If I have to take a job driving transport or digging ditches, I will. We'll survive. Together."

At that moment, any inkling of jealousy I'd felt after seeing Sylvie hug him was blasted from my head. Ray might not be perfect, but he loved me. He was trying with every cell in his body to make this right.

I pulled my head back, looking into his eyes. "You're a good man, Ray."

He wiped a tear from my cheek. "We'll make this place even better than it was before, MJ. If we have to leave, we'll leave with our heads high. That's who we are."

The door opened again and I sighed. What now? Didn't people know we were closed for business? We had to start locking that door.

When I turned, Steve Murphy stood there gazing around at the bar and dining room. He carried a grease-speckled brown bag in one hand and a bucket with sponges, cleaners, and rags in the other.

He shot us a lopsided grin. "I brought dinner as well as cleaning supplies. I made some phone calls, and a few more people are going to be here soon to help."

Oh shit! Would the tears never stop? But this time, it was

from happiness. I walked over to Steve. "I can't believe you're doing this! I...I..." Words failed me, and I turned to grab more tissues.

"We're friends, MJ. Besides, no one makes meals as good as you can. The town isn't the same without this restaurant. So, I've got my ulterior motives to get you back in business." He handed the bag of takeout to Ray.

The door opened again, and Zoe, Jack, and Libby entered. When Stan followed right on her heels, my mouth fell open. Libby came over and put her arm around my shoulders, whispering into my ear, "I did it, MJ! I joined Stan this afternoon on a hike."

What she didn't mention was the fact that they'd held hands on the way back from the stream. That came through with her touch. I squeezed her hand. "Good for you. Thanks for coming over to help us."

When I looked at Steve handing out cleaning rags and joking with the kids, I smiled. It warmed my heart that he'd gone to this much trouble. That he cared! Hell! They all cared enough to pitch in.

"Hey, Mom!" Give me a hand with these curtains." I laughed as I went over to help my daughter strain for the rod. She was my daughter all right.

THIRTY FIVE

Shannon

As I drove home, I mentally planned the piece I would write about the fire in Mary-Jane's restaurant. I had to get something in about Devon's plans. Even though he hadn't specifically told me what they were, it looked bad for MJ. How could someone be so driven for money and power? Sure, big shots on Wall Street screwed people over all the time, but these people were Devon's neighbors, people he'd known for years! Did he have NO conscience?

When my phone rang, I saw Cynthia's name come up on the screen above the radio. I pressed the button on my steering wheel to answer her call. "Hi, Cynthia. Sorry, I meant to call you. I guess I got distracted by my argument with Devon Booker."

"You talked to him about this? What'd he say? Is he buying the Cousins' estate?"

I took a deep breath. "He didn't say that exactly but, I'm pretty sure he's going to. That'll spell trouble for MJ. I took some files from Devon's office that I'm going to comb through tonight to see what he's up to."

"Oh my God. Won't he miss them? You took one hell of a chance doing that."

"If you saw his boardroom, you'd know it won't be missed.

The guy's a slob when it comes to paperwork and filing. After I go through them, I'll figure out some way of getting them back before he figures out they're missing."

My forehead tightened remembering how sad MJ had been when I'd told her about Devon. "This is the third bad thing to ricochet back at Mary-Jane. She'll probably end up closing. I'm glad I got to her before they booked contractors and wasted that insurance money."

"Wait. What? They're going ahead with the repairs? Steve Murphy called me, asking if I'd volunteer to help with the cleanup when I'm finished work."

My forehead tightened. He'd said as much to me, asking me to pitch in, but now that we knew about Devon, it didn't make sense. "Well, that's a waste of time and money."

"Hang on, Shannon. It's not like they have a choice. Well, I suppose they could just give Ed Cousins the insurance money to square things up. It's his building that got damaged."

Shit! I hadn't thought of that! Of course, I was only thinking of MJ's welfare. But what Cynthia said made sense. It was either do the repairs or hand that check over to the landlord.

"So they're going through with fixing the place up and reopening."

"Yeah. I'm going to pop by. It sounds like quite the crew there helping out. Since I started my day there, I might as well end it there. Besides, it could be fun. The smoke never damaged their bar or liquor supply."

I pictured all of them together, especially Steve and Cynthia. Was it totally over between them? Maybe something would reignite. Not sure I liked the sound of that. Then I wasn't sure if I had the right to feel like that. But THEN I wasn't NOT sure! Argh! MEN!

I took a quick breath before offering, "Maybe I should join you guys." And yeah, I wasn't sure why I offered. I sighed. This being single sure had its complications.

Cynthia paused before replying, "No. I've got an idea. The way so many people have volunteered to help out, there might be an angle there, I mean for the newspaper piece. You know, that whole community-spirit thing I pushed with the adjuster. What's happening with Steve and the people helping just proves it. Your time is best served writing a piece about that. Let *us* do the grunt work."

I almost missed my driveway as I thought about what she'd said. I slammed on the brakes and made the turn. "But in the end, Devon is just going to own the building. I mean it's great to see people come out to support MJ and Ray but it's short-term, Cynthia. There has to be something else we can do to stop him."

"*Intention*, Shannon. We send out strong intention to the universe and cross our fingers that it will bend in our favor. Don't underestimate the power of intention and magic. I don't know how this will solve MJ's problem, but I've got a good feeling about it. I'll call you later to let you know how it went with the cleanup."

With that, the line went dead. As I pulled into the drive I could see Bob sitting by the front door. He got up, sauntering across the porch and back to the front door. If I didn't know better, I'd say he was acting like I was his daughter, breaking the curfew deadline.

I got out of the car and grabbed the file folder and binder. Holding it out to show him, I said, "See, Bob. THIS...this is the kind of thing I need you to steal for me. Not pension checks, not wallets. This is going to help Mary-Jane and Ray."

His eyes narrowed, and he let out a few screeching yowls, grinding my last nerve. I stopped before opening the door, scowling down at him. "You don't like being scolded, do you? Well, I didn't appreciate the snide comments you made to Libby about me."

I tucked the paperwork from Devon's office under my arm and unlocked the door, casting a sneer over at the cat. "Watch and learn, Bob. You've got to start earning your supper and a place at my fire."

THIRTY SIX

Shannon

The next morning...

I arrived at the spot in front of Mary-Jane's restaurant bright and early. It was another mild day with the sun beaming down from a clear, cloudless sky. When my phone rang, I scooped it from my purse: Cynthia. I'd been so busy the night before that I'd forgotten she'd promised to call me back.

"Hey, Cynthia. What's up?"

"Sorry I didn't call. I didn't get home until almost eleven, and by then...How'd you make out writing the article? Did you find anything in Devon's files you took home?"

I sank back into the seat, running my fingers through my hair. "I confess, a lot of the things in Devon's binder and correspondence was Greek to me. But one thing I picked up on was that this Project Cousins involves MJ's building. There's also a ton of money on the line! I'm talking millions, if not billions!"

"What?" There was a pause. "Hmm... If I had to venture an educated guess, I'd say that MJ's building is worth maybe half a mil. Did you say *billions*? And even if you're right, where would Devon get his hands on that kind of capital?"

I pictured the pages of spreadsheets, entries that, to me, were little more than hieroglyphics and short forms. The only thing that had jolted me back on my heels were the dollar amounts with an "A," a "J," and an "H" noted next to each. "Outside investors? Some consortium?"

"Ed Cousins owns a lot more property than MJ's building. He's got about forty acres where the old lumber mill was located. There are also the ruins of a hydroelectric plant that was put out of business in the sixties. That land might be worth a few mil but hardly *billions!* I don't understand that. What about the article you're writing? Did you get a start on it?"

I smiled. It had been years since I'd done any journalism, and it had felt good to get writing again. "That's why I'm sitting out front of MJ's restaurant, Cynthia! If Devon buys that building, it'll be little more than a toy he can turn upside down, spilling out the lives and businesses of everyone in it. All for the almighty buck. I'm going to interview the residents and do a human-interest piece like you suggested."

"Shit. The Jenkins family has lived in that building for two generations. The old lady is still there, but the kids always make a point of checking in on her. Jennie in the flower shop took it over from her dad and he carried on from his dad. Your article should really play that up, Shannon. This isn't just MJ, this is a whole host of people, not to mention the history of that building."

"You read my mind, Shannon. I'm going to shoot tons of photos as well. We may not be able to stop Devon, but by the time I'm through, he'll be a social pariah. He'll be lucky if the town doesn't run him out on a rail, let alone approve some billion-dollar scheme."

"Go get him, Shannon! I'd better get back to work now, or they'll send out a search team. I'll call you later."

I clicked off the phone and grabbed my camera. When I got out of the truck, I gazed at MJ's restaurant with the striped burgundy awnings perched over the windows. I'd never noticed the ornate brickwork over the entry and above, framing each window of the apartments there. It showed true craftsmanship and character, not some cookie-cutter box that was Devon's specialty.

I'd just pop in to see how MJ and Ray were doing before I started the rounds of interviews with the other tenants. When I stepped inside, it even smelled better than the day before with the astringent scent of lemon and pine cleaning products. The windows were bare of their coverings, and the tables and chairs had all been moved to one corner of the room where Steve and a bunch of high school kids were busy wiping them down.

Amid the drone of the carpet cleaner that Mary-Jane was using, I managed to lean in to say hi to Ray, who was wiping down the cabinets of the bar.

I walked over to Mary-Jane and tapped her on the shoulder. She started and then flipped the switch, turning the carpet cleaning machine off. But before she could even say anything, a series of bangs resounded from the area of the kitchen. She grabbed my hand, leading me farther away from the din.

"I guess you can tell that the contractor didn't waste time sending his crew. They're ripping out the mess right now. Are you here to help, Shannon?"

"I would if I could, MJ. I can't believe how much progress you've made. But I'm writing that article for the paper on your story and this building. When I think of the lives that will be destroyed when Devon gets this property, it makes me sick."

"Did I hear my name? What lies are you spreading about me, now, Shannon?"

I spun around to face him. I hadn't even heard the door open, and there he was in his cashmere overcoat, the suit, and tie, his eyes hard chips of steel glaring at me. My pulse kicked up about a gazillion notches.

"What are you doing here? Nice coat, by the way, the tailoring and color is sexy." My hand shot to my mouth! Shit! THAT SPELL!

His eyes opened wider while the room became so still you

could hear a pin drop. And then anger clouded his face. "I came in to see how Ray and Mary-Jane were doing! I've eaten here for years and…"

He took a step closer, peering at me like I was an alien. "What is WRONG with you? I gave you a job, did you a favor, and…" He shook his head. "Hell! You teased me, led me to believe that you wanted to jump my bones, and then…you not only leave me high and dry, but you're also spreading *rumors* about me!"

His finger rose, making a circular motion next to his temple. "You're acting CRAZY, Shannon."

Ray took a step closer to Devon. "There's no call to insult anyone, Devon. We don't—"

Devon turned on Ray, "I don't know WHAT that psycho told you about me, Ray, but whatever it is…consider the source! She throws herself at me like some pole dancer angling for a lap dance, and the next minute she's sticking a knife in my back!"

I'd heard enough of his bullshit, the sneak! When I went to take a step closer to him, Mary-Jane gripped my wrist, whispering, "No, Shannon. Let it go. The spell…remember?"

I yanked my hand away, facing off with Devon. "You bastard! Even though you're so hot I'd like to rip your clothes off… you're still a bastard. You're going to get this building and—"

"SEE?" Devon threw his hands up. "She's *still* doing it!" He looked around the room, at Ray, MJ, Steve, the high school kids, and even to the doorway to the kitchen, where guys in hardhats stood gaping. "You're all witnesses to her PSYCHOSIS!"

I stomped my foot. "At least I'm not a sneak, trying to ruin people's lives! If I didn't want to run my hands through your hair and climb all over you, smothering you with kisses, I'd HIT you!"

"What the hell is going on? Booker! You'd better leave! Right now." Steve crossed the floor until he was about five feet from Devon. His jaw muscle twitched while the fingers of his hands at his sides curled and uncurled.

Devon dismissed him with a sweep of his hand. "She's not worth it, buddy! Sure she's got a great body and pretty face but inside that HEAD? She's batshit BONKERS! She's yours if you want her, but I'd run for the hills, brother. She's dangerously deranged."

"Never mind him, Steve. I can handle this creep. And handle is definitely the word for what I want to do." I looked up at the ceiling, fisting my hands in my hair. SHIT and DOUBLE SHIT! That damned spell! And to have to do this out in *public!* Could I ever show my face in town again?

Devon's eyes narrowed. "Cuckoo, cuckoo! You're not only off your meds, you're a THIEF! You stole a binder and some files from my office, Crazy Lady! I want them back!"

Devon looked at Mary-Jane and Ray. "If we weren't neighbors and you weren't friends of Ms. Whackjob, I'd call the police right now." He turned to me again. "I'm giving you twenty-four hours to return what you stole. Those files better be on my desk by nine o'clock tomorrow or I'm calling the cops!" He snorted, "You'd cinch an insanity plea though."

He looked around at the others, finishing with Ray. "Good luck with the cleanup, man. But take my advice, try to keep your wife away from her nutbar friend before it catches." With that, he left the restaurant.

Mary-Jane let out a long sigh. "Well, that went well, didn't it?"

I looked around the room. Steve never met my eyes, staring down and off to the side as if the carpet was suddenly riveting. The high school kids, Jack and Zoe among them, huddled together, giggling and casting glances over at me. The three guys bunched together in the doorway to the kitchen shook their heads, smirking, before slipping away.

Ray came over to me and put his hand on my shoulder. "I know it's early, Shannon, but I could get you a whiskey. After all that, you probably need one."

All I could think about was running from the restaurant and never looking back! If only the floor would open and swallow me up. To have said all those ridiculous come-on lines to Devon when we were alone in his office was bad enough! But to say that crap in front of Ray and Steve and the guys in the construction crew—and high school kids! It's going to be all over this town by sunset, for sure. I was a laughing stock. Devon looked like the sane one, not me!

Mary-Jane's voice sounded behind me. "Hey, everyone. Shannon…she just came from the dental office. I think they must have given her laughing gas, otherwise known as the truth serum."

My mouth fell open when I looked at her. She was making this worse if anything, not better. The *truth* serum? I watched Steve turn to the kids and herd them over to the chairs, trying to restore order from the chaos Devon and I had created. As I watched his broad shoulders in the plaid shirt and the jeans that highlighted muscular thighs, I couldn't help but wonder.

Why Devon? Why did he have that effect that I'd blab all those sexy thoughts to him? Why not with Steve?

I headed for the door. "I'll talk to you later, MJ! I've got to get some fresh air."

THIRTY SEVEN

Libby

Four a.m., the next morning...

As I zipped my coat up, walking across the ward to the nursing station, I noticed Sharon, the aide, working with me, stifling a yawn.

"That's contagious, y'know. That's why I'm stepping outside to get some fresh air to revive myself."

She smiled, patting her mouth before she replied. "Four a.m.'s the witching hour. Always a battle to stay awake. Go ahead. It's quiet. I can manage if I stay awake."

I nodded. "I won't be long." I went over to the main door and stepped out into the cold air. Above me, the sky was a black canvas painted with twinkling stars while the half-moon grinned at me.

I grinned back like a sixteen-year-old kid in high school who just spent time with a boy.

I took a deep breath, my mind once again tripping back to that hike with Stan. After the initial awkwardness of being with him, something melted inside me as we walked from the stream. We talked like old friends and laughed. A lot.

To feel like this again? That was a blessing, wasn't it? It had felt wonderful being with him. What had he said? That it felt so "familiar" to him?

"Yowwwwwllllll!"

My head turned at the high-pitched wail coming from the trees on the edge of the lawn. I peered at Shannon's bobcat as he hopped from the cover of the pine and loped closer. Bob! My eyes opened wider; I could feel them straining to pop right out of my skull. Well, I was completely awake now! What the heck was *he* doing here?

He stopped in the shadow of the picnic bench and screeched again.

But this time, it came through as a command.

"Come here, please. I need to talk to you."

I looked behind me at the glass door and at each side to make sure no one was around. What the hell? Bob had chosen the wee hours of the morning to come visit me? And then a bolt of fear shot through my veins.

Shannon. Was something wrong? I hurried through the drifts of snow, soaking my scrub pants but not caring. This had to be important for him to show up here, at the hospital.

"Bob! I mean, Robert! What is it?" I hunkered down on bended knees, peering at the tawny feline. "Is Shannon okay?"

"Physically yes! Mentally...?" He opened his mouth, revealing long incisors as he growled. *"She's TOTALLY inept! I've had some neophyte witches, but she takes the proverbial cake!"*

My gut sank like an anchor. "What's she done?" When he lowered onto his back haunches, lifting his head to sniff the air, I had to ask, "Did you two have a fight? Did she toss you outside?"

"She's made a total mess of things!" His paw lifted and scraped across my thigh. *"You must let her know. I'm going to dictate what you will tell her, since she's not talented enough to COMMUNICATE!"*

My head popped back as I stared at him. Dictate? What did he think I was, his personal assistant? "I can't. I mean I don't have paper or a…" I scooped my cell phone out of my pocket. "I'll record it! That way you can be sure I won't misquote you, Robert!" And knowing how prickly Robert could be…

For the next fifteen minutes, I froze my ass off playing secretary to a bobcat.

Shannon's very *pissed off*, and long-winded familiar.

THIRTY EIGHT

Shannon

Later that morning...

W here the hell is it?" I plucked the cushions up from the sofa, trying to see if that black binder and the files had somehow gotten buried there. Nada. I grit my teeth and hissed. "I HAVE to find them! They were right here, last night!"

I turned to Bob only to see him rolling on his back, gyrating from side to side, massaging his back in front of the fireplace. "YOU'RE supposed to HELP me! What good are you, anyway? You eat my food and then complain about the quality! And now when I need your help, you just suck up the heat that I'M paying for!"

His big yap opened and he yawned, blinking slowly at me. Great. Now, I'm getting attitude from an overgrown housecat.

"Aunt Maeve! If you'd deign to materialize, NOW might be a good time! If I don't find Devon's stuff and return it by nine, he's calling the cops on me! How'd you like to see your favorite niece in jail?"

I looked around the room but no change in the air, no

shimmering. Argh! I marched to the stairway to check my bedroom for the THIRD time.

Pounding at my front door stopped me dead in my tracks! Shit! Was that Devon? My heart leaped into my throat. With the amount of money cited in that binder, it could even be hitmen, sent to get his records and leave me beaten to a pulp… or worse.

"Shannon!"

All the air in my chest whooshed out at the sound of Libby's voice. Thank God. But what would she be doing here at this time of the morning? When Bob rubbed his side against my leg, I looked down at him. If I didn't know better, I'd swear that cat was preening!

I nudged him away with my knee, muttering, "Useless! That's what I'm going to start calling you! Now, find that file, while I see what Libby wants!"

When I opened the door, Libby brushed by me, holding her cell phone in the air.

"What are you doing here? Look, I don't have time to look at any photos you've taken or—"

"You'll want to hear this." She leaned over and scratched behind Bob's stump of an ear.

As if her familiarity with MY familiar wasn't goading enough, she was wasting precious time! "What? What's so important? You'd better make it fast because—"

Her head tipped to the side, smirking at me. "Because you need to deliver a package to Devon?"

My mouth fell open, gawking as her finger touched the phone's screen. Immediately a high-pitched yowl pierced the air, like fingernails scraping a chalkboard.

Libby's tinny voice followed from the cell phone, "Shannon crossed a line when she took that binder from Devon's office."

Libby grimaced, pausing the phone's recording. "This is all dictation from your familiar, Shannon! Bob, I mean Robert, visited me at four this morning when I was working. I stepped outside for a breath of air and there he was! It seems I'm now Robert's secretary and messenger all rolled into one!"

She tapped the screen again, resuming the recording, her voice coming up from her phone. "You must tell my witch that it is I who will provide for *her*! If… it is an item that will benefit my witch. The consequence of her foolhardy attempt to right a wrong is an unmitigated DISASTER! To prevent pure calamity and a possible jail sentence, I was FORCED to act."

I held up my hand, looking at Bob. He leaned into Libby's leg as he sat next to her, casually licking his paw. "What did you do, fleabag? You KNOW where that binder IS! I know it! Hand it over before I skin you and wear your coat as a muff!"

Libby held her finger up, wagging it as she scolded. "Nuh-uh. He's not done, Shannon! Not by a long shot! I was late getting back from my break with the earful that Mr. Eloquent dictated!"

She brushed the screen and the recording started again.

"I, *me personally!* I returned the binder and files to Devon's office! At great personal discomfort, I might add. I dislike being in town. The smells and cold concrete, not to mention cracking a nail jimmying the lock!"

My head fell back, and I felt the weight of the world lift from my shoulders. Thank goodness. Or Bob. The rest of his lecture almost fell on deaf ears with the relief seeping through me.

"I am *not* a delivery cat! Do I look like the return desk at Wal-Mart, where I'm sure she purchases her hideous clothes? Next time, Shannon must convey what she needs *me* to do for *her*. SHE may not understand me, but I've been around the block with *her* kind for centuries, you know. She needs to step her witch game up a few notches."

My gaze dropped to Bob and we stared at each other. Neither one of us blinking. It went on for a few moments before Libby let out a long sigh.

"I've got to get home! After working a twelve-hour overnight shift, I really don't have time for this childish nonsense." As her feet thudded to the door, she called over her shoulder, "Work it out, you two! I'm not a secretary or some weird marriage counselor."

When the door banged shut, I sank down onto my haunches, my gaze never wavering from Bob's. "Thanks."

His eyes slowly closed and opened again.

Was that a "You're welcome"? Something told me it was.

I looked to the side, hating what I was about to say but knowing it had to be said if there was ever going to be peace between us.

"I'm sorry, Robert."

This time his head dipped lower as he blinked. My eyes popped open wider, peering at him. "That was 'apology accepted,' right?"

Again, he repeated his action, dipping and blinking. I reached out my hand, going slowly until my fingers touched his head. His chin lifted, and he pressed into my touch, a purr starting to rumble in his throat.

A warm tingle started in my chest, spreading out and up until there was a big grin on my lips. "We're good? We're friends now?"

The air behind Robert shimmered, and my aunt's form glittered before becoming solid. She extended her hand and scratched Robert's stump of an ear. "So mote it be."

THIRTY NINE

Libby

A week later...

"Hey, Libby! You're reading the piece about the Cousins' building?" I jerked back before I noticed it was Steve wheeling a shopping cart ahead of him. "Shannon wrote one hell of an article, didn't she?"

Wanda, the cheery cashier ringing Ida Watkins's groceries through chimed in, "I read it this morning at breakfast! I can't imagine that I've lived here all my life and never knew the history of that building! It's a sad day when you don't learn something!"

"For sure." I'd just finished reading the article and was skimming through it once more, standing in line with my groceries.

Grinning, I turned to Steve. "She made it sound like that building is the cornerstone of this town, even more historic and important than the old courthouse. And the stories of all the tenants in that building. I never knew the Jackson family were the original tenants. Imagine living in an apartment that your great-grandfather first rented."

Steve nodded "Yeah, I know. But it's the part about MJ's restaurant that tugs the heartstrings. Shannon must have visited poor Ed Cousins to get all those details, although how she managed that with him being so sick…"

I nodded. "Yeah, some of my coworkers have been moonlighting, taking care of the poor man. It's a shame that everything his family built will get sold off when he dies. Shannon really laid some big hints about that. She omitted Devon Booker's name, but it's pretty obvious to anyone with half a brain that he'll end up buying everything up."

The smile fell from Steve's face and was replaced with a scowl. "Don't mention that jerk's name, not to me. I'm glad that Shannon finally saw through that bastard." His forehead tightened and he looked down for a moment. "From the way I saw Shannon talking to Devon at MJ's restaurant… it seems like these reporters…they sure do some oddball stuff to get the story."

I'd heard all about that horrible scene from both MJ and Shannon themselves. Even my son, Jack, had sniggered about Shannon's insane and sexy comments to Devon as she argued with him! How much longer until whatever powers in the well would lift the hex from Shannon—and Mary-Jane, for that matter?

I was saved from replying when Wanda finished ringing Ida through. Smiling at Steve, I shifted a head of lettuce onto the conveyor belt. "Looks like it's my turn."

"Yeah. I should get going too. I have to pick up Byron from the ex's house. We're doing a movie marathon weekend *Guardians of the Galaxy One* and *Two*. Just what I don't need, a cuteness overload of that tree creature and the talking raccoon." He waved his hand and left to get his groceries.

Hmm…talking raccoon? I got one of those! I smiled as I finished loading my groceries on the belt and listened to Wanda still singing the praises of Shannon's piece in the *Wesley Weekly*.

Fifteen minutes later, I found a parking space in front of MJ's restaurant. If she hadn't read the newspaper, she needed to. When I entered the building, I couldn't believe my eyes! The dining room was set up exactly the way it had been before the fire damaged it. Well, except for the wall at the far end of the room. Instead of tables and chairs, a stage dominated, with burgundy, floor-length curtains framing it on each side.

At the sound of MJ's laughter, I turned to see her and Cynthia emerge from the kitchen door. Cynthia held a copy of the *Wesley Weekly* in her hand.

"Great minds think alike, I see." I held up my copy, flourishing it with a wave of my hand.

"Libby!" MJ practically beamed as she hurried over to greet me. "As I was just telling Cynthia, the phone and computer have been buzzing all morning! Everyone wants to secure a table for the grand reopening! And not only that, but they're also booking for Tuesday night! A TUESDAY! That's when the high school is doing *The Mousetrap* play!"

"Oh my God! I didn't know you were back up and running! I thought it wasn't happening until tomorrow!" But looking around, and the smell of something delicious cooking in the kitchen made me wonder.

Cynthia chimed in, "The grand reopening is still tomorrow. But MJ wanted to give the new equipment a test run. We were just about to give you a call. Shannon's on her way now. How does Cornish hen on a bed of wild rice with garlic-glazed green beans sound? MJ and Ray are christening the restaurant with lunch just for us."

"Don't forget us! We're not missing this." Ray and Zoe stepped out from behind the curtains next to the stage.

Zoe gushed, "I can't wait to show Jack the sound system for the play. It's totally dope!" She walked over to MJ. "I asked Jack to join us for lunch, Mom. That's okay, right?"

Wow! The progress in the restaurant wasn't the only thing moving fast. It looked like Zoe and my son were hitting it off well too. Not that I minded. Zoe was a good kid, unlike that shifty gang he'd hung around with at the start of the school year.

MJ nodded. "Of course it's okay. Jack's done a ton of work to help us with the cleanup. But he'd be welcome anyway."

Ray stepped closer to me. "You're staying, right? Can I get

you a drink?" He looked over at Cynthia. "And your money is no good here, Cynthia. Not after all the help and the crazy flirting with the insurance adjuster. What are you drinking?"

I put my hand on Ray's shoulder. "Can you give me twenty minutes? I've got to get my groceries home before the ice cream melts. I'll be right back for lunch. Who can resist MJ's cooking?"

"I'll walk you to your car, Libby." After saying this, Cynthia turned to Ray. "Make it a double Jack Daniels on ice, please." She then led the way past the bar and out the door.

When I stepped outside, the woman of the hour was just getting out of her truck. Shannon grinned as she walked over to Cynthia and me.

"Did you read it? Tell me there weren't any typos!" She gathered her mane of dark hair in one hand, nervously glancing at Cynthia and me.

It was hard to say who got to Shannon first, me or Cynthia. Both throwing our arms around her shoulders.

"Are you kidding? You wrote a great piece! The whole town is talking about it!"

Cynthia weighed in after me, "You hit all the high notes, Shannon! I don't think Devon is going to want to touch this place with a ten-foot pole after the job you did with that article! At the very least, if he does buy it, he'll encounter some serious opposition if he changes anything…like boosting the rent or evicting people."

Shannon giggled and did a fist pump to the sky! "Yes! I was so worried that I'd overdone it!"

"No way!" After one final squeeze of her hand, I stepped away. "I'll be back in a flash." Turning and pointing my finger at them, I added, "Don't drink all the liquor."With that, I got in my car to drive home.

Shannon had done a great job and possibly a big favor to MJ. Things were going well between all of us. Those damn spells were reversed now.

Right?

FORTY

Mary-Jane

The next day

"Mary-Jane, I think you should get your ass in here right now. Debbie and Sylvie are working like slaves preparing for our reopening. We need you here, not out jogging around town!"

I held the phone out from my ear before Ray's bark busted my eardrums. It had been well over a week since I'd jogged. I had to do this! The scale that morning hadn't been good. I'd gained two pounds! Not only that, but I *really* missed running in the fresh air.

"I won't be long, Ray. it's such a glorious day that I can't resist. I'll only go half a mile, okay?" Not to mention this was a test. Our coven, my sisters in magic, were finally working together, and the voice in the well had said that once that happened, the spell would be reversed. There was only one way to know for sure and that was by exercising. If it stirred the hormonal stew, I'd stop straight away.

His voice was lower when he replied, "I'm not leaving work, Mary-Jane. This day is too important to screw around with. I mean that quite literally."

"I get that. Don't worry. I'll be there in an hour." I clicked the phone off and shoved it in my pocket. After a few stretches, I started off at a fast walk. If this worked, I'd pour a whole bottle of Jack Daniels down that Witching Well on Monday night! I just wanted to be normal again. Shannon's spell had helped me shed a ton of weight, and healthy habits were now ingrained in me, but the case of the hornies HAD to go.

So far so good. I picked up the pace as I sprinted across the street. The sun's rays were whittling away at the snow, and patches of brown lawn showed through in my neighbor's yards. An approaching red truck slowed down and honked its horn. The window rolled down, and Stan Jones waved to me.

I waved back and wondered if he was on his way to see Libby. They'd been out on a few more dates according to her, and things were going well. There was hope for Libby after all.

I'd gone about a quarter of a mile, but the only result was a tightening of my quads. This was terrific! I'd never made it this far without the "other" thing happening. I broke out into a full-on run, racing past the high school to reach the midpoint of my route, the Episcopal church.

As I rounded the parking lot there, heading back, the first tingle started. My feet pounded more slowly on the concrete until I slumped against the side of the stone structure. SHIT! It was still there! That damned spell might have diminished a bit, but it was still affecting me. What the hell was it going to take to *finally* be rid of that stupid spell?

I fished my phone from my pocket and called the cab company. No way was I going to get into a lather... not today! There was too much riding on the reopening. I'd tested the spell, and I'd bet wrong.

Forget about pouring a bottle of Jack Daniels down that damned well! I would smash it against the stones first!

***

Later, I lost all thought of the run as the prep work in the restaurant's kitchen demanded my attention. This was a big day with waves of reservations for dinner on our reopening.

The kitchen door swung open and Ray stepped in. "Mary-Jane! You're not going to believe who just called."

I looked over at him, and my hand paused from folding cream into the sauce. His eyes blinked a few times, shaking his head. "What? Who called? I'm busy here, Ray. In case you didn't notice, the dining room is at capacity." Beside me, Debbie was a dervish, taking steaks from the grill and setting them on plates.

Ray took a step closer. "Ed Cousins! Well, not Ed but his caregiver! He wants us to set up a video feed so that Mr. Cousins can view the play from his bed. He also asked if we can cater his favorite dinner of mustard salmon to eat while he watches."

I stared at Ray. "I wouldn't have thought he was well enough! Is he in remission? Wow! I sure hope so." I'd make the very best mustard salmon with…

But this was followed by another thought. "Can we do that, Ray? We're kind of challenged when it comes to technical computer stuff, y'know."

Zoe stepped over from her spot at the dishwasher. With arms akimbo, she looked from her father to me. "This is the guy who owns the building, right? The same one who is letting it slip into Devon Booker's hands. Why would we do him any favors?"

Ray's voice was low, gently chastising when he answered. "Because he's always been fair with us, Zoe. And because he's dying. It may be the last time he can engage with the town, even if it's just vicariously."

I sighed. "Your father's right. If we can do anything to make Mr. Cousins' final days a bit better, then we do it. Maybe Steve can help us—"

"Leave it to me, Mom. I'm good at computer tech stuff. I'll touch base with his caregiver, and we'll get it set up. I can see that this means a lot to you guys too." She turned and went back to the cleanup area, submerging her hands in a sink full of dirty pots.

I grabbed a tissue to wipe the tear building in my eye. But whether it was sorrow for Ed Cousins or the fact that our daughter had stepped up to help was a toss-up.

We'd make sure Ed had a great meal along with our best liquor as he watched the opening performance of the school play. It might be the last kindness we could extend to the old gentleman, but as Ray had said... That was who we are. We could leave this place with our heads held high.

Ray came over to me. "You okay, MJ? You've been pretty quiet since you came in today. Was it the run? How'd that go?"

I rolled my eyes. "You were right. I should have skipped it." Smiling, I added, "You'd better get back out there. We haven't seen a night like this in a very long time. We've probably got Shannon's article to thank for that."

He kissed my forehead. "Personally, I think it's your cooking more than anything. But whatever, we'll take it."

Tomorrow night was going to be memorable; we have Esbat tonight to make sure.

FORTY ONE

Libby

Monday Esbat

So, give us the dirty details on your dates with *Stan*, Libby." Mary-Jane took a seat next to me on Shannon's sofa and put her hand on my arm.

I pushed her hand away like it was a hot ember. "No way! I'm not letting you read me like an open book! Some things are private, MJ. If I wanted to tell you, I would." Sheesh! I was still figuring all this out without her probing touch.

Shannon came in from the kitchen with Bob at her heels. "There's no sign of Cynthia. She's twenty minutes late. I wonder what's keeping her?" She flopped down on the chair across from us and looked over at MJ. "I'm really sorry that the spell is still affecting you. I guess that means that I'm not out of the woods either."

Bob took a seat next to me and I absently scratched behind his ear. "I take it you haven't heard anything from Devon. That's kind of surprising considering the article you wrote. I would have thought he'd threaten you with a lawsuit or something."

Bob yawned and turned to me. *"He probably can't find his lawyer's phone number. Have you seen his office? Hurricanes leave tidier places."*

I shook my head. "Nope. I'll take a pass on that, thanks." I noticed Shannon watching the cat closely as he spoke to me. But unlike before, she didn't look upset about the fact that only I could understand him. The way that Bob now shadowed her, it looked like they'd come to some kind of truce, if not friendship.

Mary-Jane rose to throw another log on the fire. "Well, for what it's worth, we had one of the busiest nights we've ever had, thanks to your article, Shannon." She grinned when she turned to go back to her spot. "I've got a table front-row center for you guys for the play. It looks like you'll be able to do another article for the paper on it."

Shannon's eyebrows rose. "I'll need to. Don't forget I still have an enormous tax bill to pay. That job at Devon's office would have taken care of the bulk of that but…"

A series of taps on the front door was followed by a cheery, "I'm here! Sorry I'm late."

Shannon rose. "Don't take your coat off, Cynthia. I want to get out to the well. Something's not working with these spells lifting, and I want to know why."

MJ and I rose to follow Shannon to the front of the house. Bob was right behind us, muttering, *"Just when I get toasty warm, and then I'm back outside freezing my whiskers off. Why didn't I choose a witch in Florida?"*

I bent to scratch his head. "You'd probably get eaten by an alligator if you were there. Now, hush."

Cynthia smiled. "I was half tempted to take a pass on coming. My spells are back up and working. It's a great night to lounge in the hot tub, y'know."

Mary-Jane scowled. "Must be nice. I agree with Shannon. We bonded, working together, and that damned spell still has me in its clutches. I barely made it a quarter-mile running before I had to quit."

"That's weird. I wonder if something else is interfering with you two?" Cynthia looked over at me. "How about you, Libby? How are things going with you?"

I shrugged. "I'm good. Actually, better than good. The other day when I was coming out of the drugstore, an Irish wolfhound some guy was walking, started chatting me up. It's like these animals can sense I'm different, that I can understand them. Although the dog had a serious brogue."

"Argh!" Shannon shoved her arms into her jacket and handed me and MJ satchels with the magic items. "So it's just Mary-Jane and me! Tonight I want to focus all our energy on us, okay?"

Cynthia and I exchanged a look before we swept the wool capes over our shoulders.

Mary-Jane nudged Shannon. "You packed the Jack Daniels, didn't you? This time the bottle and not some measly flask?"

"Well, yeah! I'm willing to do whatever it takes to get this damned spell removed. Although it's curious that it's only worked with Devon and Stan but not Steve." Shannon opened the door and stepped out into the wintry night.

"I've got a theory about that, Shannon. I've been giving this some serious thought, and I think it's because you're attracted to Steve and not Devon. That there's a connection between the two of you." Cynthia fell into step beside Shannon.

Her theory didn't sound plausible. I weighed in, "What about what happened with Stan? No. It's got to be something else about Steve. I saw him at the grocery store the other day. I think it hurt him hearing you say those flirty things to Devon."

Shannon looked over her shoulder at me. "Yeah. You should have seen his face that day. It was bad. But once this spell is lifted, I'll make it up to him. Maybe invite him for dinner or something."

"Over my dead body."

My gaze flew to the bobcat walking beside me. "What'd you say, Robert? You don't like Steve? *Everyone* likes Steve." But his good ear had flattened, and a low growl rumbled in his throat.

Shannon's face took on a curious expression as she looked wide-eyed at her familiar. "It's because Steve said animal control should get rid of him. I can't blame Robert for disliking Steve after that comment."

"Don't forget the gun! He threatened to shoot me!"

I leaned over and rubbed my fingers through his thick mane of hair. "Poor Robert. I wouldn't like him either if I were you."

Mary-Jane cleared her throat. "Speaking of Devon… he's coming to the play tomorrow night. I just wanted to give you a heads-up, Shannon."

Shannon turned on her heel, peering at MJ. "Are you kidding me! After all we've gone through with that jerk, and you're letting him come to see the play at your restaurant? MJ! Now, *I* can't go!"

"I put him at a table close to the kitchen. He won't be anywhere near you! To be frank, he requested that when he spoke to Ray. We squeezed him in with the newspaper guy and his wife since we're so booked."

Cynthia put her arm over Shannon's shoulders. "I'm sitting with you, doll. Don't worry. I'll keep Devon away if I have to put a double hex on him. You HAVE to be there! Just don't look at Devon or Stan, and keep your eyes on the performance. You'll be fine."

"Famous last words. I'd wire my mouth shut except I'd miss out on MJ's meal. I'm not doing that for anyone!"

"Yowl! Tell her to bring home a kitty bag! I miss out on all the good stuff. It's tough being her familiar, although the menu's somewhat improved lately. It helps that I raid her fridge every night."

Shannon looked back at me. "What'd Robert say?"

I laughed. "He says he'd like to sample MJ's meal, although he's sure it can't compete with your wonderful cooking."

She looked down at Robert. "You didn't say that, did you? I might not understand the exact words, but I sure as hell can detect your tone. You might try the butcher shop on your next raid instead of scooping up people's parcels from their porch."

Mary-Jane snickered. "Is he *still* doing that? Anything as good as what he stole from Libby?"

I elbowed her. "Don't go there. I tossed the pink parcel out after all your teasing." My cheeks warmed thinking of that embarrassing night.

She snorted. "Riiight. So dating Stan wouldn't have *anything* to do with that? And by the way, giving me that jab with your elbow? I GOT the dirty details."

Shaking my head, I stepped into the clearing of trees. The well was just ahead, still untouched by snow, although a few strands of ivy clung to it.

Cynthia's gaze took in all of us in a sweep. "Well, bitches, let's do it right this time!"

FORTY TWO

Shannon

The Mousetrap Debut at The Cat's Whiskers Restaurant

Shannon! Wow. You clean up pretty well, girlfriend!"
Cynthia grinned as her gaze took in my hair swept up
into a messy bun, the pearl earrings, the little black dress,
and the spiked leather boots.

I couldn't help the shoulder shimmy, smiling at her
compliment as we stood in the entrance of MJ's restaurant.
Coming from Cynthia, this was high praise! I'd spent over an
hour getting ready for this evening. It was fun getting dolled up
for a change!

"You look pretty hot yourself, Cynthia!" The emerald-green
satin hugged every curve while accentuating her red hair and
blue eyes. She could have stepped off the cover of *Vogue*
magazine.

I looked across the room, giving a finger wave at the few
people in town I knew but secretly trying to see if Devon was
there yet. My stomach tightened when I saw him at the table
with Wayne Silver and his wife. Well, this was *awkward*. I

should stop by to at least say hi to my boss and his wife, but there was no way I could chance it. Not with Devon sitting there.

Cynthia leaned in and whispered, "C'mon. Ignore him. Let's go join Libby and her kids." She took my hand, leading the way, as we threaded through packed tables with people already enjoying their meals.

I noticed Steve sitting with his son, Byron, and two women. From the way the cuddly brunette leaned close to Byron, that had to be Steve's ex. The other woman had spiky, blonde hair and an angular face above a high-necked, black blouse.

"Hi, Shannon!"

I turned at the woman's voice and waved back at Ida Flaming-Red-Car Watkins. She was there with her husband and a few couples who looked familiar from the disastrous Halloween party I'd thrown last year. Yikes. I'd barely lived that down before that scene with Devon Booker made the rounds.

It was a relief to see Libby and her two kids sitting at a table of six near the stage. Kevin jumped to his feet, holding chairs out for Cynthia and me.

"Hi, Shannon, Cynthia. Good timing, the play's going to start pretty soon." When we were seated, Kevin introduced Dahlia's friend Rita, who was the only one I didn't know.

Libby's face was almost as pink as her dress as she beamed at her son being so gentlemanly seating Cynthia and me and doing the introductions. She'd gone to some trouble with her makeup, and even her hair was different, the curls straightened and held up on one side by a rhinestone clip.

She leaned over the table to speak to Cynthia and me, "I can't believe how nervous I am. I mean, I've never seen Jack in a play before, and he's got the *lead*!" She held up her hand, crossing her fingers. "What is it they say… break a leg! Weird coming from a nurse, right?"

"Thank God I don't have to listen to him rehearsing anymore! I swear, I've heard it so much, I could be up on that stage." Kevin shook his head, but it was clear he was proud of his brother from the wide grin.

Ray appeared at our table before I could comment. "What are you lovely ladies drinking? The usual? Jack on ice?"

"Of course!" Cynthia beat me to it.

Ray nodded and leaned closer. "Now that you're here, the server will be around with appetizers and, of course, the main course: prime rib roast beef au jus. Mary-Jane's outdone herself."

"I can't believe how packed this place is!" I looked around and noticed a young guy adjusting a cell phone attached to a tripod. "You're videoing this? Awesome! I'd like a copy to send along to my kids. They'll get a kick out of seeing Jack and Zoe."

Ray smiled. "Of course. That's the live feed for Ed Cousins. I hope the poor man enjoys it." With that, he left to get our drinks.

I could feel eyes watching me. It had to be Devon, but there was no way I was going to look back. He was probably giving an earful to Wayne Silver about me. I'd be lucky if I didn't lose THAT job too. I saw Libby's gaze drift over to the kitchen door next to where he was seated, confirming my suspicions.

Cynthia must have noticed, too, as she tried to distract us. "So Libby, I thought Stan would be here with you."

Libby's eyes flashed wider before casting a pointed glance at me. "He's working tonight, which is just as well if you get my drift."

Cynthia's mouth formed an "O" as it sunk in. "Gotcha."

Ray came back with the drinks, and as he set them in front of us, he leaned close. "These drinks are compliments of Wayne Silver. He told me to tell you he expects a good article on this evening's play."

I swallowed. There was no way I could avoid acknowledging Wayne's kind gesture. Turning, I lifted the drink in my hand, smiling my thanks at the old editor. He nodded and lifted his glass.

Try as I might, I couldn't help but see Devon, a smirk

curling his lips while his eyes narrowed. If he could kill me with a look, I'd be dead meat. Thank goodness I didn't have to go anywhere near him and open my mouth.

The server, a young teen, arrived carrying plates of steaming roast beef with a variety of oven-roasted vegetables. Before he set the plate down, he asked if I'd prefer vegetarian.

Cynthia looked over at me. "MJ decided that the only way she could serve this many people at one sitting was by limiting the choice to roast beef or vegetarian. As it is, I think she's worked hard to pull this off."

I signaled for the beef, before smiling at Cynthia. "This is perfect. Remind me to wrap up a slice for Robert."

The lights dimmed, and a barrel-chested man walked onto the stage.

Kevin leaned over and whispered, "That's Mr. Conley, the drama teacher. I guess the show's about to start."

***

The kids did such a great job during act one that I almost forgot to eat, let alone give Devon Booker another thought. When the lights brightened, many smiling people got up from their spots, making a mad dash for the restrooms or going outside for a cigarette.

Libby gave a big sigh of relief before a wide grin became plastered on her face. "Jack did an *amazing* job, didn't he? I think he may have finally found his niche in life. And Zoe!" She grabbed a tissue from her bag and dabbed the corner of her eye.

You should be so proud, Libby! And for this to happen here, in MJ's restaurant. Wow!" I pushed my chair back and started to rise. "I'm going to take my spot in line for the bathroom. I'll get to eavesdrop on people's comments for my article."

Cynthia nodded. "I'll order us coffee with Bailey's while I wait for the mad rush to calm down."

I took my time heading to the ladies' room on the other side of the bar. People were raving about the performance everywhere I looked. And not only that, they thought the dinner theater should have been done years ago! I couldn't wait to pass all this along to MJ.

The lineup for the bathroom was out the door, and I took my spot behind Wanda from the grocery store. I was just getting my phone from my purse to send a text to my kids when fingers gripped my upper arm.

My head turned and I gasped. Devon Booker's flinty eyes peered at me, but there was a forced smile on his lips.

"I want to talk to you. It'd be best if we stepped outside. Or I can make a scene if you'd prefer."

I looked around, but there was no one to help me avoid this. Nodding, I stepped out of the line. Even though I'd determined to keep my trap shut, the spell had other plans. "There're lots of things I'd prefer, but having you manhandle me is a good start on that."

He rolled his eyes as he pushed the door to the outside open. "You never quit, do you? Psycho."

He herded me past a group of people lost in a fog of cigarette smoke. When we were out of earshot from them, he spun me to face him. "How'd you do it?"

I looked up into his eyes, while his woodsy aftershave drifted into my nostrils. The muscle in his jaw twitched under the dark shadow of beard growth. I took a deep breath. "Do what?" But before I could breathe a sigh of relief that nothing more had popped out of my mouth, it did. "There are lots of things I'd like to do with you. Ever read *The Kama Sutra*?"

"Oh, for *God's* sake! Try to be sane for just one minute, will you!" His fingers threaded through his hair, glaring his exasperation with steely eyes. "You BROKE into my office to return those files! You even damaged my lock so that I had to get it replaced!"

My mouth fell open. "Not me. Robert did that!" My hand flew to cover my mouth but it was out before I even knew it. Was this spell getting worse? Before it had just been sexual double entendres, but now…there was absolutely NO FILTER?

"What? Who's Robert?" His face morphed from confusion to smugness, nodding. "Of course he did. Robert's one of those people who live in your head, isn't he, Shannon?" He snorted, "You're never alone when you're a schizophrenic, right? Except I think this is an act. You can't be as crazy as you let on."

At this point, I didn't even care about the spell. If he thought I was pulling his leg, that this was an act... why not go for broke? "Robert is real. He's my bobcat. And you better be nice to me or—"

Devon broke away from me, walking back to the restaurant's door. He called over his shoulder. "Stay away from me and my office or I'll get a restraining order."

"Restraints? I've never tried handcuffs, but I'm interested!" I called back. Oh man... well, at least he ignored me and went back inside.

I leaned back against the brick wall. That went well. NOT! The cold seeped from the wall straight through me, and I pushed away, rubbing my upper arms.

As I walked back to the entrance, I noticed Steve Murphy standing a few feet away, watching me. He looked angry. How long had he been there watching the argument between Devon and me?

He stepped over and before he opened the door for me, he commented. "You should stay away from him, Shannon. I know I've told you before, but I think you're starting to get the picture. He's bad news."

"You're telling me. Don't worry, Steve. Point taken."

Even though the rest of the play was as good as the first part, the encounter with Devon ruined it for me. I couldn't help thinking that the spell had amped up rather than dwindling. And that was even after our Esbat at the well the night before.

Shit.

FORTY THREE

Mary-Jane

Four days later...

As Ray wheeled the car through the iron gates of the
cemetery, I wiped a tear from my eye. We had hardly
gotten over the excitement of the dinner theater,
making plans for the next week when we got the news.

Ed Cousins had passed away the day after the play.

Ray reached over and cupped his hand over mine. "I'm so
glad we did that thing with the video, so he could see it. He
passed in his sleep, MJ, and that's better than lingering on in
pain."

I nodded. "That poor man." As Ray parked the car at the
end of what was a VERY long line, I noticed the black Lincoln
Town Car stop close to the gravesite and Ed's daughter
emerge.

Hmph! The pointy-nosed bitch hadn't shown her face in
town when Ed had been alive, but now she was playing it up,
with the black dress, and netting from her hat covering her
pinched face. Her brother, Barry, got out the other side and
hurried over to take her arm.

When I got out, we joined the throng of neighbors and friends walking to the grave to pay our respects. The church had been packed, and that crowd hadn't dwindled much. At the touch on my arm, I turned and saw Libby, with Stan next to her.

"It's a dreary day for a funeral. That's appropriate, I guess."

I sighed. "I think there's a saying about that, but yes, you're right." When I turned my head slightly, I saw Libby's kids, and behind them, Cynthia with Shannon almost lost in the sea of people.

We huddled close together, feeling the rain turn to sleet, biting our faces as the preacher spoke.

Finally, it was over.

As we walked back to our car, a tall, spindly man fell into step beside us. It was one of the three lawyers in town, Mr. Harding.

"Mr. and Mrs. Matthews?"

I turned my head to look at him. "Yes, but it's Ray and Mary-Jane. Can we help you?" Was that force of habit, my saying that after years of working in a restaurant? How could I help him? Gosh.

A ghost of a smile lifted his lips. "Ray, Mary-Jane, then. Normally, my office would contact you but as this matter is being expedited…" He gave a slight shake of his head. "TODAY, in fact. Mr. Cousins' will is being read in my office at four this afternoon. His children requested this as they are returning to Albany today."

A jolt of fear shot through my chest. Immediately my mind went to the lease. Were his children in that big of a rush that they wanted to evict us right away? What else could it be? Had Devon asked for vacant premises before he'd buy the building?

Ray paused and looked the lawyer in the eye. "What's this about, Mr. Harding? Why are you telling us this?"

The lawyer's gray eyebrows arched. "Your presence is optional but I urge you to attend." He pulled his business card from the pocket of his overcoat and handed it to Ray. "Four o'clock." With that, he joined his wife, heading for their car.

My eyebrows knitted together as I watched him. "Should we go? Be at his office for the reading?"

Ray shrugged. "If it's bad news, I'd rather know than have this hanging over our heads, MJ. At least then we can personally tell that pair of gold diggers to go screw themselves."

"Fair enough." I took his hand and squeezed it as we walked to the car.

***

When Mr. Harding's assistant escorted Ray and me into the lawyer's office, Laura and Barry, with their respective spouses, looked at us like we were aliens dropped from Mars.

The lawyer stood up and with a sweep of his hand asked us to have a seat. Before he could say another word, Laura spoke.

"I'm sorry, but this should be just family at the reading. If these people are mentioned in the will at all, could it not wait until after? This is, after all, a private *family* affair." She pulled herself more erect, looking down her long nose at the lawyer.

"Yes. My sister is correct." Barry turned to Ray. "Would you mind stepping outside? This won't take long I'm sure."

I felt like my eyes were going to pop out on my cheeks listening to the condescension in their tones. We were being relegated like hired help to the waiting room. Before I could say anything, Ray squeezed my hand and held my chair for me. "Take a seat, MJ." He turned to the lawyer, ignoring Barry and Laura. "Please proceed, Mr. Harding."

"Well! I never—"

The lawyer also ignored the heirs when he spoke. "We will deal with the portion of the estate that pertains to Mr. and Mrs. Matthews first. It is a short section. They will then leave so that we can deal with your portion, Laura and Barry. But I felt it was important that you all be present for this."

My mouth fell open as I tried to process his words. *Our portion of the estate?* I looked over at Ray and saw his eyes were as round as my own.

The lawyer started, rhyming off the legalese…being of

sound mind and body, etcetera., but I was still in a state of shock.

When Ray gave my hand a sharp tug, I tuned in.

"I hereby bequeath the property at 46 Mountain View Avenue and its entirety, to Raymond Matthews and his wife, Mary-Jane Matthews. The building is not only a historical monument to my family's legacy, it serves the interests of the community from the focal point of the restaurant, the inter-generational flower shop, the dental office, and the tenants of the apartments who have raised their families there. The restaurant, in particular, holds fond memories for me and my deceased wife. While Mary-Jane and Ray are free to manage or dispose of the property, it is my deepest hope that they will continue the current use."

The lawyer paused and looked at Ray and me. I sat still as a statue, barely breathing, while Ray softly muttered, "Holy shit."

"This is outrageous! My father must not have been thinking clearly to leave that building to them!" Laura fixed her beady eyes on Ray and me. "What did you do? You must have wheedled and taken advantage of his drugged state."

The lawyer cleared his throat. "Your father summoned me the day before he died. His caretaker was present as well as the nurse. He was entirely lucid, let me assure you. He'd become quite concerned after reading an article in the *Wesley Weekly* about the building and its tenants. It was clear to him that with his passing, the building would share the same fate, eventually."

The son blustered, "We'll contest that part of the will! I don't know what you're trying to pull here, Harding, but it's obvious that you're in cahoots with this shifty pair!"

Ray stood up and nudged me with his hand to join him. He practically snarled when he looked at Laura and Barry. "You aren't as good as your father. He was a fine and decent man. You don't give a damn about this town or the people in it! You two are vultures, fighting over the poor man's carcass!"

I turned to Laura, echoing Ray's sentiments. "Don't *ever* darken the door of OUR building, or we'll have you thrown out." I cast a grim smile at the lawyer. "Thank you, Mr. Harding."

Ray's hand was on my waist as we left the lawyer's inner sanctum. We had hardly reached the reception area before my legs turned to meringue. I fell into the nearest chair, fanning my hand before my face.

"I think I'm having a stroke, Ray." I looked up at him and grinned. "Holy Shit! We OWN the building?"

FORTY FOUR

Shannon

Monday Esbat

I had barely opened the door when Mary-Jane thrust a huge bouquet of red roses forward.

"For you, Shannon!" Her eyes twinkled above a mile-wide grin. "Thanks to your article in the paper, Ray and I now own the building! I still can't believe it!"

I took the flowers from her, inhaling the heady aroma. She wasn't the only one in a state of shock. When she called me the night of Ed Cousins' funeral, it was a good thing I was sitting down. "Mary-Jane, these roses are gorgeous, but you didn't have to do that!"

Libby laughed, "She bought every red rose in the shop! Are you kidding me? You *totally* deserve the flowers after how this turned out!"

I signaled for them to follow me as I walked to the kitchen to get a vase. "I'm so happy that everything worked out for you and Ray. No more worries about Devon scooping your building up and making trouble for you."

"Nope! It's all ours, lock, stock, and barrel! We had a

celebration last night with the other tenants in the building. Everyone was so relieved when we told them that things are going to be exactly the way Ed Cousins managed things."

MJ squee'd while her feet tapped fast in a victory jig. "And that's not all! The spell you wished on me is GONE! I went out for a mile run today! The only side effect was sore muscles! Yay!"

I spun around to face her, watching Libby give her a big hug. If the spell was off MJ, then... "It's because we *worked* together! The well said that the spells would be reversed if we all bonded and helped each other. Mine must be gone too! I'm FREE of the dirty, flirty mouth!"

Libby scratched her head, and her smile fell. "Too bad you can't test it like MJ did. There's no way that Devon is ever going to let you within a million miles of him."

She looked over at me. "Although I'm not crazy about the idea, you could try having a conversation with Stan."

"That would be weird, don't you think?" MJ looked over at Libby. "What if the spell isn't reversed on Shannon? She's liable to say all kinds of smutty things to your guy. You okay with that?"

"No!" Libby rolled her eyes. "I'm totally NOT okay with that, but what choice do we have? The only stipulation I'm making is that I have to be there when Shannon talks to Stan." She looked over at me. "One word out of line, lady, and I'm hauling your ass outta there. Okay?"

I nodded. "Absolutely! If Devon hadn't threatened me with a restraining order, I'd go see him to test this. I feel kind of uncomfortable using Stan as the guinea pig."

Mary-Jane was still on cloud nine from everything, the grin still plastered on her face. "I bet the spell on you is gone, Shannon. I can't wait to get to the well tonight and celebrate! I feel like I owe that well *big time*!"

After a few taps on the door, Cynthia called to us, "Hi! Sorry I'm late again!" She poked her head into the kitchen and asked, "Is Robert here? I saw a bobcat about a mile away running into the forest. I didn't get a good look at his ear though."

I thought of how strange the cat had been acting that day. Normally he lounged in front of the fire sucking up every bit of heat he could get. But as the day had been sunny and mild, I didn't think too much of him going out that afternoon. "It could have been. I would have thought he'd be back by now. He knows this is Esbat."

Mary-Jane muttered, "It's spring. Maybe he's out tomcatting around, y'know. There could be a female cat around that caught his eye. He'll probably show up at the well."

She brightened, smiling at Cynthia. "I've been thinking of having a party for us. Y'know, to celebrate us getting the building. Would it be too nasty to invite Devon, to gloat?"

Cynthia loosened her scarf, grimacing at each of us. "About Devon… I ran into him at the coffee shop on my lunch. He's pretty thrilled that Ed Cousins left the building to you and Ray."

I couldn't believe my ears. That made no sense at all after what I'd seen in those files. "What do you mean he was *thrilled?* He had plans all drawn up for some Project C, the Cousins' estate."

"According to him, he's in the process of purchasing the land and homestead from Laura and Barry. But he never wanted the building or even the homestead. He only wanted the forty acres and those old, abandoned factories on it, but the heirs insisted on selling everything as a package."

This time it was Mary-Jane expressing disbelief. "All this time we were worried he'd get our building and toss us out. And he never even *wanted* it!"

"Sounds like Ed Cousins not only did you guys a favor, but he also helped Devon." Libby's forehead knotted as she processed this new development.

I peered into Cynthia's eyes. Was she pulling our legs? "You believe him? He was genuinely happy he didn't have to buy the building?"

She nodded. "I know Devon. He could hardly contain

himself, he was so excited. I have no idea what he plans to do with the acreage, but something tells me it's huge! As in those dollar amounts you saw in his files, Shannon. Billions!"

"Oh, shit."

At Mary-Jane's soft curse, we all looked at her. "What? What else is going on?"

She took a deep breath. "When I was out jogging, I saw a black Tahoe stop in front of Devon's office this afternoon. Three suits got out and went into his office. They weren't from around here."

Another penny dropped for me. I gasped. "Those guys have to be outside investors. There were massive financial entries on the spreadsheet with initials next to each one. What is Devon up to with that land?"

Libby murmured, "And what about the homestead? Didn't you say that the spirit haunting his building…Wasn't Estelle worried about that falling into his hands? But he doesn't want it."

Cynthia sighed. "Whatever plans he has will soon come to light. And I'm in the right spot working for the town to find out what that is. He'll have to file if he plans on changing the use of the land. There are environmental regulations and all kinds of zoning hoops for him to jump through."

I turned to Libby. "How soon can we meet with Stan? If this spell is reversed from me, I want to interview Devon about his plans. It's going to affect the town. Plus, I want to try to persuade him to do something decent with Estelle's old homestead."

My stomach fell at the next thought. "I also owe Devon an apology. I called him every name in the book when I thought he was a threat to MJ and Ray. Turns out, I was wrong about that." But I knew I had a snowball's chance in hell of him agreeing to meet with me. Still, I had to try.

FORTY FIVE

Shannon

The next day

When I pulled into the fire station the next afternoon, I saw Libby holding a golden retriever puppy in her arms while Stan and two other firefighters stood next to her. Stan looked at me and immediately turned away. Shit. That wasn't a good sign. No doubt he thought the same way that Devon did—batshit-crazy Shannon. Who could blame them after all the insane, flirty talk?

Steeling myself for the worst, I got out of the truck and walked over to join them. "What's this? You get a new dog, Libby?" I looked at her, trying not to smirk. Only she and I knew about her 'special' gift of communicating with animals. I wondered what the little pup was saying to her.

"Isn't this a sweet little guy?" Libby smiled at me and then went back to tickling the pup's chin. "I wish I could keep you, Ruff. Such a good boy!"

Stan took a deep breath and thrust his hands deep into his pockets. "Libby said you wanted to speak to me, Shannon?"

I nodded, silently praying to the Divine Mother that the

blasted spell was gone. "Yeah, I did. When I saw you at MJ's restaurant the day of the fire, I said some pretty strange things to you."

"Yup." He looked over at Libby who handed the pup back to the two other firefighters. "I told Libby all about that, but she explained you weren't yourself."

Libby brushed the hair from her jacket. "Yes. It was dental issues, right? Sodium Pentothal. Shannon should have gone straight home from the dentist but she wanted to cover the fire for the newspaper."

I heard both of them but my mind was doing cartwheels! I'd spoken to Stan like a *normal* person! No flirty talk or coming onto him. And considering how hot he looked in the tight T-shirt and jeans, that was saying something! I was free from MJ's spell!

Libby prodded me with her elbow, getting my full attention. My eyes opened wider and I blurted, "Yes! That's right. Still, I wanted to apologize for acting so ridiculous. Especially since you and Libby are dating. You two make a great couple."

Stan brightened when he looked over at Libby. "We do, don't we?" He put his hand on my shoulder, "No harm done, Shannon. You weren't yourself and we'll leave it at that, okay?"

"Thanks, Stan! You have no idea how much this means to me." And he really didn't! It was only then that I noticed Libby was dressed in business clothes, with a gorgeous navy full-length coat and leather boots rather than the usual jeans and jacket.

My face fell, "Don't tell me there's another funeral, Libby. Who died this time?" She even had her hair pinned up and was wearing makeup.

"Today's the day, Shannon!" She looked at her watch. "I've got that interview for head nurse in another hour."

"Oh my God! Good luck! I hope you get that job." I crossed my fingers holding my hand up. But the furrow in her brow as she took a deep breath was an odd response. "What's wrong? You aren't ready for the interview?"

Her mouth pulled to the side. "Yeah, I think I am. But…

This job is so far out of my bailiwick of patient care that I'm having second thoughts. It would mean more money but it would also mean a lot more responsibility and work. I'm not a businessperson, Shannon. I like patient care."

Stan interjected, "I think Libby would be great at anything she does. But a job should be fulfilling. If she's having second thoughts, there's a reason." He sighed. "You talk to her, Shannon. I've got to get back to work."

He hugged Libby and then walked back to the station house. Libby watched him enter the building and then she turned to me. "I'm torn in so many directions. I think I want to work with animals. I mean, I've got this gift now, so shouldn't I be making better use of it? Think of how we have to second-guess whether our pet is in pain or sick. Unlike other people, I *know* what's wrong."

As I looked into her eyes, I knew how important this was to her. Hell! I'd seen her talk to Bob… Robert! I placed my hand on her arm. "You need to do what will make you happiest, Libby. I agree with Stan."

Her head tipped back and she groaned, "I know! But this job… Being a head nurse pays waaay more than I earn now. It could take years to make any money working at a Vet clinic. I've got Kevin going to college in a year and then Jack in another couple. I have to think of that."

"Nothing important is ever easy, is it?" My head tipped to the side as I gazed at her, "For what it's worth, I agree with Stan. You deserve to be happy, Libby. You've been given an amazing gift which would be a shame to squander."

"There's a 'but' coming. I know it's the same one I've been wrestling with." Libby sighed. "I'm going to do my best to get the head nurse job. But y'know, one thing I'm learning is that I don't always have all the answers. I mean, I *want* to work with animals but I *need* to provide for my family."

I shook my head slowly before replying. "One thing I've learned is that it's not always up to you how things play out. There's the universe hearing your wants and needs and helping you get to where you should be." I rolled my eyes thinking of all that had happened recently, "But of course, that path is full of hills and valleys when you aren't careening out of control around a hairpin turn."

She smiled as she reached to hug me. "The voice of experience. You've certainly come a long way from where you started. And you're still traveling that crazy world of magic, as am I. It'll all work out."

When she pulled back, looking me in the eye, she added, "So you're free of the spell now and ready to face Devon. It'll be okay, Shannon."

"I hope so. We were so wrong about him. He never wanted to take MJ's building or the homestead. I just hope he'll accept my apology for all that I said and did to him."

"If he doesn't, he's the one who's crazy." She shook her head, "I don't understand it but there IS something between you. Even if it's just plain old sexual attraction."

"That's not plain and certainly not old." I gave a pointed smile over at the fire hall. "It worked for you and Stan...finally." I stepped back and gave her a thumbs-up sign, "You're going to ace that interview, Libby. And after that, we'll see."

"Totally. I'll call you later to find out how it went with Devon."

As I got in my truck and started it up, I wondered about Libby and her job interview. There was no doubt in my mind she would do well, but it would still be a loss. She had so much to offer the world than sitting behind a desk doing administration would never come close to fulfilling. I said a silent prayer that things would work out for her.

And for me. With Devon.

***

I sat in the truck staring at the window of Devon's office for a few minutes, rehearsing what I would say to him. That is if he didn't call the cops to have me thrown out first.

Closing my eyes, I silently prayed. *'Please Divine Mother help me get through this to make things right.'* It helped center me even though my fingers still trembled opening the truck's door.

When I entered his office, I could hear his voice. But no other voices, so he was probably on the phone. I crept across the burgundy carpet never making a sound before I tapped on the doorframe. His back was to me, but at the knock, he swung around. His face transformed from a wide smile to a scowl in a nanosecond when his eyes locked with mine.

"Hang on, Eric. I'll call you right back." He set the phone on his desk and stood up. "I thought I told you not to come anywhere near me!" His gaze flitted over my body from the slouch boots to my leather jacket. "Are you armed? God knows you're dangerous, but mostly to yourself, I suppose."

I swallowed, feeling my rehearsed words dry up in my mouth. "Devon, I came in to apologize. I misjudged you and I'm sorry." My breath was shallow, waiting for the explosion from him. "You didn't deserve the way I treated you."

His eyes narrowed. "You back on your meds, Shannon? You almost sound sane today. But I'm not banking on that. Why are you *really* here?"

"Because I like you? Hell, who am I kidding? Judging by everything I said to you, it's clear that I'm attracted to you." My lips snapped shut. Oh my God! I'd been FINE with Stan but was this spell still lingering with Devon? The attraction part was true but why did I say it? Nope. It was that damned spell! I had to get out of there. FAST!

"There you *go*, again! I knew you'd try your tricks on me! How can you sound normal one second and like some kind of vamp the next? What the hell is your *game*, Shannon? Just GO, will you?"

My gut plummeted to my knees, but I had to give it one more try before I hightailed it out of there. My hand fell from my mouth and I did my best to keep my voice steady. "I heard you were happy that the building went to Ray and MJ, that you never wanted it in the first place. So what is it you want with the Cousins' home and land? Asking as a reporter, Devon."

His eyebrows rose. "Well, at least that's honest, unlike you sneaking my files out of the office and blabbing your half-baked ideas about my business all over town. But you are the *last* person I would ever... *ever* confide in. It's not just that you're certifiable, I can no longer trust you. That ship has sailed."

My eyes welled with tears as I listened. What could I say? He had every right to think the way he did. I'd jumped to conclusions and upset everyone in the process. Especially him.

"I'm truly sorry, Devon." I practically ran out of his office and jumped into my truck. He hated me and I couldn't blame him. As I drove out of town, I swiped at the tears which were blinding me. This hurt. A Lot. Much more than whenever I'd fought with Steve.

It was at that moment that I realized. It was more than just an attraction to Devon. I *cared* about him. Cared what he thought of me. He'd been kind to me and he certainly didn't deserve the devious way I'd treated him. I mean, that whole episode about the septic tank was his buddy over-reaching, not a plot by Devon. And the tax thing wasn't due to any shenanigans by him; in fact, he tried to help me out of that financial hole.

But I'd blown it. Or magic had blown it. But did it matter? The end result was the same.

FORTY SIX

When I pulled up to my house, a fresh set of tears bubbled out of me, seeing my familiar sitting next to the door, on my porch. My friend Robert. His ear perked forward and he stood up, walking down the steps to come over to me.

I sank down on my knees and hugged him, letting my tears fall onto his fur. "Oh, Robert. Why do I always make such a mess out of things? Devon hates me. To make matters worse, I'm not sure this spell is even removed. Why can't magic work out for me the way it does for MJ and Libby?"

At the sensation of his dry tongue scraping on my neck, I pulled back. Robert blinked slowly, and his tongue disappeared back into his mouth. Robert! Robert was trying to console me, licking my neck? A purr rumbled in his throat, and he leaned forward to lick my cheek. More tears blurred my vision as I hugged the big cat again, openly sobbing.

"I wish you could help me, Robert. If you could find a way so that I could at least be friends with Devon. I feel so rotten after what I did to him."

Robert's answer was to tilt his head to the side, rubbing his cheek against mine.

I whispered into his good ear. "We got off on the wrong foot, but I'm glad you're here with me. I'm not sure how our magic jives, but you're a sweet guy." Pulling back, I smiled at him. "If I am destined to be a cat lady for the rest of my days, I'm glad it's with you."

Again, he rubbed his head against me, purring even more loudly. I may not have Libby's gift, but that cat was doing everything he could to comfort me.

"Are you hungry, Robert? I missed you last night. Did you find a lady cat? C'mon. Let's go inside, and see if we can find us something decent to eat." I stood up and rubbed behind his ear. "You can tell me all about it even if I don't understand what you're saying. I hope you had better luck with your love life than I'm having with mine."

He walked beside me, rubbing along my legs. But before I reached the first step, he spun, leaped into the air, and let out a high-pitched *yowww!*

When I turned, I saw Steve's truck barreling down my driveway. I reached for Robert. "Go! Go into the woods until he leaves! You know he doesn't like you. From the looks of it, the feeling is mutual."

Steve was only twenty feet away from us, but Robert stood his ground! Shit! "Robert! As your witch, I *command* you. GO!" My fingers dug into the fur on his neck. "Now!"

Robert let out another yowl before bounding through the snow in my yard, headed for the trees. I turned to see Steve emerge from his truck, staring at the woods and then back at me.

"Shannon! Are you okay? That cat...he was right next to you! I tell you, there's something not right about that bobcat! He must be rabid. He's *dangerous*!" Steve kept walking over as he shouted at me.

I was in no mood to be lectured to, especially about Robert! Not to mention the fact that Steve's timing sure as hell sucked after the fiasco with Devon.

"We've had this discussion before, Steve. Nothing's changed. That cat is fine, and he's on *my* property." I jabbed a finger at him."You're the only one who has an issue with him hanging around." I took a step closer, scowling up into his face. "Now is not a good time to visit, Steve. I've had a horrible day."

For just a moment he just at me with a wide-eyed open-mouthed gawp. Then his eyes narrowed. "You'll have an even worse day if you let that cat hang around. He's gonna turn on you, Shannon! That's what wild animals do. He'll attack you, and no one will find you for a week!"

"NO, he won't! He's completely tame around me! Now, if you don't mind, I'm going inside. Alone! You can't just stop by and lecture me, y'know! This is my house and my cat."

Steve's eyebrows arched to his hairline. "That's *crazy*, Shannon!"

"Ha!" I snorted. "That's the word going around about me. *Crazy*! You and Devon should get together and compare notes." I turned and marched up the stairs and into the house.

I'd give it a few minutes after he left to call Robert in for dinner. At least there was one male I could get along with.

After I got the fire going and the teakettle plugged in, I rummaged around in the fridge trying to figure out what we could eat for dinner.

At the loud screech from outside, Robert was letting me know he was back. I went to the front door and opened it.

I did a double-take seeing Devon Booker getting out of his SUV. What the hell was *he* doing here? I stepped outside and my jaw fell open. Robert sat in the center of the lawn staring at Devon. He wasn't hissing or snarling, just calmly watching him. A glance at Devon showed surprise...even awe in his face?

Devon finally noticed me standing on the verandah. His eyes were big marbles when he looked at me. "What the hell? That bobcat! You weren't lying when you said you had a bobcat! This is amazing! He's just sitting there!"

"Yeah, I know. That's Robert, my bobcat."

Folding my arms over my chest, I examined Devon's face. "Why are you here?" If he'd driven out to give me more shit, there was no way I could take anymore. The bruise from my last encounter with him still stung too much.

"I can't believe this! He's just sitting there as calm as a house cat!" Devon took more tentative steps closer to Robert.

My gaze pinged from the cat to Devon. It was amazing that Robert wasn't kicking up a fuss, screeching or growling. Instead, he looked as placid as if it were me or Libby walking over to him. What was up with Robert? He hadn't acted that way at all with Steve.

I walked down the steps and over to Devon. "He's pretty cool, isn't he? Have you ever been this close to a bobcat?"

Even more astounding was the fact I'd spoken normally to Devon. Maybe I was *wrong* about that spell. Oh God, it was so confusing!

"Are you *kidding* me? No! I've never even *seen* a bobcat! I'm totally in awe!" He looked at me. "You can get close to it? *Touch* it?"

"Yeah." I looked over at the bobcat. "Is it okay if Devon comes closer with me, Robert?"

He did that slow-blink thing, lowering his head a smidge, his way of saying yes. I nodded my head to Devon. "C'mon. Robert's cool with it."

But then I stopped, looking up at him. "Wait. You didn't answer me, Devon. Why did you come out here?"

He took a deep breath, looking away for a moment. "I was rude to you. I made you cry, like some big bully. I guess it's my turn to say I'm sorry."

My chest felt like the elephant sitting on it had vaporized. "It's okay, Devon. What you said, I deserved it. I've acted crazy and judged you without knowing all the facts. I *meant* it when I said I'm sorry."

He looked down at the ground for a moment. When he looked at me again, a smile twitched his lips. "I believe you meant it. My only question is, did you mean any of the other crazy stuff you said? Do you know about being attracted to me? 'Cause that would be okay. Just letting you know that."

I took a step closer to him, meeting his eyes. "I meant that, too, even if saying it was completely inappropriate. It just popped out of my mouth before I could help it. I'm sorry that it was awkward."

His eyebrows bunched, and he scoffed. "It only got awkward when you took my files. Other than that... well, I liked it." His eyebrows arched. "A lot."

Now I felt so light, I could float away! "It's all true. I will freely admit, I'm attracted to you." There. It was out there, and MJ's spell had nothing to do with me saying it.

Robert let out another high-pitched howl, jolting Devon and me back to reality. He'd sprung to his feet, hissing at something behind me.

At the crunch of gravel and the low rumble of an engine, I spun around and saw Steve's truck once more, driving down my laneway. What the hell, now? Talk about shitty timing!

Devon touched my arm, and his words were stiff:" I'm sorry. I shouldn't have just dropped in. I guess you were expecting company."

Steve was close enough now that I could see the hard set of his jaw, the glare in his narrow eyes.

Something wasn't right. My gut tightened, and a chill went up my spine.

FORTY SEVEN

N o. Please don't leave, Devon." I never took my eyes off Steve, slamming his brakes on and shutting the engine off.

"What's going on, Shannon?"

Ignoring Devon's question, I watched Steve get out of the truck and then reach back inside. When he straightened, there was a shotgun in his fists.

My heart leaped into my throat and I yelled, "No! You can't—"

"I'm going to do what I should have done before! You don't know what you're dealing with, Shannon." Holding the gun across his chest with both hands, he kept striding forward.

Steve glared over at Devon. "What the hell are you doing here? Stay back, Booker!"

Robert's high-pitched scream tore through my ears. A series of snarls and growls followed, coming closer by the second.

I spun around, shouting at the big cat, "Run, Robert! Go! Get out of here!"

Time slowed, playing out heartbeat by thundering heartbeat.

Stepping away from my side, Devon shouted at Steve, "Drop that gun, Steve! You can't do this!"

Steve raised the gun, aiming it at the bobcat. All the while the cat's growls and his pounding feet raced across the yard straight at Steve.

I hurtled over to push Steve away, but my feet felt like I was wading through sludge, not nearly fast enough to reach him in time. A blur of Devon's navy coat passed by me as he leapt to tackle Steve.

BOOM!

The shot blasted the air, ricocheting through the still woods and over the lake. I gasped, watching Devon's body spin and fall to the ground.

A screech of pain from Robert sliced through my heart. When I spun to check, plumes of snow kicked up as the cat raced for the trees. A trail of crimson dotted the white powder behind him. Oh shit! Robert was hit! How bad? But before that thought flew through my head, I heard Devon.

A hoarse groan sounded from him laying on his side, curled almost to a fetal position. Oh God, no! I rushed over to him. His shoulder was a mass of red but his head and chest weren't touched. Thank God he was alive!

I knelt, hovering over Devon before turning my gaze to Steve.

Wide-eyed, the bastard's mouth had fallen open as he stared dumbfounded at Devon. "I... I... He shouldn't have tried to—"

"GET THE HELL OFF MY LAND! Get out of here, Steve!" My voice broke, I yelled so hard.

When he still stood there like a mannequin, my body trembled with rage. My fingers clenched and unclenched. I wasn't even aware that I'd stood up until my hands rose, fingers splayed, pointing at him.

Everything around me faded as a miasma of fury thundered in my head. White-hot energy filled my chest, jolting down like a bolt of lightning through my arm. My thoughts were laser-sharp, focused on destroying that god-damned gun!

Closing my eyes, letting the energy fly from my fingers. KNOWING, FEELING, SEEING the target. A flash of light snapped before Steve's yelp of pain. The clang of metal on metal was next.

When I opened my eyes, the gun was in pieces on the ground in front of Steve's truck. He held one hand with the other as he scuttled away, almost tripping to get to his truck.

The life force which had ripped through my body drained. I fell to my knees as I watched Steve flee in his truck, careening to each side of the lane before a screeching turn onto the main road.

"Shannon." This was followed by a low moan.

When I turned, Devon's hand was pressed to his wounded shoulder as he struggled to sit up. I scrambled over to him. "Devon! I'm so sorry! I've got to call 9-1-1."

His hand left the wound, gripping my arm. "No. Help me get up. If... if I can get to my car, it'll be faster to drive to the hospital." His breathing was labored, and a bead of sweat rolled down his temple. "Thank God it was birdshot. But it stings like a bastard."

His eyes became wider. "What about the bobcat?"

Shit! I let go of Devon and ran through the snow following Robert's trail of blood. It went into the woods. I ran in, shouting his name over and over. I lost the trail and cupped my hands to my mouth. "Robert! Come back!" There was no response. SHIT! Devon was shot, too, and he wasn't magical! "Robert! I have to help Devon! I'll come back for you!" I shouted, before running back to Devon.

He was sitting on the ground, struggling to stand up.

"Where's the cat?" he gasped.

I looked at him dumbly. He'd just been shot and he was concerned about my bobcat?

I'd think about that later.

Squatting down, I curled my arm around him, lifting his good arm over my shoulders. "He's alive. Now, you gotta help me, Devon! Come on!" I shifted my legs, bracing myself to help lift a guy that was over six feet tall. "Now!"

He moaned. I grunted. He groaned. I strained. But inch by inch, we got him to his feet. Now that he was up, the worst was over, guiding and steadying him to the passenger side of his SUV. When he was inside, I grabbed a blanket that was folded on the back seat and pressed it into his bloody shoulder.

"Hold that tight, Devon! It'll slow the bleeding." I sprinted to the driver's side and started the vehicle. My drive down the laneway was almost as erratic as Steve's. That overbearing BASTARD!

Devon looked over at me, and a ghost of a smile lifted his lips. "Never a dull moment with you, is there, Shannon?" He shook his head. "What the hell was Murphy *thinking*? Coming onto your property with a gun!"

As I floored the big SUV heading to town, a coldness seeped into my gut. That could have ended so much worse.

And what had happened to me? I'd become another person... some kind of wizard, zapping Steve's gun. It'd been like a jolt of lightning. Where had that come from? What had happened to me?

As if I needed to ask.

Magic.

FORTY EIGHT

Shannon

Later that evening...

I looked up when the hospital door opened and Libby came through. Behind her were Mary-Jane and Cynthia. They rushed over to where I sat in the waiting room.

"How is he?" Mary-Jane took the seat next to me, leaning close and putting her hand on my arm. For a second, she was silent, and then her eyes became round. She'd seen everything play out like it was 3-D. "Shit. And double shit."

Libby bent lower, peering into my eyes. "I'll go check with the nursing station to see how much longer he'll be. I'm sure he's going to be fine, Shannon. It was birdshot from a shotgun, not a .357 Magnum."

When she hurried off, Cynthia slipped into the chair on my other side. A worried look came over her face. "You're sure Robert is okay?"

I could barely get the words past the lump in my throat, fighting tears. "I think so. He took some of the pellets though. I heard him yelp, and then he ran into the woods. Should we ask Libby to go out there to check on him? I hate the thought of him lying alone out there, bleeding and in pain."

She nodded. "I'll go with her. I can't *believe* that Steve Murphy showed up at your house like that! That stupid jerk! And to shoot Devon as well! He's going to pay big time for that, I'm sure! Devon will have him charged or sue his ass off."

Cynthia's eyes narrowed, as she edged closer. "What was Devon doing there? I thought he hated you. The last I heard, he was going to get a restraining order against you."

Mary-Jane huffed, "You don't know the *half* of it!" She squeezed my arm before letting go of it. "Much as I'm totally in awe of your newfound powers, Shannon, you've really opened a can of worms this time."

Cynthia leaned forward, peering at MJ. "I hate being the last to know!" She gripped my hand and closed her eyes. She gasped, and then her eyes flew open after "reading" me. "Oh. My. God. You busted his gun! And Steve saw all that happen... the whole *Wonder Woman* schtick?"

MJ muttered, "I was thinking Supergirl myself, but yeah, I guess she does kinda look like Lynda Carter."

"Who's that?" Cynthia asked.

"A TV show we watched as kids on Nickelodeon," MJ replied.

I felt myself shrink into myself. "What am I going to do?" I tugged the bloodstained blanket from Devon's vehicle higher up until it was just under my chin. In all the craziness, I had left the house without my jacket, and now that the adrenaline, or whatever it was that exploded through my body, was gone, I was shivering like a leaf.

Libby came back from the inner sanctum of the hospital. "They're taking Devon to a private room now. He's fine. He got hit with just a few pellets, and they got them all. They're keeping him overnight. He's a bit groggy from the anesthesia."

"Can I see him?" I pushed the blanket off and stood up. "Take me to his room, Libby." This whole mess was once again MY fault! Thanks to me going to see Devon, he'd taken a bullet or pellet or whatever, trying to stop Steve.

Libby looked away for a moment. "Okay. Technically, you

aren't family, but I have some pull around this place. C'mon."

As I followed next to her, I asked her if she'd try to find Robert to fix him up, making her promise to let me know that she'd found him.

She paused at one of the doors in the corridor. "He's in there, Shannon. Much as I've always disliked Devon, I have to give him credit for trying to save Robert. I guess there's a bit of good in everyone." She sneered, "Maybe not Steve. I'm so pissed with him, I could *spit*!"

"Let one fly at him for me too, will ya?" I leaned closer, lowering my voice even though there was no one close by. "MJ and Cynthia will update you on all that happened, Libby. It's not good, I'm afraid."

She rolled her eyes. "Why am I not surprised? I'll call you later about Robert."

When she walked away, I opened the door to Devon's room.

FORTY NINE

Devon's eyes opened when I walked over to the side of the bed. Tucked under the blue sheet, with the injury hidden by the hospital gown, it was hard to tell that he'd been shot. His eyes opened wider when his gaze met mine.

"How are you doing, Devon?" I patted his hand, taking a place at the side of the bed. Concern for him waged with guilt that he was here because of me. I didn't even want to think about what he might have seen me do with Steve's gun. Hell, I was still trying to process that.

"I'm tired. I can't believe everything that happened. If it weren't for the fact that I'm laying here in the hospital, I'd say this was all a bad dream. A genuine nightmare." He moved his hand away from mine and stared at the ceiling, avoiding me. "I should have stayed in town… away from the craziness that is your life. A moment of weakness…"

I felt my gut sink down to my toes as I stood there peering at him. Oh God. I couldn't blame him for feeling this way. He'd tried to help me and ended up getting shot. "I'm so sorry for what happened, Devon."

His eyes were icy when he looked over at me. "What the hell was going on with Steve Murphy and you? The only one I feel sorry for… aside from me, is that bobcat. Somehow, both of us get caught up in your bullshit drama with Steve, and we end up the worse for it."

"It wasn't like that, Devon. Steve did this all on his own. I had no idea that he'd do this." Shit! I could understand him being angry but he wasn't being fair. "I didn't know he was coming back to my place with a shotgun to shoot Robert."

"Coming *back* to your place? So, something was going on between you two that I just stumbled into?" Devon shook his head from side to side. "I should have known better. I've been thinking about all this, since I woke up, Shannon. Ever since I tried to help you out, giving you a job at my office, things have sure gone off the rails."

"No. Things will get better. It's Steve's craziness this time, not mine." Just as we'd begun to talk reasonably with one another, with MJ's spell lifted, my friendship with Devon was slipping through my fingers.

"Well then, you and Steve make a good pair. But leave me out of it. It's better for my health and sanity." His gaze returned to the ceiling, and his voice was flat when he added, "Just go. I hope your bobcat's okay, but I don't want you here."

As I stared at his profile, I thought of how he'd tried to help me save Robert. Hell, he'd come out to visit me to apologize for making me cry. Despite what he was saying now, there was a spark between us. He'd admitted it before Steve had shown up to ruin everything.

"I'll leave you to rest, Devon. But this isn't over. Too much has happened for me to give up on you." I risked putting my hand on his arm before I continued, "And if you weren't so shaken up right now after getting shot, you'd agree. We have some unfinished business, Devon. I'll see you later."

His gaze flitted to me for a moment before his eyes closed. I turned and walked out of the room, defeated for now, but definitely not destroyed. Another man had left me down and out but I'd been okay. And that guy hadn't been half the guy Devon was. Devon had proved that when he'd tried to save

Robert.

If Devon and I could only ever be friends, that would be okay. Not ideal but I'd live with it.

When I reached the waiting room, Cynthia stood up and came over to me. "How is he?"

"Of course he's pissed, and he asked me to leave." I squeezed her hand. "But he'll be okay, and if not… but that's a battle for another day." I shrugged. "Any word on Robert?"

"I just spoke to Libby. They followed the spots of blood in the snow but then it just ended. They're still combing the area."

"I'm going to join them and find Robert. I can't stand the thought of him out there hurt and bleeding." When I turned to leave, Cynthia was right on my heels.

FIFTY

When I parked Devon's vehicle in my driveway, Cynthia turned to me."We'll find him, Shannon. And then after we do, we're going to tear a strip off Steve Murphy for shooting him."

As I got out of the SUV, I grimaced. "Steve's gonna have his hands full with Devon. He'll be lucky if he doesn't end up in jail."

"He deserves that. Poor Robert. What the hell was Steve thinking, coming onto your land and shooting your cat? For two cents I'd put such a hex on that guy he wouldn't ever show his face in public again!" She looked over at me and rolled her eyes. "But I can't. That goes against the code of magic."

"Steve will get his just desserts." I started for the front door to go get my parka and snow boots. "I'll be right back. I'll bring a flashlight." This was going to be even harder to find Robert now that it was dark. The only saving grace was the half-moon in the sky lighting the snow-covered ground.

After getting warm winter gear on, I stepped back outside. Movement at the edge of my yard near the trees caught my eye. My chest sank, seeing Libby and Mary-Jane step out from the forest. No Robert.

"We followed his trail, but then it just stopped." Libby kept walking toward Cynthia and me. "It was the damnedest thing. It wasn't even like there was a burrow or cave that he could have disappeared into, to lick his wounds."

"Let me see. Show me." I started off toward the trees, but as I came abreast of MJ, her hand reached out to stop me.

Even in the low light, I could see the look of wonder in her dark eyes. "He's alive, Shannon. I held drops of his blood in my fingers, trying to catch a clue where he is. I felt him. I felt his heartbeat and the pain in his neck from the pellets. He's angry and hurt, but he's safe, wherever he is."

My heartbeat ratcheted up a few notches, and I itched to get out there to hold Robert. "So where is he? You felt him. You *have* to know where he is." Good goddess and powers that be! Hurry up and get on with it. I had to help Robert!

She shook her head, and her voice was barely above a whisper, "That's just it. I don't know. I feel him but I can't see his surroundings. The only thing I pick up is a green mist. Well, more like a cloud or waves than mist."

I blinked a few times, staring at her like she was talking Greek. "What do you mean, a green cloud? We're in the mountains! He's got to be here, even if he's dug himself into a snowdrift! C'mon! Let's go. We need to find him!"

Cynthia tugged at my sleeve. "Look, we want to find the bobcat as much as you do, Shannon! But there's more to this." Her gaze flew to MJ, "Green? Do you sense Robert in a cloud of green? A sickly green, or more like the color of grass?"

I threw my hands in the air. "Why the hell does THAT matter? We need to get to Robert! He's out there, probably in shock, bleeding and cold."

"He's sending you a *message*, Shannon! He's alive! The green color is symbolic. It's life!"

Mary-Jane nodded. "It was vibrant, the color of new leaves or the grass. It gave me a sense of peace, now that I think of it."

Libby stepped over, blocking my path to the forest. "You said earlier today that the universe takes care of us. The path is not linear and neither is finding Robert. He's alive but he's hidden. Robert is magic, Shannon. When he's ready, he'll come back to you. You have to trust in that."

"I believe that too, Shannon." Mary-Jane stepped to my side. "Remember that you have us. We may bicker and snipe at each other, but when we're threatened, we're shoulder to shoulder. Robert is just away from us for a time. We have to trust that."

"Trust intention and the universe. It's worked for us before and it will again. We have each other and we have the well. For now, that's enough." Cynthia took her place on my other side. "As long as we're together and keep the faith, we'll be okay. Robert's part of us, so we have to trust that he'll return."

I looked at each of my friends in turn. When things had looked bleak for Mary-Jane and me, we'd overcome the problems by sticking together. The well had demanded it and we'd done it. This was another hurdle that we'd survive. Plus, our magic was growing.

"That's it, then? We sit back and wait for things to work out. As hard as that's going to be, what choice do I have?" The ache inside for Robert and for how things were between Devon and me, was hard. But then, magic had never been easy. It had flipped my world upside down, to put it mildly.

I'd have to wait and see where this latest trial would end up, keeping faith in myself and my coven. I looked up at the half-moon almost hidden by clouds skittering across its face. By the light of that moon, the mysticism of the well, and the bond with my sisters, Robert would be okay and find his way back.

Devon might be another story, but I'd deal with that in good time.

So mote it be.

The END

AUTHOR'S NOTE

Well, well well… (sorry, I couldn't resist LOL)

These 'Magick' gifts Shannon and her besties have received sure came with some strings attached, eh? I was able to draw on more than a few memories when I wrote about their being bitchy to each other.

Shannon's ultimately loving when MJ's confessed about hexing her wasn't something I was mature enough to come up with on my own. It was a lesson I learned from a dear, dear friend when we had a falling out. Writing that scene swept me back to a time long ago. I've been so blessed in my life with friends as aggravating and ultimately loving as MJ is with Shannon.

Yes, there's more in store for these three ladies, let me tell you. The third book in this series is well in hand and I plan to release it this summer!

The title is 'The Devil In The Details', and things take a bit of a darker turn…

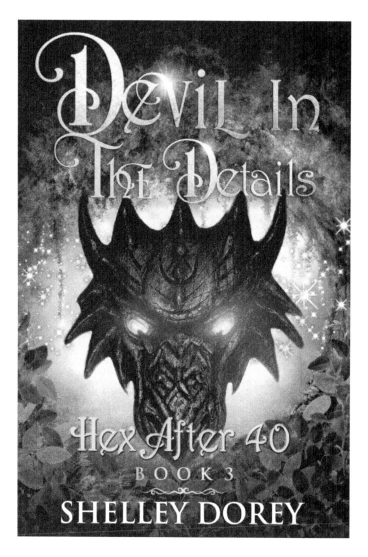

The Book Club meets Hocus Pocus in midlife, magical mayhem.
Are these four women the worst witches ever, or what?

You would think that Shannon and her coven really ought to have their act together by now—especially after Cynthia, who is waaay more experienced in the magical realm, joins them.

Nope.

Shannon's familiar, Robert the bobcat, is still missing in action after being shot by Steve. Which also shot that budding romance between Shannon and Steve all to hell, by the way.

Libby hates her new job, but it looks like every four-legged creature in Wesley is in love with her!

Mary-Jane? Oh boy. What's so great about having magical powers if your marriage is on the rocks?

And dear Cynthia, who is only in her mid thirties, can no longer hit the snooze button on her biological clock, not if she ever wants to have a daughter.

Despite all they've learned, practising charms and trying to figure out the contents of Shannon's Grimoire, their magic is still messed up.

- Shannon's spell to kick-start her love life ends up screwing over Mary-Jane's marriage.
- When Libby enlists the help of wildlife to locate Robert the bobcat, her entire neighbourhood is transformed into some sort of Critter Spa.
- Mary-Jane? Oh boy…almost burning her restaurant down was the least of her challenges. Now she's coping with a jealous husband…who is too busy hanging with his new buddy than making time with her. What the hell…?

These four witches can't get their collective asses in gear, despite the Spanx.

Wait.

A.

Minute…

There's no way they're still this crappy at magic. It has to be something else.

*Or **someone** else? But who would want to hex them up?*

Coming Summer of 2021!

ABOUT THE AUTHOR

Michelle Dorey, writing as 'Shelley Dorey' is the author of more than a dozen spine-chilling novels featuring ghosts, haunted houses and the supernatural. She has been on the Amazon best seller list many times throughout her career.

A voracious reader of the masters like Stephen King and Dean Koontz, she decided to try her hand at writing after going on a Ghost Walk in the enigmatic city of Kingston, Ontario, Canada where she lives. Her first book, Crawley House was inspired by a true tale of a family's nightmare, living in a home owned by Queen's University.

"Expect the supernatural when the bedrock of a city is limestone. Throw in the fact it is bordered on three sides by the mighty St. Lawrence River, The Rideau River and Lake Ontario and you are in for some thrills and chills of the paranormal variety--which of course is my cup of tea."

Does she love Kingston? You bet! Her husband Jim, a transplanted native New Yorker born and raised in the Bronx, agrees. Michelle and Jim like nothing better than spoiling their two pugs with treats and long walks in their neighborhood. Funny, but the slightly neurotic dogs always refuse to go for a stroll in the cemetery nearby.

OTHER WORKS

All of Michelle Dorey and Shelley Dorey books are
exclusively available on Amazon

Women's Paranormal Fantasy By Shelley Dorey

The Mystical Veil Series
Hex After 40 Series
Celtic Knot Series

Ghosts And Hauntings By Michelle Dorey

The Hauntings Of Kingston Series
The Haunted Ones Series
The Haunted Cabin

Printed in Great Britain
by Amazon